ERSKINE CALDWELL, the son of a Presbyterian minister, left his Georgia home at the age of fourteen to wander through the Deep South, Mexico, and Central America. Later, while attending the University of Virginia on a scholarship, he began to write short stories. One of his novels, *God's Little Acre*, has been called by the *Saturday Review* "one of the finest studies of Southern poor whites that has ever come into our literature."

Mr. Caldwell's most recent books include *Annette, Miss Mamma Aimee, Summertime Island, The Weather Shelter,* and *The Earnshaw Neighborhood.*

The stories in this book were selected by Carvel Collins, Professor of English at the University of Notre Dame, who has arranged them so they progress in subject matter from youth to old age. The first stories are concerned with the perplexities of childhood and adolescence; the next with love and courtship, marriage and family life; and the final ones with age and death.

Erskine Caldwell's Men and Women

A SIGNET MODERN CLASSIC
NEW AMERICAN LIBRARY
TIMES MIRROR
NEW YORK AND SCARBOROUGH, ONTARIO

Library of Congress Catalog Card Number: 61-12810

Published by arrangement with the author.

 SIGNET CLASSIC TRADEMARK REG. U.S. PAT. OFF. AND FOREIGN COUNTRIES
REGISTERED TRADEMARK—MARCA REGISTRADA
HECHO EN CHICAGO, U.S.A.

SIGNET, SIGNET CLASSICS, MENTOR, PLUME AND MERIDIAN BOOKS are published in the United States by
The New American Library, Inc.,
1301 Avenue of the Americas, New York, New York 10019,
in Canada by The New American Library of Canada Limited,
81 Mack Avenue, Scarborough, 704, Ontario.

FIRST PRINTING, NOVEMBER, 1962

3 4 5 6 7 8 9 10 11

PRINTED IN THE UNITED STATES OF AMERICA

Contents

Introduction

In ADDITION TO his many novels Erskine Caldwell has published a hundred and fifty short stories. When he recently asked whether I would read his stories and select those I thought best, I was pleased to have the opportunity to reexamine an important part of the work of the world's most popular author of fiction.

Several of his stories, "Kneel to the Rising Sun" and "Candy-Man Beechum" and "Country Full of Swedes" among them, are classics of what Budd Schulberg calls "the one cultural expression in which our country seems to have excelled—the short story." And I knew that Erskine Caldwell takes great pleasure in writing short fiction, for in an *Atlantic Monthly* interview in 1958 he told me, "I don't think there is anything to compare with the short story. I think it's the best form of writing there is." When I had asked why he thought it was a better form than the novel, he had replied, "Well, I think you can tell as much in a story as you can in a novel, but it's more difficult to do. It's hard to accomplish a good short story because you have to concentrate it so much. So I like the discipline of it." The pleasure Caldwell takes in his stories obviously has been shared by readers, for short stories make up a significant portion of the fiction published in his thirty-eight books—of which over sixty-one million copies have been sold!

There has been much speculation about the reason for this immense response to Caldwell's work. Sex has been one of the standard answers, and many writers seem to have tried that route in an attempt to reach Caldwell's popularity. Kenneth Burke possibly explained their failure when he remarked that "unendowed" writers "might strain to engross us by lurid description of the sexual act—and the result would be negligible . . . By an astounding trick of oversimplification, Caldwell puts people into complex situations while making them act with the scant, crude tropisms of an insect—and the result is cunning, where Lawrence, by a variant of the same pattern, is as unwieldy as an elephant in his use of vulgar words for romantic love-making." And a writer for the New York *Herald Tribune* has observed that though some consider the sexual behavior of Caldwell's characters looser than that of real people, the "Kinsey report has seemed to indicate that the Caldwell men and women behave much as actual men and women do" in comparable levels of our population, and that possibly "many thousands of readers find in Caldwell what seems to them the first realism about sex they have ever encountered in print."

But something other than its treatment of sex must account for the astonishing popularity of Caldwell's fiction. The psychoanalyst Dr. Lawrence S. Kubie, dealing with this point in an essay on Caldwell, says that as long as there are "people who cannot be fooled or consoled by romance, whether it be cheap and tawdry or delicate and sophisticated; as long as there are those who refuse to content themselves with the cold comfort of an ironical sneer; and as long as those who reject either of these escapes have courage and honesty, there will be a literature which seeks to write its way out of confusion and restraint into some pathway of passionate relief and happiness." And both Dr. Kubie and Kenneth Burke may have touched on an additional reason for the popularity of Caldwell's fiction by relating it to dreams. Burke denies "that Caldwell is a realist. In his tomfoolery, he comes closer to the Dadaists; when his grotesqueness is serious, he is a Superrealist. We might compromise by calling him over all a Symbolist (if by a Symbolist we mean a writer whose work serves most readily as a case history for the psychologist and whose plots are more intelligible when interpreted as dreams)." Dr. Kubie, making a comment on *God's Little Acre* which can apply to other Caldwell works, supports this view by saying that in Caldwell's fiction just as "in many dreams, one may recognize two groups of characters . . . some shrouded and ominous figures who hover dimly in the background like those unseen persons in a dream . . . others who stand out with all the hallucinatory vividness of the lions and tigers of a child's nightmare. Their clarity is a tribute to the author's skill, particularly because, despite their sharp outlines, they retain their fantastic and unreal quality; and when closely examined . . . fuse until they seem to become different aspects of a single human spirit, split up by a legitimate and effective literary artifice into the semblance of separate things." Holding a similar opinion, the poet and critic Horace Gregory says of Caldwell that "like all writers of the first rank he has an instinct for converting a casual episode into a symbol that carries profound meaning."

Another feature of Caldwell's fiction which surely accounts for some of its popularity is the power of its social protest. While "A Woman in the House," "Meddlesome Jack," and "A Small Day" may appeal to us by their humorous treatment of sexual unconventionalities, Caldwell's outrage at injustice, with his effective understatement of that outrage, has made such stories as "Kneel to the Rising Sun" and "Candy-Man Beechum" rank well in the fiction of man's inhumanity to man. This must give satisfaction to Caldwell, for in one of his autobiographical books he responded to the question, "Why don't you write about the pleasant things in life?" by replying, "Those enjoying the pleasant things in life are fewer than those enduring the unpleasant. When this social condition no longer exists, I'll feel there is no longer any purpose in writing about the effects of poverty on the human spirit."

Caldwell's fiction not only shows man's inhumanity to man but the astonishing ability of some men to rise, with great nobility, above their muddy circumstance. In "Horse Thief" the hero will go to jail rather than put the slightest stain on the name of the girl he loves. Candy-Man Beechum, facing the stupid officer, dies with as much flair as he has lived. Though the defeated tenant in "Kneel to the Rising Sun" shows the depths of appalling weakness to which too many of us can descend, the braver tenant, Clem, is magnificent in his support of the right and in his dignity when confronting the most extreme viciousness. In "A Short Sleep in Louisiana" the aged traveler proves indomitable despite his years.

Another aspect of Caldwell's fiction high on the list of probable reasons for its popularity is its humor, now ironical, now wry, now wild. Here too, even in the stories with the wildest humor, Caldwell, as the poet Randall Jarrell says, "generally depends on understatement and repetition, rather than exaggeration." And readers in their thousands seem to have shared Mr. Jarrell's belief that the "best thing one can do with Mr. Caldwell's peculiar variety of humor is to accept it with gratitude."

Closely related to this humor for which we are grateful is Caldwell's ability to dupe us. "Soquots," "The Growing

Season," and "Country Full of Swedes" illustrate that talent
at its best. Showing Jesse's mounting frenzy under the stress
of heat and frustrated labor, "The Growing Season" gives us
a psychological study, almost an explanation, of violence.
But as Jesse moves toward his frenzied, therapeutic killing
of Fiddler, the story turns into a masterpiece of duping the
reader: partly for humor of an extreme kind and partly to
present Jesse's frenzy in almost laboratory isolation and
clarity, the author skillfully keeps Fiddler unidentified and
unidentifiable (although one critic, I find, has mistakenly assumed Fiddler to be a dog; and another, especially fooled,
has assumed Fiddler to be a "donkey"). "Country Full of
Swedes" also dupes us skillfully: at the start it seems to be
setting the stage humorously to demonstrate the falsity of
the inhibited farmers' prejudices against their neighbors; at
the end the ebullient Swedes live up to part of the farmers'
fearful expectations, and the reader is tricked again. In longer works this sort of thing can easily get out of hand and
lose effect, but in short stories such as "Country Full of
Swedes" and "The Growing Season" many readers find it
extremely welcome. Apparently, though, editors at first did
not like "Country Full of Swedes"; for Caldwell has said it
"was rejected by practically every magazine in the United
States" and that "editors, not content with merely turning it
down, felt called upon to accompany their refusals with ad-
vice that the story was (a) not true to life, (b) a denial of
man's nobility, (c) injurious to my reputation, (d) an incita-
tion to violence, (e) not understandable to readers (Hello,
Bill!), and (f) evidence of a disordered mind." Then *The
Yale Review* not only published it but gave it an important
award, and it has been reprinted in anthologies and text-
books ever since.

The order of appearance of the stories selected for this
volume is not that of their composition or first publication
but loosely follows their subject matter as it moves from
youth to old age. Caldwell often shows great perception of
adolescent awakening to awareness of the love of men
and women, and he has well presented it in the opening
stories, "Maud Island" and "Indian Summer." The arrangement of stories then moves on to present Caldwell's perception of the tribulations of youthful courtship in "Horse
Thief," "A Day's Wooing," and the bizarrely humorous
"Where the Girls Were Different." Marriage and various
aspects of love and life in maturer years are the subjects of

further stories, among them the unique and effective "Midsummer Passion." The volume ends by glancing at old age and death with "A Short Sleep in Louisiana" and the fantastic story of the fly in the coffin.

Erskine Caldwell, born in 1903 in Georgia of sophisticated parents, his father a pastor and secretary of a Home Missions Board and his mother a former teacher of Latin and French who turned her pedagogical talent to the education of their son, has had a rich opportunity to observe men and women in many stations of life in many parts of the world. After a youth spent in the backcountry South and at college in Georgia, Virginia, and Pennsylvania, Caldwell lived for several years in Maine expressly to observe and share a quite different way of life, a sojourn which produced such stories as "A Woman in the House," "Midsummer Passion," "Country Full of Swedes," and "The Corduroy Pants." Since leaving Maine he has not only lived in other parts of this country, most recently in Tucson and San Francisco, but has traveled widely and thoroughly both here and abroad. Observations of life in these varied scenes he has reworked with imagination into his many stories, the best of which certainly bear out Otis Ferguson's judgment that a "good story is the easiest thing to read there is, and the damnedest thing to write; and while there are many writers who can take a day off now and then and do a story, there are very few storywriters. Erskine Caldwell is one of these rare birds."

CARVEL COLLINS

Maud Island

UNCLE MARVIN was worried. He got up from the log and walked toward the river.

"I don't like the looks of it, boys," he said, whipping off his hat and wiping his forehead.

The houseboat was drifting downstream at about three miles an hour, and a man in a straw hat and sleeveless undershirt was trying to pole it inshore. The man was wearing cotton pants that had faded from dark brown to light tan.

"It looks bad," Uncle Marvin said, turning to Jim and me. "I don't like the looks of it one whit."

"Maybe they are lost, Uncle Marvin," Jim said. "Maybe they'll just stop to find out where they are, and then go on away again."

"I don't believe it, son," he said, shaking his head and wiping the perspiration from his face. "It looks downright bad to me. That kind of a houseboat never has been out for no good since I can remember."

On a short clothesline that stretched along the starboard side, six or seven pieces of clothing hung waving in the breeze.

"It looks awful bad, son," he said again, looking down at me.

We walked across the mud flat to the river and waited to see what the houseboat was going to do. Uncle Marvin took out his plug and cut off a chew of tobacco with his jackknife. The boat was swinging inshore, and the man with the pole was trying to beach it before the current cut in and carried them back to mid-channel. There was a power launch lying on its side near the stern, and on the launch was a towline that had been used for upstream going.

When the houseboat was two or three lengths from the shore, Uncle Marvin shouted at the man poling it.

"What's your name, and what do you want here?" he said gruffly, trying to scare the man away from the island.

Instead of answering, the man tossed a rope to us. Jim picked it up and started pulling, but Uncle Marvin told him to drop it. Jim dropped it, and the middle of the rope sank into the yellow water.

"What did you throw my rope in for?" the man on the houseboat shouted. "What's the matter with you?"

Uncle Marvin spat some tobacco juice and glared right back at him. The houseboat was ready to run on the beach.

"My name's Graham," the man said. "What's yours?"

"None of your business," Uncle Marvin shouted. "Get that raft away from here."

The houseboat began to beach. Graham dropped the pole on the deck and ran and jumped on the mud flat. He called to somebody inside while he was pulling the rope out of the water.

The stern swung around in the backwash of the current, and Jim grabbed my arm and pointed at the dim lettering on the boat. It said *Mary Jane,* and under that was *St. Louis.*

While we stood watching the man pull in the rope, two girls came out on the deck and looked at us. They were very young. Neither of them looked to be over eighteen or nineteen. When they saw Uncle Marvin, they waved at him and began picking up the boxes and bundles to carry off.

"You can't land that shantyboat on this island," Uncle Marvin said threateningly. "It won't do you no good to unload that stuff, because you'll only have to carry it all back again. No shantyboat's going to tie up on this island."

One of the girls leaned over the rail and looked at Uncle Marvin.

"Do you own this island, Captain?" she asked him.

Uncle Marvin was no river captain. He did not even look like one. He was the kind of man you could see plowing cotton on the steep hillsides beyond Reelfoot Lake. Uncle Marvin glanced at Jim and me for a moment, kicking at a gnarled root on the ground, and looked at the girl again.

"No," he said, pretending to be angry with her. "I don't own it, and I wouldn't claim ownership of anything on the Mississippi, this side of the bluffs."

The other girl came to the rail and leaned over, smiling at Uncle Marvin.

"Hiding out, Captain?" she asked.

Uncle Marvin acted as though he would have had something to say to her if Jim and I had not been there to over-hear him. He shook his head at the girl.

Graham began carrying off the boxes and bundles. Both Jim and I wished to help him so we would have a chance to go on board the houseboat, but we knew Uncle Marvin would never let us do that. The boat had been beached on the mud flat, and Graham had tied it up, knotting the rope around a young cypress tree.

When he had finished, he came over to us and held out his hand to Uncle Marvin. Uncle Marvin looked at Graham's hand, but he would not shake with him.

"My name's Harry Graham," he said. "I'm from up the river at Caruthersville. What's your name?"

"Hutchins," Uncle Marvin said, looking him straight in the eyes, "and I ain't hiding out."

The two girls, the dark one and the light one, were carrying their stuff across the island to the other side where the slough was. The island was only two or three hundred feet wide, but it was nearly half a mile long. It had been a sandbar to begin with, but it was already crowded with trees and bushes. The Mississippi was on the western side, and on the eastern side there was a slough that looked bottomless. The bluffs of the Tennessee shore were only half a mile in that direction.

"We're just on a little trip over the week end," Graham said. "The girls thought they would like to come down the river and camp out on an island for a couple of days."

"Which one is your wife?" Uncle Marvin asked him.

Graham looked at Uncle Marvin a little surprised for a minute. After that he laughed a little, and began kicking the ground with the toe of his shoe.

"I didn't quite catch what you said," he told Uncle Marvin.

"I said, which one is your wife?"

"Well, to tell the truth, neither of them. They're just good friends of mine, and we thought it would be a nice trip down the river and back for a couple of days. That's how it is."

"They're old enough to get married," Uncle Marvin told him, nodding at the girls.

"Maybe so," Graham said. "Come on over and I'll introduce you to them. They're Evansville girls, both of them. I used to work in Indiana, and I met them up there. That's where I got this houseboat. I already had the launch."

Uncle Marvin looked at the lettering on the *Mary Jane,*
spelling out *St. Louis* to himself.

"Just a little fun for the week end," Graham said, smiling.
"The girls like the river."

Uncle Marvin looked at Jim and me, jerking his head to one
side and trying to tell us to go away. We walked down to the
edge of the water where the *Mary Jane* was tied up, but we
could still hear what they were saying. After a while, Uncle
Marvin shook hands with Graham and started along up the
shore towards our skiff.

"Come on, son, you and Milt," he said. "It's time to look
at that taut line again."

We caught up with Uncle Marvin, and all of us got into
the skiff, and Jim and I set the oarlocks. Uncle Marvin turned
around so he could watch the people behind us on the
island. Graham was carrying the heavy boxes to a clearing,
and the two girls were unrolling the bundles and spreading them on the ground to air.

Jim and I rowed to the mouth of the creek and pulled
alongside the taut line. Uncle Marvin got out his box of
bait and began lifting the hooks and taking off the catfish.
Every time he found a hook with a catch, he took the cat
off, spat over his left shoulder, and dropped it into the
bucket and put on a new bait.

There was not much of a catch on the line that morning.
After we had rowed across, almost to the current in the
middle of the creek mouth, where the outward end of the
line had been fastened to a cypress in the water, Uncle
Marvin threw the rest of the bait overboard and told us to
turn around and row back to Maud Island.

Uncle Marvin was a preacher. Sometimes he preached in
the schoolhouse near home, and sometimes he preached in a
dwelling. He had never been ordained, and he had never
studied for the ministry, and he was not a member of any
church. However, he believed in preaching, and he never let
his lack of training stop him from delivering a sermon
whenever a likely chance offered itself. Back home on the
mainland, people called him Preacher Marvin, not so much
for the fact that he was a preacher, but because he looked
like one. That was one reason why he had begun preaching at the start. People had got into the habit of calling him
Preacher Marvin, and before he was forty he had taken up
the ministry as a calling. He had never been much of a
farmer, anyway—a lot of people said that.

Our camp on Maud Island was the only one on the river for ten or fifteen miles. The island was only half a mile from shore, where we lived in Tennessee, and Uncle Marvin brought us out to spend the week end five or six times during the summer. When we went back and forth between the mainland and the island, we had to make a wide circle, nearly two miles out of the way, in order to keep clear of the slough. The slough was a mass of yellow mud, rotting trees, and whatever drift happened to get caught in it. It was almost impossible to get through it, either on foot or in a flat-bottomed boat, and we kept away from it as far as possible. Sometimes mules and cows started out in it from the mainland to reach the island, but they never got very far before they dropped out of sight. The slough sucked them down and closed over them like quicksand.

Maud Island was a fine place to camp, though. It was the highest ground along the river for ten or fifteen miles, and there was hardly any danger of its being flooded when the high water covered everything else within sight. When the river rose to forty feet, however, the island, like everything else in all directions, was covered with water from the Tennessee bluffs to the Missouri highlands, seven or eight miles apart.

When we got back from baiting the taut line, Uncle Marvin told us to build a good fire while he was cleaning the catch of catfish and cutting them up for frying. Jim went off after an armful of driftwood while I was blowing the coals in the campfire. Jim brought the wood and built the fire, and I watched the pail of water hanging over it until Uncle Marvin was ready to make the coffee.

In the middle of the afternoon Uncle Marvin woke up from his midday nap and said it was too hot to sleep any longer. We sat around for ten or fifteen minutes, nobody saying much, and after a while Uncle Marvin got up and said he thought he would walk over to the other camp and see how the people from Caruthersville, or Evansville, or wherever they came from, were getting along.

Jim and I were up and ready to go along, but he shook his head and told us to stay there. We could not help feeling that there was something unusual about that, because Uncle Marvin had always taken us with him no matter where he went when we were camping on the island. When Jim said something about going along, Uncle Marvin got excited and told us to do as he said, or we would find ourselves being sorry.

"You boys stay here and take it easy," he said. "I've got to find out what kind of people they are before we start in to mix with them. They're from up the river, and there's no telling what they're like till I get to know them. You boys just stay here and take it easy till I get back."

After he had gone, we got up and picked our way through the dry underbrush toward the other camp. Jim kept urging me to hurry so we would not miss seeing anything, but I was afraid we would make so much noise Uncle Marvin would hear us and run back and catch us looking.

"Uncle Marvin didn't tell them he's a preacher," Jim said. "Those girls think he's a river captain, and I'll bet he wants them to keep on thinking so."

"He doesn't look like a river captain. He looks like a preacher. Those girls were just saying that for fun."

"The dark one acted like she's foolish about Uncle Marvin," Jim said. "I could tell."

"That's Jean," I said.

"How do you know what their names are?"

"Didn't you hear Graham talking to them when they were carrying their stuff off that houseboat?"

"Maybe he did," Jim said.

"He called that one Jean, and the light one Marge."

Jim bent down and looked through the bushes.

"Uncle Marvin's not mad at them now for coming here to camp." he said.

"How can you tell he's not?" I asked Jim.

"I can tell by the way he's acting up now."

"He told Graham to get the houseboat away from here, didn't he?"

"Sure he did then," Jim whispered, "but that was before those two girls came outside and leaned over the railing and talked to him. After he saw them awhile he didn't try to stop Graham from landing, did he?"

We had crawled as close as we dared go, and fifty feet away we could see everything that was going on in Graham's camp. When Uncle Marvin walked up, Graham was sitting against the trunk of a cypress trying to untangle a fishing line, and the two girls were lying in hammocks that had been hung up between trees. We could not see either of them very well then, because the sides of the hammocks hid them, but the sun was shining down into the clearing and it was easy to see them when they moved or raised their arms.

Five or six cases of drinks were stacked up against one of the trees where the hammocks were, and several bottles had already been opened and tossed aside empty. Graham had a bottle of beer beside him on the ground, and every once in a while he stopped tussling with the tangled fishing line and grabbed the bottle and took several swallows from it. The dark girl, Jean, had a bottle in her hand, half full, and Marge was juggling an empty bottle in the air over her head. Everybody looked as if he was having the best time of his life.

None of them saw Uncle Marvin when he got to the clearing. Graham was busy fooling with the tangled fishing line, and Uncle Marvin stopped and looked at all three of them for almost a minute before he was noticed.

"I'll bet Uncle Marvin takes a bottle," Jim said. "What do you bet?"

"Preachers don't drink beer, do they?"

"Uncle Marvin will, I'll bet anything," Jim said. "You know Uncle Marvin."

Just then Graham raised his head from the line and saw Uncle Marvin standing not ten feet away. Graham jumped up and said something to Uncle Marvin. It was funny to watch them, because Uncle Marvin was not looking at Graham at all. His head was turned in the other direction all the time, and he was looking where the girls lay stretched out in the hammocks. He could not take his eyes off them long enough to glance at Graham. Graham kept on saying something, but Uncle Marvin acted as though he was on the other side of the river beyond earshot.

Jean and Marge pulled the sides of the hammocks over them, but they could not make Uncle Marvin stop looking at them. He started to grin, but he turned red in the face instead.

Graham picked up a bottle and offered it to Uncle Marvin. He took it without even looking at it once, and held it out in front of him as if he did not know he had it in his hand. When Graham saw that he was not making any effort to open it, he took it and put the cap between his teeth and popped it off as easily as he could have done it with a bottle opener.

The beer began to foam then, and Uncle Marvin shoved

the neck of the bottle into his mouth and turned it upside down. The foam that had run out on his hand before he could get the bottle into his mouth was dripping down his shirt front and making a dark streak on the blue cloth.

Jean leaned out of her hammock and reached to the ground for another bottle. She popped off the cap with a bottle opener and lay down again.

"Did you see that, Milt?" Jim whispered, squeezing my arm. He whistled a little between his teeth.

"I saw a lot!" I said.

"I didn't know girls ever did like that where everybody could see them," he said.

"They're from up the river," I told him. "Graham said they were from Evansville."

"That don't make any difference," Jim said, shaking his head. "They're girls, aren't they? Well, whoever saw girls lie in hammocks naked like that? I know I never did before!"

"I sure never saw any like those before, either," I told him.

Uncle Marvin had gone to the tree at the foot of one of the hammocks, and he was standing there, leaning against it a little, with the empty bottle in his hand, and looking straight at them.

Graham was trying to talk to him, but Uncle Marvin would not pay attention to what Graham was trying to say. Jean had turned loose the sides of the hammock, and Marge, too, and they were laughing and trying to make Uncle Marvin say something. Uncle Marvin's mouth was hanging open, but his face was not red any more.

"Why doesn't he tell them he's a preacher?" I asked Jim, nudging him with my elbow.

"Maybe he will after a while," Jim said, standing on his toes and trying to see better through the undergrowth.

"It looks to me like he's not going to tell them," I said. "It wouldn't make any difference, anyway, because Uncle Marvin isn't a real preacher. He only preaches when he feels like doing it."

"That doesn't make any difference," Jim said.

"Why doesn't it?"

"It just doesn't, that's why."

"But he calls himself a preacher, just the same."

"He doesn't have to be a preacher now if he doesn't want to be one. If he told them he was a preacher, they'd all jump up and run and hide from him."

Uncle Marvin was still standing against the tree looking at the dark girl, and Graham was a little to one side of him, looking as if he didn't know what to do next.

Presently Uncle Marvin jerked himself erect and turned his head in all directions listening for sounds. He looked towards us, but he could not see us. Jim got down on his hands and knees to be out of sight, and I got behind him.

The three others were laughing and talking, but not Uncle Marvin. He looked at them a while longer, and then he reached down to the top case against the cypress and lifted out another bottle. Graham reached to open it for him, but Uncle Marvin bit his teeth over the cap and popped it off. The beer began to foam right away, but before much of it could run out, Uncle Marvin had turned it up and was drinking it down.

When the bottle was empty, he wiped his mouth with the back of his hand and took three or four steps towards the dark girl in the hammock. Jean kicked her feet into the air and pulled the sides of the hammock around her. The other girl sat up to watch Uncle Marvin.

All at once he stopped and looked towards our camp on the other side of the island. There was not a sound anywhere, except the sucking sound in the slough that went on all the time, and the sharp slap of water against the sides of the houseboat. He listened for another moment, cocking his head like a dog getting ready to jump a rabbit, and broke into a run, headed for our camp. Jim and I just barely got there before Uncle Marvin. We were both puffing and blowing after running so fast, but Uncle Marvin was blowing even harder and he did not notice how short our breath was. He stopped and looked down at the dead fire for a while before he spoke to us.

"Get ready to go home, son, you and Jim," he said. "We've got to leave right now."

He started throwing our stuff into a pile and stamping out the ashes at the same time. He turned around and spat some tobacco juice on the live coals and grabbed up an armful of stuff. He did not wait for us to help him, but started for our skiff on the mud flat right away with a big load of stuff in both arms. Jim and I had to hurry to catch up with him so he would not forget and leave us behind.

He took the oars from us and shoved off without waiting for us to do it for him. When we were out of the mouth of the creek, he took his hat off and threw it on the bottom of the skiff and bent over the oars harder than ever. Jim and I could not do a thing to help, because there were only two oars and he would not turn either one of them loose.

Nobody said a thing while we were rowing around the slough. When we got within a hundred feet of shore, Uncle Marvin started throwing our stuff into a heap in the stern. We had no more than dragged bottom on shore when he picked up the whole lot and threw the stuff on the dried mud. The pans and buckets rolled in every direction.

Both of us were scared to say a word to Uncle Marvin because he had never acted like that before. We stood still and watched him while he shoved off into the river and turned the skiff around and headed around the slough. We were scared to death for a while, because we had never seen anybody cut across so close to the slough. He knew where he was all the time, but he did not seem to care how many chances he took of being sucked down into the slough. The last we saw of him was when he went out of sight around Maud Island.

We picked up our things and started running with them towards home. All the way there we were in too much of a hurry to say anything to each other. It was about a mile and a half home, and upgrade every step of the way, but we ran the whole distance, carrying our heavy stuff on our backs.

When we reached the front gate, Aunt Sophie ran out on the porch to meet us. She had seen us running up the road from the river, and she was surprised to see us back home so soon. When we left with Uncle Marvin early that morning, we thought we were going to stay a week on Maud Island. Aunt Sophie looked down the road to see if she could see anything of Uncle Marvin.

Jim dropped his load of stuff and sank down on the porch steps panting and blowing.

"Where's your Uncle Marvin, Milton?" Aunt Sophie asked us, standing above me and looking down at us with her hands on her hips. "Where's Marvin Hutchins?"

I shook my head the first thing, because I did not know what to say.

"Where's your Uncle Marvin, James?" she asked Jim.

Jim looked at me, and then down again at the steps. He tried to keep Aunt Sophie's eyes from looking straight into his.

Aunt Sophie came between us and shook Jim by the shoulder. She shook him until his hair tumbled over his face, and his teeth rattled until they sounded as if they were loose in his mouth.

"Where is your Uncle Marvin, Milton?" she demanded, coming to me and shaking me worse than she had Jim. "Answer me this minute, Milton!"

When I saw how close she was to me, I jumped up and ran out into the yard out of her reach. I knew how hard she could shake when she wanted to. It was lots worse than getting a whipping with a peach-tree switch.

"Has that good-for-nothing scamp gone and taken up with a shantyboat wench again?" she said, running back and forth between Jim and me.

I had never heard Aunt Sophie talk like that before, and I was so scared I could not make myself say a word. I had never heard her call Uncle Marvin anything like that before, either. As a rule she never paid much attention to him, except when she wanted him to chop some stovewood, or something like that.

Jim sat up and looked at Aunt Sophie. I could see that he was getting ready to say something about the way she talked about Uncle Marvin. Jim was always taking up for him whenever Aunt Sophie started in on him.

Jim opened his mouth to say something, but the words never came out.

"One of you is going to answer me!" Aunt Sophie said. "I'll give you one more chance to talk, Milton."

"He didn't say where he was going or what he was going to do, Aunt Sophie. Honest, he didn't!"

"Milton Hutchins!" she said, stamping her foot.

"Honest, Aunt Sophie!" I said. "Maybe he went off somewhere to preach."

"Preach, my foot!" she cried, jamming her hands on her hips. "Preach! If that good-for-nothing scalawag preached half as many sermons as he makes out like he does, he'd have the whole country saved for God long before now! Preach! Huh! Preach, my foot! That's his excuse for going off from home whenever he gets the notion to cut-up-jack, but he never fools me. And I can make a mighty good guess where he is this very minute, too. He's gone chasing off after some shantyboat wench! Preach, my foot!"

Jim looked at me, and I looked at Jim. To save our life

we could not see how Aunt Sophie had found out about the two girls from Evansville on Maud Island.

Aunt Sophie jammed her hands on her hips a little harder and motioned to us with her head. We followed her into the house.

"We're going to have a house cleaning around this place," she said. "James, you bring the brooms. Milton, you go start a fire under the washpot in the back yard and heat it full of water. When you get it going good, come in here and sweep down the cobwebs off the ceilings."

Aunt Sophie went from room to room, slamming doors behind her. She began ripping curtains down from the windows and pulling the rugs from the floor. A little later we could hear the swish of her broom, and presently a dense cloud of dust began blowing through the windows.

Indian Summer

THE WATER was up again. It had been raining for almost two whole days, and the creek was full to the banks. Dawn had broken gray that morning, and for the first time that week the sky was blue and warm.

Les pulled off his shirt and unbuckled his pants. Les never had to bother with underwear, because as soon as it was warm enough in the spring to go barefooted he hid his union suit in a closet and left it there until fall. His mother was not alive, and his father never bothered about the underclothes.

"I wish we had a shovel to dig out some of this muck," he said. "Every time it rains this hole fills up with this stuff. I'd go home and get a shovel, but if they saw me they'd make me stay there and do something."

While Les was hanging his shirt and pants on a bush, I waded out into the yellow water. The muck on the bottom was ankle deep, and there were hundreds of dead limbs stuck in it. I pulled out some of the largest and threw them on the other bank out of the way.

"How's the water, Jack?" Les asked. "How deep is it this time?"

I waded out to the middle of the creek where the current was the strongest. The yellow water came almost up to my shoulders.

"Nearly neck deep," I said. "But there's about a million dead limbs stuck in the bottom. Hurry up and help me throw them out."

Les came splashing in. The muddy water gurgled and sucked around his waist.

"I'll bet somebody comes down here every day and pitches these dead limbs in here," Les said, making a face. "I don't see how else they could get here. Dead tree limbs don't fall into a creek this fast. Somebody is throwing them in, and I'll bet a pretty he doesn't live a million miles away, either."

"Maybe Old Howes does it, Les."

"Sure, he does it. He's the one I'm talking about. I'll bet anything he comes down and throws limbs in every day."

Les stepped on a sharp limb. He held his nose and squeezed his eyes and ducked under and pulled it out.

"You know what?" Les said.

"What?"

"Old Howes told Pa we scared his cows last Saturday. He said we made them run so much he couldn't get them to let down their milk Saturday night."

"This creek bottom isn't his. Old Howes doesn't own anything down here except that pasture on the other side of the fence. We haven't even been on the other side of the fence this year, have we?"

"I haven't seen Old Howes's cows all summer. If I did see them, I wouldn't run them. He just told Pa that because he doesn't want us to come swimming in the creek."

Pieces of dead bark and curled chips suddenly came floating down the creek. Somewhere up there the trash had broken loose from a limb or something across the water. I held my arms V-shaped and caught the bark and chips and threw them out of the way.

Les said something, diving down to pull up a dead limb. The muck on the bottom of the creek was so deep we could not take a step without first pulling our feet out of the sticky mud; otherwise we would have fallen flat on our faces in the water. The muck had a stink like a pig pen.

Les threw the big limb out of sight.

"If Old Howes ever comes down while we're here and tells us to get out of the creek, let's throw muck at him. Are you game, Jack? Wouldn't you like to do that to him just once?"

"That's what we ought to do to him, but we'd better not, Les. He would go straight and tell my folks, and your pa."

"I'm not scared of Old Howes," Les said, making a face. "He hasn't got me buffaloed. He wouldn't do anything. He's scared to tell anybody. He knows we'd catch him some time and mud-cake him."

"I don't know," I said. "He told on me that time I caught his drake and put it in that chicken run of his."

"That was a long time—" Les stopped and listened.

Somebody had stepped on a dead limb behind the bushes. The crack of the wood was loud enough to be heard above the splashing and gurgling of the creek.

"What's that?" both of us said.

"Who's that?" Les asked me.

"Listen!" I said. "Duck down and be quiet."

Behind the bushes we could hear someone walking on dead twigs and dry leaves. Both of us squatted down in the water until only our heads were above it.

"Who is it?" Les whispered to me.

I shook my head, holding my nose under the water.

The yellow water swirled and gurgled through the tree roots beside us. The roots had been washed free of earth by the high waters many years before, and now they were old-looking and covered with bark.

Les squatted lower and lower until only his eyes and the top of his head were showing. He held his nose under the water with both hands. The water was high, and its swiftness and muddy-heaviness made gurgling sounds that echoed up and down the creek.

Suddenly the bushes parted, and Jenny came through. When Les saw her, his eyes popped open and he jerked his head above the water to get his breath. The noise he made when the water bubbled scared all three of us for a moment.

Jenny was Old Howes's daughter. She was about our age, possibly a year or two older.

Les saw her looking at our clothes hanging on the bushes. He nudged me with his elbow.

"What are you doing down here?" Les said gruffly, trying to scare her.

"Can't I come if I want to?"

"You can't come down here when we're in swimming. You're not a boy."

"I can come if I wish to, smarty," Jenny said. "This creek doesn't belong to you."

"It doesn't belong to you, either," Les said, making a face. "What are you going to do about that?"

"All right," Jenny said, "if you are going to be so mean about it, Leslie Blake, I'll take your clothes and hide them where you'll never find them again as long as you live. What are you going to do about that?"

Jenny reached for the clothes. She grabbed Les's pants and my shirt and union suit.

Les caught my arm and pulled me towards the bank. We couldn't hurry at first, because we had to jerk our feet out of the muck before we could move at all.

"Let's duck her, Jack," Les whispered. "Let's give her a good ducking. Come on."

We crawled up the bank and caught Jenny just as she was starting to run through the bushes with our clothes. Les locked his arms around her waist and I caught her arms and pulled as hard as I could.

"I'll scream!" Jenny said. "If you don't stop, I'll scream at the top of my lungs. Papa is in the pasture, and he'll come right away. You know what he'll do to both of you, don't you?"

"We're not afraid of anybody," Les said, scowling and trying to scare her.

I put my hand over her mouth and held her with one arm locked around her neck. Together we pulled and dragged her back to the bank beside the creek.

"Don't you want to duck her, Jack?" Les said. "Don't you think we ought to? She's been telling Old Howes tales about us. She's a tattletale tit."

"We ought to duck her, all right," I said. "But suppose she goes and tells on us about that?"

"When we get through ducking her, she won't tell any more tales on us. We'll duck her until she promises and crosses her heart never to tell anybody. She's the one who's been throwing dead limbs into the creek every day. I'll bet anything she's the one who's been doing it."

Jenny was helpless while we held her. Les had her around the waist with both arms, and I still held her neck locked in the crook of my left arm. She tried to bite my hand over her mouth, but every time she tried to hurt me, I squeezed her neck so hard she had to stop.

I was a little afraid to duck Jenny, because once we had ducked a colored boy named Bisco, and it had almost drowned him. We ducked Bisco so many times he couldn't breathe, and he became limp all over. We had to stretch him out on the ground and roll him over and over, and all the time we were doing that, yellow creek water was running out of his mouth. I was afraid we might drown Jenny. I didn't know what would happen to us if we did that.

"I know what let's do to her, Les," I said.

"What?"

"Let's mud-cake her."

"What's the matter with ducking her? It will scare her and make her stop throwing dead limbs into the creek. It'll stop her from telling tales about us, too."

"We'd better not duck her, Les," I said. "Remember the

time we ducked Bisco? We nearly drowned him. I don't want anything like that to happen again."

Les thought a while, looking at Jenny's back. She was kicking and scratching all the time, but she couldn't begin to hurt us, and we had her so she couldn't get loose.

"All right," Les said. "We'll mud-cake her then. That's just as good as ducking, and it'll teach her a lesson. It'll make her stop being a tattletale tit."

"She's going to tell on us anyway, so we'd better do a good job of it this time. But it ought to make her stop throwing dead limbs into the swimming hole, anyway."

"She won't tell on us after we get through with her," Les said. "She won't tell anybody. She won't even tell Old Howes. Ducking and mud-caking always stops kids from telling tales. It's the only way to cure it."

"All right," I said. "Let's do it to her. She needs ducking or mud-caking, or something. Somebody has got to do it to her, and we're the right ones to make a good job of it. I'll bet she won't bother us again after we get through with her."

Les threw Jenny on the ground beside the bank, locking her arms behind her back and holding her face in the earth so she couldn't make any noise. Les had to straddle her neck to keep her still.

"Take off her clothes, Jack," Les said. "I've got her. She can't get away as long as I'm holding her."

I reached down to pull off her dress, and she kicked me full in the stomach with both feet. When I fell backward and tried to sit up, there was no breath left in me. I opened my mouth and tried to yell at Les, but I couldn't even whisper.

"What's the matter, Jack?" Les said, turning his head and looking at me.

I got up on both knees and doubled over, holding my stomach with both arms.

"What's the matter with you, Jack?" he said. "Did she kick you?"

Les's back had been turned and he had not seen what Jenny had done to me.

"Did she kick me!" I said weakly. "It must have been her, but it felt like a mule. She knocked all of the wind out of me."

"Sit on her legs, then," Les said. "She can't kick you if you do that."

I ran down to the side of the creek and came back with a double handful of yellow muck. When I dug it out of the creek, it had made a sucking sound, and the odor was worse than any that ever came out of a pig pen. The muck in the creek stank worse than anything I had ever smelled. It was nothing but rotted leaves and mud, but it smelled like decayed eggs and a lot of other things.

I got Jenny's dress off and tossed it on the bushes so it would not get covered with muck. Les was able to hold her arms and cover her mouth at the same time by then, because she was not nearly so strong as either of us.

"She's got underwear on, Les," I said.

"Sure she has," Les said. "All girls wear underclothes. That's what makes them so sissy."

"You're not talking about me, are you?" I said, looking at him. "Because if you are—"

"I'm talking about her," Les said. "I know you have to wear the stuff because your people make you do it. But girls like to have it on. They don't want to go without it. That's why girls are so sissy."

"All right," I said, "but don't try to get nasty with me, because I'll—"

"You won't do anything, so shut up. Hurry and take her clothes off."

"Are we going to strip her naked?" I said.

"Sure," Les said. "We've got to. We can't mud-cake her if we don't strip her, can we?"

"I know that," I said, "but suppose Old Howes came down and saw us—"

"Old Howes wouldn't do nothing but spit and slip up in it. Who's scared of him, anyway? I'm not."

After we had struggled with Jenny a while longer, and after her underclothes were finally off, Les said he was tired of holding her. He was puffing and blowing as if he had been running five miles without stopping to rest.

I took Jenny's arms and put my hand over her mouth and sat on her neck. Les picked up a big handful of muck and threw it at her. The muck struck her on the stomach, making a sound like slapping water with a plank. He threw another handful. It splattered all over us.

While Les was running to the creek for another load, I turned Jenny over so he could smear some on her back. She did not struggle any more now, but I was afraid to release my grip on her arms or to take my hand off her mouth. When I had turned her over, she lay motionless on the ground, not even kicking her feet any more.

"This'll fix her," Les said, coming back with his hands and arms full of yellow muck. "She's had it coming to her for a long time. Maybe it'll stop her from being a tattletale tit."

He dropped the mass on her back and ran back for some more.

"Rub that in while I'm getting another load, Jack," he said. "That's what she needs to make her stop throwing dead limbs into the creek. She won't tell any more tales about us, either."

I reached over and with one hand smeared the muck up and down Jenny's back, on her legs, and over her arms and shoulders. I tried not to get any of it in her hair, because I knew how hard it was to try to wash it out with yellow creek water.

"Turn her over," Les said, dropping down beside us with a new load of muck. "We're just getting started on her."

I turned Jenny over again, and she did not even try to get loose from me. Les had begun to spread the muck over her, rubbing it into her skin. He took a handful and smeared it over her legs and thighs and stomach. Then he took another handful and rubbed it over her shoulders and breasts. Jenny still did not attempt to move, though she squirmed a little when Les rubbed the most tender parts of her body with the mass of rotted leaves and mud. Most of the time she lay as still as if she had been sound asleep.

"That's funny," I said.

"What's funny?" Les asked, looking up.

"She's not even trying to get loose now."

"That's because she's foxy," Les said. "She's just waiting for a good chance to break away. Here, let me hold her awhile."

Les took my place and I picked up a handful of muck and began spreading it over her. The muck was not sticky any longer, and when I smeared it on her, it felt slick and smooth. When my hands moved over her, I could feel that her body was much softer than mine, and that parts of her were very soft. When I smeared the slick mud over her breasts, it felt so smooth and soft that I was afraid to touch her there again. I glanced at her face, and I saw her looking at me. From the way she looked at me, I could not help thinking that she was not angry with us for treating her like that. I even thought that perhaps if Les had not been there she would have let me mud-cake her as long as I wished to.

"What are you doing, Jack?" Les said. "That's a funny way to spread muck on her."

"We've got enough on her, Les. Let's not put any more on her. Let's let her go home now. She's had enough."

"What's the matter with you?" Les said, scowling. "We're not half finished with her yet. We've got to put another coat of muck on her."

Jenny looked up when Les said that, and her eyes opened wider. She did not have to speak to tell me what she wished to say.

"That's enough, Les," I said. "She's a girl. That's enough for a girl."

I don't know, but somehow I believed that Les felt the same way I did, only he did not want to admit it. Now that we had stripped her and had smeared her all over with muck, neither of us could forget that Jenny was a girl. We had treated her as though she were a boy, but she remained a girl still.

"If we let you up now, will you promise not to tell?" Les asked her.

Jenny nodded her head, and Les dropped his hand from her mouth.

We both expected to hear her say what she was going to do, and what she was going to tell, because of the way we had treated her; but the moment she was freed she sat up quickly and tried to cover herself with her arms, without once speaking.

As soon as we saw that she was not going to call for Old Howes, Les and I ran to the creek and dived head-on into it. We squatted down until only our heads were showing above the water and began scrubbing the muck off us. Jenny looked at us, covering herself as much as she could.

She still had not said anything to us.

"Let's get dressed and run for home," Les said. "Pa would tear me up into little pieces if he caught me down here now, with her like that."

Jenny covered her eyes while we dashed out of the water and grabbed our clothes. We ran behind the bushes to dress. While we were standing there, we could hear Jenny splashing in the creek, scrubbing the muck from her.

Les had only his shirt and pants to put on, and he was ready to go before I could even straighten out my union suit. He buckled his pants and started backing off with his shirt tail hanging out while he tried to find the right buttons for the buttonholes. I had been in such a hurry to jump in the creek when we first came that I had tangled my union suit, and when I would get the arms straight, the legs would be wrong side out. Les kept backing farther and farther away from me.

"What's the matter?" he said. "Why don't you hurry?"

"I can't get this union suit untangled."

"That's what you get for wearing underclothes in summer."

"I can't help it," I said, "and you know it."

"Well it's not my fault, is it?"

"Aren't you going to wait for me?"

"I can't, Jack," he said, backing away faster. He suddenly turned around and began running. "I've got to go home."

"I thought you said you weren't scared of Old Howes, or of anybody else!" I yelled after him, but if he heard me, he pretended not to understand what I had said.

After Les had gone, I took my time. There was no need to hurry, because I was certain that no matter what time I got home, Jenny would tell Old Howes what we had done to her, and he would come and tell my folks all about it. I wished to have plenty of time to think of what I was going to say when I had to face everybody and tell the truth.

Jenny had left the creek by the time I was ready to button my shirt, and she had only to slip her underclothes over her head and to put on her dress to be ready to go home. She came through the bushes while I was still fumbling with my shirt buttons.

"What's the matter, Jack?" she asked, smiling just a little. "Why didn't you run off with Leslie?"

"I couldn't get dressed any quicker," I said.

I was about to tell her how my union suit was so tangled that I had had to spend most of the time struggling with that, but I thought better of saying it.

She came several steps closer, and I started to run from her.

"Where are you going?" she said. "What are you running for?"

I stopped, turned around, and looked at Jenny. Now that she was dressed, she looked the same as she had always looked. She was the same in appearance, but somehow I knew that she was not the same, after what had happened beside the creek. I could not forget the sensation I had felt when my hands, slick with mud, had touched the softness of her body. As I looked at her, I believed I felt it again, because I knew that without the dress and the underclothes she would always remain the same as she was when I had first touched her.

"Why don't you wait for me, Jack?" she said.

I wanted to run away from her, and I wanted to run to her. I stood still while she came closer.

"But you're going to tell, aren't you? Aren't you going to tell what we did to you?"

She had come to where I stood, and I turned and walked beside her, several feet away. We went through the bushes and out through the woods to the road. There was no one in sight, and we walked together until we reached her house.

Just before we got to the gate I felt my hand touch hers. I don't know, but somehow, whether it was true or not, I believed she had taken my hand and held it in hers for a moment. When I suddenly looked to see, because I wanted to know if she really had taken my hand and squeezed it, she turned the other way and went through the gate.

I waited in the middle of the road until she walked up the front steps and crossed the porch. She stopped there a moment and brushed her dress with her hands, as if she wanted to be sure that there was no muck clinging to it. When she opened the door and went inside, I was not certain whether she had glanced at me over her shoulder, or whether I merely imagined she had. Anyway, I believed she had, because I felt her looking at me, just as I was sure that she had held my hand for a moment.

"Jenny won't tell," I said, running up the road towards home. "Jenny won't tell," I kept saying over and over again all the way there.

Where the Girls Were Different

Nobody could ever explain why it was, but the girls who lived in all the other parts of Oconee County were different from the ones in our section. All the girls in Woodlawn, which was the name of the town where we lived, were the sassy kind. They were always slapping and biting, too. I suppose all of them were tomboys. That's about the worst thing you can call a girl when she is growing up. But the girls who lived at Macy's Mill, and at Bradford, and especially in Rosemark, were a different kind. We used to talk about it a lot, but nobody knew why it was.

"How are the Rosemark girls different?" I asked Ben, when we were talking about it one day.

"Jiggers," he said, "I don't know exactly."

I never went around like Ben and the other boys did, because I had a girl who lived in town and I went to see her two or three times a week, and that was as many nights as my folks would let me go out. They did not believe in letting me go all over the county to see girls. So I stayed at home and went to see Milly pretty often.

But those girls in other parts of the county were not like the ones at home. The other boys used to go off nearly every night to see girls at Bradford and Macy's Mill and Rosemark, Rosemark especially. I don't know why that was, either. There was just something about those girls down in Rosemark that made a man act kind of funny.

Ben went down to Rosemark three or four nights every week to see girls. The strange part of it was he rarely went to see the same girl more than once. He had a new girl almost every time he went down there. The other boys did the same way, too. They had a new girl every time. Shucks, I had to stay at home and go to see Milly and nobody else.

I asked Ben in a confidential way what it was about the

34

girls down in Rosemark that made them so different from the ones around home.

Ben was my first cousin and I didn't mind asking him personal questions.

"Jumping jiggers!" he said, "You've never been down there to see a Rosemark girl, have you, Fred?"

I told him how it was about Milly. I did not want to go to see her all the time, but I never had a chance to go down to Rosemark like the other boys.

"Well," he said, "you are a fool to go to see her all the time. She's just like all the other girls around here. You've got to go down to Rosemark and see some real girls. They're not like these around Woodlawn."

"What are they like, Ben?" I asked him again. Everybody said they were different, but nobody ever said in what way they were different. "What do they do that's different?"

"Well, that's hard to say. They act just like all girls do —but they are different."

"Tell me about them, Ben."

"I'll tell you this," he said. "You got to be careful down there. Every girl in Rosemark that's got an old man or a brother is watched pretty close. I guess that's because they are pretty wild."

"How are they wild?" I asked him. "What do they do?"

"That's hard to say, too. You can't put your finger on it, exactly—they are just different. You've got to go down there."

"But how can I get a date with one of them?"

"Oh, that's easy," he said. "You just go down there some Sunday night and wait outside a church until they come out. Then pick one out and ask her to let you take her home. That's the way to do it."

"Can I do that? Would she let me take her home?"

"Sure. That's one way they are different. You can get any girl you want if you ask her before somebody else does. You go down Sunday night and try it. Jiggers, Fred, you got to see those Rosemark girls! The ones around here aren't fit to fool with."

I hated to tell my folks the next Sunday night that I was going to see Milly when I wasn't, but—gee—I had to go down to see those girls in Rosemark. I drove the old car down and got there just before the churches let out.

I picked out the biggest church I could find and waited outside the door. I figured that the bigger the church the better chance I would have because there would be more girls in it.

Shucks, it wasn't any trouble at all. I asked the first girl that came out by herself if I could take her home and she said, "Sure," just as nice. Gee, this was the way to see girls. Up at home the girls acted sassy about letting you take them home. These Rosemark girls were different that way.

"Where do you live?" I asked her.

"About five miles out in the country," she said. She talked nice and soft like all girls would if they knew what was good for themselves. "Do you want to take me?"

"You bet I do," I told her. "I don't care how far it is."

Five miles wasn't anything. It was fine, because I'd have a longer time to find out about her. I could tell right away she was different.

She showed me the way to go and we started out. The old car was running good, but there was no hurry to get there.

"What's your name?" I asked her.

"Betty," she said.

No girl up in Woodlawn had a name like that. I was beginning to see why all the boys at home liked to come down to Rosemark.

Gee, she was different! She sat real close to me and sort of hunched her shoulders forward like she was awfully pleased. I had never seen a girl act so nice in all my life. She put her arm through mine and sort of leaned against me a lot and I had a devil of a time trying to keep our old car in the road.

As soon as we got outside of town a little distance another automobile came up behind us real close. I drew over to the side of the road so it could pass, but whoever was running it wouldn't try to pass. I thought that was funny, because I was driving only about ten miles an hour and making a lot of dust behind, too. The man who was running the other car was crazy not to pass us and go on ahead.

Betty sat closer and closer all the time and was so nice I didn't know what to make of it.

"The devil," I said to myself, "I'm going to take a chance and kiss her."

That was a reckless thing to do, because all the girls I knew up home were pretty particular about things like that and they didn't mind slapping you good and hard, either.

Gee whiz! I reached down and kissed her and she wouldn't let me stop. That old car rocked from one side of the road to the other as dizzy as a bat. I couldn't see to steer it because Betty wouldn't let me stop kissing her, and I had to wait until we ran into a ditch almost before I knew which way to turn the wheel. Gee whiz! The girls in Rosemark were certainly different, all right.

Finally I got away from her and got back my breath and saw which way to guide the old car.

"Don't you like to kiss me?" she asked, hunching her shoulders forward again like a girl does when she wants to make you feel funny.

Shucks, I couldn't let her get away with that! I reached my right arm around her and kissed her as hard as I could. She didn't mind how rough I was, either. I guess she liked it, because she put both of her arms around my neck and both of her legs across my lap and hugged the life out of me. *Gee whiz!* I didn't know girls did like that! Ben said the girls down in Rosemark were different, but I didn't expect anything like this to happen to me. Holy cats! The girl was sitting on my lap under the steering wheel and I was having a devil of a time trying to kiss her for all I was worth and steer the old car at the same time.

Right then I knew I was coming down to Rosemark again as soon as I could get away. Ben sure knew what he was talking about when he said the girls down here were nothing like the ones at home. Shucks, those old girls up at home were not anything.

By this time we had got to the place where she lived and she looked up just at the right moment to tell me where to turn in. Before I could steer the old car into the driveway the automobile that had been behind us all the time beat me to it and I had to jerk on the brakes to keep from running smack into it.

"Who is that fool?" I asked Betty.

"That's Poppa," she said.

I started to say something pretty mean about him for doing a thing like that but I thought I had better not if I wished to come back to see her. I was going to ask her for a lot of dates as soon as we got in the yard.

She took her arms down and moved over to her side of the seat just as if nothing in the world had happened.

I shut off the engine and reached over and opened the door for her. She jumped out just as nice and I was right behind her. I got as far as the running board when the man who had beaten us to the gate pushed me back into the seat. He shoved me so hard I hurt my spine on the steering wheel.

"Where do you think you're going?" he growled at me. "Start up that car and get away from here and don't ever let me see you again."

He came closer and shoved me again. I then saw for the first time that he had a great big rusty pistol with a barrel about a foot and a half long in his other hand.

"If I ever catch you around Betty again I'll use this gun on you," he said.

I didn't lose any time getting away from there. I hated to go away and not see Betty again, so I could ask her for a lot of dates next week, but it wouldn't do any good to have dates if I couldn't come back.

I drove the old car back home and went to bed. I knew now why Ben never went to see the same girl twice. He knew what he was doing, all right. And I knew why he said the girls down there were different. They sure were different. It was hard to say what the difference was, but if you ever went down there it was easy to feel it all over yourself.

The next morning I saw Ben and told him about going down to Rosemark the night before. After a while I told him about the way Betty kissed me and how she wanted to sit on my lap under the steering wheel.

"What!" he said, his eyes wide open.

I told him about it again, and how she wouldn't let me stop kissing her and how she put her legs across my lap.

"Jumping jiggers, that's funny. None of them ever let me kiss her, and none of them ever sat on my lap."

"Gosh, Ben," I said, "then why did you think they were different?"

"Jumping jiggers!" he said again, frowning all over. "I don't know."

time I got as far as the milking shend when the man
had gone to the gate paused my foot line the post
spoon me up until my spine on the struggle

Horse Thief

I DIDN'T STEAL Lud Moseley's calico horse.

People all over here been trying to make me out a thief, but anybody who knows me at all will tell you that I've never been in trouble like this before in all my life. Mr. John Turner will tell you all about me. I've worked for him, off and on, for I don't know exactly how many years. I reckon I've worked for him just about all my life, since I was a boy. Mr. John knows I wouldn't steal a horse. That's why I say I didn't steal Lud Moseley's, like he swore I did. I didn't grow up just to turn out to be a horse thief.

Night before last, Mr. John told me to ride his mare, Betsy. I said I wanted to go off a little way after something, and he told me to go ahead and ride Betsy, like I have been doing every Sunday night for going on two years now. Mr. John told me to take the Texas saddle, but I told him I didn't care about riding saddle. I like to ride with a bridle and reins, and nothing else. That's the best way to ride, anyway. And where I was going I didn't want to have a squeaking saddle under me. I wasn't up to no mischief. It was just a little private business of my own that nobody has got a right to call me down about. I nearly always rode saddle Sunday nights, but night before last was Thursday night, and that's why I didn't have a saddle when I went.

Mr. John Turner will tell you I'm not the kind to go off and get into trouble. Ask Mr. John about me. He has known me all my life, and I've never given him or anybody else trouble.

When I took Betsy out of the stable that night after supper, Mr. John came out to the barnyard and asked me over again if I didn't want to take the Texas saddle. That mare, Betsy, is a little rawboned, but I didn't mind that. I told Mr. John I'd just as lief ride bareback. He said it was all right with him if I wanted to get sawn in two, and for me to go ahead and do like I pleased about it. He was stand-

39

ing right there all the time, rubbing Betsy's mane, and trying to find out where I was going, without coming right out and asking me. But he knew all the time where I was going, because he knows all about me. I reckon he just wanted to have a laugh at me, but he couldn't do that if I didn't let on where I was headed. So he told me it was all right to ride his mare without a saddle if I didn't want to be bothered with one, and I opened the gate and rode off down the road towards Bishop's crossroads.

That was night before last—Thursday night. It was a little after dark then, but I could see Mr. John standing at the barnyard gate, leaning on it a little, and watching me ride off. I'd been plowing that day, over in the new ground, and I was dog-tired. That's one reason why I didn't gallop off like I always did on Sunday nights. I rode away slow, letting Betsy take her own good time, because I wasn't in such a big hurry, after all. I had about two hours' time to kill, and only a little over three miles to go. That's why I went off like that.

II

Everybody knows I've been going to see Lud Moseley's youngest daughter, Naomi. I was going to see her again that night. But I couldn't show up there till about nine-thirty. Lud Moseley wouldn't let me come to see her but once a week, on Sunday nights, and night before last was Thursday. I'd been there to see her three or four times before on Thursday nights that Lud Moseley didn't know about. Naomi told me to come to see her on Thursday night. That's why I had been going there when Lud Moseley said I couldn't come to his house but once a week. Naomi told me to come anyway, and she had been coming out to the swing under the trees in the front yard to meet me.

I haven't got a thing in the world against Lud Moseley. Mr. John Turner will tell you I haven't. I don't especially like him, but that's to be expected, and he knows why. Once a week isn't enough to go to see a girl you like a lot, like I do Naomi. And I reckon she likes me a little, or she wouldn't tell me to come to see her on Thursday nights, when Lud Moseley told me not to come. Lud Moseley thinks if I go to see her more than once a week that maybe we'll take it into our heads to go get married without giving him a chance to catch on. That's why he said I couldn't come to his house but once a week, on Sunday nights.

He's fixing to have me sent to the penitentiary for twenty years for stealing his calico horse, Lightfoot. I reckon he knows good and well I didn't steal the horse, but he figures he's got a good chance to put me out of the way till he can get Naomi married to somebody else. That's the way I figure it all out, because everybody in this part of the country who ever heard tell of me knows I'm not a horse thief. Mr. John Turner will tell you that about me. Mr. John knows me better than that. I've worked for him so long he even tried once to make me out as one of the family, but I wouldn't let him do that.

So, night before last, Thursday night, I rode off from home bareback, on Betsy. I killed a little time down at the creek, about a mile down the road from where we live, and when I looked at my watch again, it was nine o'clock sharp. I got on Betsy and rode off towards Lud Moseley's place. Everything was still and quiet around the house and barn. It was just about Lud's bedtime then. I rode right up to the barnyard gate, like I always did on Thursday nights. I could see a light up in Naomi's room, where she slept with her older sister, Mary Lee. We had always figured on Mary Lee's being out with somebody else, or maybe being ready to go to sleep by nine-thirty. When I looked up at their window, I could see Naomi lying across her bed, and Mary Lee was standing beside the bed talking to her about something. That looked bad, because when Mary Lee tried to make Naomi undress and go to bed before she did, it always meant that it would take Naomi another hour or more to get out of the room, because she had to wait for Mary Lee to go to sleep before she could leave. She had to wait for Mary Lee to go to sleep, and then she had to get up and dress in the dark before she could come down to the front yard and meet me in the swing under the trees.

III

I sat there on Betsy for ten or fifteen minutes, waiting to see how Naomi was going to come out with her sister. I reckon if we had let Mary Lee in on the secret she would have behaved all right about it, but on some account or other Naomi couldn't make up her mind to run the risk of it. There was a mighty chance that she would have misbehaved about it and gone straight and told Lud Moseley, and we didn't want to run that risk.

After a while I saw Naomi get up and start to undress.

I knew right away that that meant waiting another hour or longer for her to be able to come and meet me. The moon was starting to rise, and it was getting to be as bright as day out there in the barnyard. I'd been in the habit of opening the gate and turning Betsy loose in the yard, but I was scared to do it night before last. If Lud Moseley should get up for a drink of water or something, and happen to look out toward the barn and see a horse standing there, he would either think it was one of his and come out and lock it in the stalls, or else he would catch on it was me out there. Anyway, as soon as he saw Betsy, he would have known it wasn't his mare, and there would have been the mischief to pay right there and then. So I opened the barn door and led Betsy inside and put her in the first empty stall I could find in the dark. I was scared to strike a light, because I didn't know but what Lud Moseley would be looking out the window just at that time and see the flare of the match. I put Betsy in the stall, closed the door, and came back outside to wait for Naomi to find a chance to come out and meet me in the swing in the yard.

It was about twelve-thirty or one o'clock when I got ready to leave for home. The moon had been clouded, and it was darker than everything in the barn. I couldn't see my hand in front of me, it was that dark. I was scared to strike a light that time, too, and I felt my way in and opened the stall door and stepped inside to lead Betsy out. I couldn't see a thing, and when I found her neck, I thought she must have slipped her bridle like she was always doing when she had to stand too long to suit her. I was afraid to try to ride her home without a lead of some kind, because I was scared she might shy in the barnyard and start tearing around out there and wake up Lud Moseley. I felt around on the ground for the bridle, but I couldn't find it anywhere. Then I went back to the stall door and felt on it, thinking I might have taken it off myself when I was all excited at the start, and there was a halter hanging up. I slipped it over her head and led her out. It was still so dark I couldn't see a thing, and I had to feel my way outside and through the barnyard gate. When I got to the road, I threw a leg over her, and started for home without wasting any more time around Lud Moseley's place. I thought she trotted a little funny, because she had a swaying swing that made me slide from side to side, and I didn't have a saddle pommel to hold on to. I was all wrought up about getting away from there without getting caught up with, and I didn't think a thing about it. But I got home all right and slipped the halter off and put her in the stall. It was around one or two o'clock in the morning then.

The next morning after breakfast, when I was getting ready to catch the mules and gear them up to start plowing in the new ground again, Lud Moseley and three or four other men, including the sheriff, came riding lickety-split up the road from town and hitched at the rack. Mr. John came out and slapped the sheriff on the back and told him a funny story. They carried on like that for nearly half an hour, and then the sheriff asked Mr. John where I was. Mr. John told him I was getting ready to go off to the new ground, where we had planted a crop of corn that spring, and then the sheriff said he had a warrant for me. Mr. John asked him what for, a joke or something? And the sheriff told him it was for stealing Lud Moseley's calico horse, Lightfoot. Mr. John laughed at him, because he still thought it just a joke, but the sheriff pulled out the paper and showed it to him. Mr. John still wouldn't believe it, and he told them there was a mix-up somewhere, because, he told them, I wouldn't steal a horse. Mr. John knows I'm not a horse thief. I've never been in any kind of trouble before in all my life.

They brought me to town right away and put me in the cellroom at the sheriff's jail. I knew I hadn't stole Lud Moseley's horse, and I wasn't scared a bit about it. But right after they brought me to town, they all rode back and the sheriff looked in the barn and found Lud Moseley's calico horse, Lightfoot, in Betsy's stall. Mr. John said things were all mixed up, because he knew I didn't steal the horse, and he knew I wouldn't do it. But the horse was there, the calico one, Lightfoot, and his halter was hanging on the stall door. After that they went back to Lud Moseley's and measured my foot tracks in the barnyard, and then they found Betsy's bridle. Lud Moseley said I had rode Mr. John's mare over there, turned her loose, and put the bridle on his Lightfoot and rode him off. They never did say how come the halter came to get to Mr. John's stable, then. Lud Moseley's stall door was not locked, and it wasn't broken down. It looks now like I forgot to shut it tight when I put Betsy in, because she got out someway and came home of her own accord sometime that night.

Lud Moseley says he's going to send me away for twenty years where I won't have a chance to worry him over his youngest daughter, Naomi. He wants her to marry a widowed farmer over beyond Bishop's crossroads who runs twenty plows and who's got a big white house with fifteen rooms in it. Mr. John Turner says he'll hire the best lawyer in town to take up my case, but it don't look like it will do much good, because my footprints are all over Lud Moseley's barnyard, and his Lightfoot was in Mr. John's stable.

I reckon I could worm out of it someway, if I made up my mind to do it. But I don't like to do things like that. It would put Naomi in a bad way, because if I said I was there seeing her, and had put Betsy in the stall to keep her quiet, and took Lightfoot out by mistake in the dark when I got ready to leave—well, it would just look bad, that's all. She would just have to say she was in the habit of slipping out of the house to see me after everybody had gone to sleep, on Thursday nights, and it would just look bad all around. She might take it into her head some day that she'd rather marry somebody else than me, and by that time she'd have a bad name for having been mixed up with me —and slipping out of the house to meet me after bedtime.

Naomi knows I'm no horse thief. She knows how it all happened—that I rode Lud Moseley's calico horse, Lightfoot, off by mistake in the dark, and left the stall door unfastened, and Betsy got out and came home of her own accord.

Lud Moseley has been telling people all around the courthouse as how he is going to send me away for twenty years so he can get Naomi married to that widowed farmer who runs twenty plows. Lud Moseley is right proud of it, it looks like to me, because he's got me cornered in a trap, and maybe he will get me sent away sure enough before Naomi gets a chance to tell what she knows is true.

But, somehow, I don't know if she'll say it if she does get the chance. Everybody knows I'm nothing but a hired man at Mr. John Turner's, and I've been thinking that maybe Naomi might not come right out and tell what she knows, after all.

I'd come right out and explain to the sheriff how the mix-up happened, but I sort of hate to mention Naomi's name in the mess. If it had been a Sunday night, instead of night before last, a Thursday, I could—well, it would just sound too bad, that's all.

If Naomi comes to town and tells what she knows, I won't

say a word to stop her, because that'll mean she's willing to say it and marry me.

But if she stays at home, and lets Lud Moseley and that widowed farmer send me away for twenty years, I'll just have to go, that's all.

I always told Naomi I'd do anything in the world for her, and I reckon this will be the time when I've got to prove whether I'm a man of my word, or not.

Candy-Man Beechum

IT WAS TEN MILES out of the Ogeechee swamps, from the sawmill to the top of the ridge, but it was just one big step to Candy-Man. The way he stepped over those Middle Georgia gullies was a sight to see.

"Where you goin', Candy-Man?"

"Make way for these flapping feet, boy, because I'm going for to see my gal. She's standing on the tips of her toes waiting for me now."

The rabbits lit out for the hollow logs where those stomping big feet couldn't get nowhere near them.

"Don't tread on no white-folks' toes, Candy-Man," Little Bo said. "Because the white-folks is first-come."

Candy-Man Beechum flung a leg over the rail fence just as if it had been a hoe handle to straddle. He stood for a minute astride the fence, looking at the black boy. It was getting dark in the swamps, and he had ten miles to go.

"Me and white-folks don't mix," Candy-Man told him, "just as long as they leave me be. I skin their mules for them, and I snake their cypress logs, but when the day is done, I'm long gone where the white-folks ain't are."

Owls in the trees began to take on life. Those whooing birds were glad to see that setting sun.

The black boy in the mule yard scratched his head and watched the sun go down. If he didn't have all those mules to feed, and if he had had a two-bit piece in his pocket, he'd have liked to tag along with Candy-Man. It was Saturday night, and there'd be a barrelful of catfish frying in town that evening. He wished he had some of that good-smelling cat.

"Before the time ain't long," Little Bo said, "I'm going to get me myself a gal."

"Just be sure she ain't Candy-Man's, boy, and I'll give you a helping hand."

He flung the other leg over the split-rail fence and struck out for the high land. Ten miles from the swamps to the top

46

of the ridge, and his trip would be done. The bushes whipped around his legs, where his legs had been. He couldn't be waiting for the back-strike of no swamp-country bushes. Up the log road, and across the bottom land, taking three corn rows at a stride, Candy-Man Beechum was on his way.

There were some colored boys taking their time in the big road. He was up on them before they had time to turn their heads around.

"Make way for these flapping feet, boys," he shouted. "Here I come!"

"Where you going, Candy-Man?"

They had to do a lot of running to keep up with him. They had to hustle to match those legs four feet long. He made their breath come short.

"Somebody asked me where I'm going," Candy-Man said. "I got me a yellow gal, and I'm on my way to pay her some attention."

"You'd better toot your horn, Candy-Man, before you open her door. Yellow gals don't like to be taken by surprise."

"Boy, you're tooting the truth, except that you don't know the whyfor of what you're saying. Candy-Man's gal always waits for him right at the door."

"Saturday-night bucks sure have to hustle along. They have to strike pay before the Monday-morning whistle starts whipping their ears."

The boys fell behind, stopping to blow and wheeze. There was no keeping up, on a Saturday night, with the seven-foot mule skinner on his way.

The big road was too crooked and curvy for Candy-Man. He struck out across the fields, headed like a plumb line for a dishful of frying catfish. The lights of the town came up to meet him in the face like a swarm of lightning bugs. Eight miles to town, and two more to go, and he'd be rapping on that yellow gal's door.

Back in the big road, when the big road straightened out, Candy-Man swung into town. The old folks riding, and the young ones walking, they all made way for those flapping feet. The mules to the buggies and the sports in the middle of the road all got aside to let him through.

"What's your big hurry, Candy-Man?"

"Take care my dust don't choke you blind, niggers. I'm on my way."

"Where to, Candy-Man?"

"I got a gal what's waiting right at her door. She don't like for to be kept waiting."

"Better slow down and cool those heels, Candy-Man, because you're coming to the white-folks' town. They don't like niggers stepping on their toes."

"When the sun goes down, I'm on my own. I can't be stopping to see what color people be."

The old folks clucked, and the mules began to trot. They didn't like the way that big coon talked.

"How about taking me along, Candy-Man?" the young bucks begged. "I'd like to grab me a chicken off a henhouse roost."

"Where I'm going I'm the cock of the walk. I gouge my spurs in all strange feathers. Stay away, black boy, stay away."

Down the street he went, sticking to the middle of the road. The sidewalks couldn't hold him when he was in a hurry like that. A plateful of frying catfish, and he would be on his way. That yellow gal was waiting, and there was no time to lose. Eight miles covered, and two short ones to go. That sawmill fireman would have to pull on that Monday-morning whistle like it was the rope to the promised land.

The smell of the fish took him straight to the fish-house door. Maybe they were mullets, but they smelled just as good. There wasn't enough time to order up a special dish of fins.

He had his hand on the restaurant door. When he had his supper, he would be on his way. He could see that yellow gal waiting for him only a couple of miles away.

All those boys were sitting at their meal. The room was full of hungry people just like him. The stove was full of frying fish, and the barrel was only halfway used. There was enough good eating for a hundred hungry men.

He still had his hand on the fish-house door, and his nose was soaking it in. If he could have his way about it, some of these days he was going to buy himself a whole big barrel of catfish and eat them every one.

"What's your hurry, Candy-Man?"

"No time to waste, white-boss. Just let me be."

The night policeman snapped open the handcuffs, and reached for his arms. Candy-Man stepped away.

"I reckon I'd better lock you up. It'll save a lot of trouble. I'm getting good and tired of chasing fighting niggers all over town every Saturday night."

"I never hurt a body in all my life, white-boss. And I

sure don't pick fights. You must have the wrong nigger, white-boss. You sure has got me wrong. I'm just passing through for to see my gal."

"I reckon I'll play safe and lock you up till Monday morning just the same. Reach out your hands for these cuffs, nigger."

Candy-Man stepped away. His yellow gal was on his mind. He didn't feel like passing her up for no iron-bar jail. He stepped away.

"I'll shoot you down, nigger. One more step, and I'll blast away."

"White-boss, please just let me be. I won't even stop to get my supper, and I'll shake my legs right out of town. Because I just got to see my gal before the Monday-morning sun comes up."

Candy-Man stepped away. The night policeman threw down the handcuffs and jerked out his gun. He pulled the trigger at Candy-Man, and Candy-Man fell down.

"There wasn't no cause for that, white-boss. I'm just a big black nigger with itching feet. I'd a heap rather be traveling than standing still."

The people came running, but some of them turned around and went the other way. Some stood and looked at Candy-Man while he felt his legs to see if they could hold him up. He still had two miles to go before he could reach the top of the ridge.

The people crowded around, and the night policeman put away his gun. Candy-Man tried to get up so he could be getting on down the road. That yellow gal of his was waiting for him at her door, straining on the tips of her toes.

"White-boss, I sure am sorry you had to go and shoot me down. I never bothered white-folks, and they sure oughtn't bother me. But there ain't much use in living if that's the way it's going to be. I reckon I'll just have to blow out the light and fade away. Just reach me a blanket so I can cover my skin and bones."

"Shut up, nigger," the white-boss said. "If you keep on talking with that big mouth of yours, I'll just have to pull out my gun again and hurry you on."

The people drew back to where they wouldn't be standing too close. The night policeman put his hand on the butt of his gun, where it would be handy, in case.

"If that's the way it's to be, then make way for Candy-Man Beechum, because here I come."

A Day's Wooing

WHEN TUFFY WEBB woke up that morning, the first thing he saw was his new straw hat hanging on the back of the cane-bottomed chair beside the bed. The red, orange, and blue silk band around the hat looked as bright in the sunshine as the decorations in the store windows in town on circus day. He reached out and felt the rough crown and brim, running his fingers over the stiff brown straw. He would never have to step aside for anybody, in a hat like that. That was all he needed, to get the world by the tail.

"Maybe that won't knock a few eyes out!" Tuffy said, throwing off the covers and leaping to the floor. "They'll all be cross-eyed from looking at it."

He placed the hat carefully on his head and walked over to the mirror on the wall. The new straw hat looked even finer Sunday morning than it had Saturday night when he tried it on in the store.

"When Nancy sees this lid, she'll come tumbling," Tuffy said, stepping back and tilting the hat a little on one side of his head and winking at himself under the brim.

He walked past the mirror several times, free and easy in his loose knee-length nightshirt, turning his eyes to see himself in passing. It was easy to get up courage in a hat like that.

"I could have all the girls after me now if I wanted them," he said to himself.

Tuffy got dressed in a hurry and made a fire in the cookstove. He pulled the hat down carefully over his head so it would not fall off and hit the floor while he was cooking breakfast.

During all the time he was in the kitchen he kept thinking to himself that he would not have to keep back much longer after that, not after Nancy saw him in his new hat. She would be tickled to death to marry him now, the first time she saw him walking up to her house with the straw sailor tilted over one ear, sort of like a cock's comb that always looked like it was going to fall off but never did.

After breakfast Tuffy had to drive the cows to the pasture on the other side of the creek because it had become time for them to have a change of feed, and the Johnson grass over there was ready for grazing.

He started off with his hat on his head, but he got to thinking about it and finally decided he ought to leave it at the house. Sometimes a yearling took to heels and bolted off into a thicket, and he did not like to think of taking any chances of having the hat fall off into the briers and mud, and maybe being trampled by the cows. Now that he was thinking about it, he remembered seeing a cow chew up a straw hat once and swallow it.

He hurried back to the house and hung the hat on the cane-bottomed chair beside the bed.

Tuffy got back from the pasture at about eleven o'clock, and he changed his clothes right away, putting on his coat and the hat. After that he still had almost an hour to wait before he could leave home, because he did not wish to get to the Millers' while they were eating dinner. If he did that, one of the Millers would be certain to say that he had got there then to get something to eat.

He walked out on the porch and leaned against the railing for a while. The sun was almost directly overhead, and there was not a cloud in sight. He knew he could not have chosen a finer day to go calling on Nancy in a new straw hat. There was not a single drop of rain in the whole sky above.

"This would be a dandy time to speak to Nancy about us getting married," he said, going out into the yard and walking first around the chinaberry tree and then around the willow. "All I'd have to do would be to ask her, and I know already what Nancy'll say. She's just as willing as I am, and she knows it. It wouldn't do her any good to try to show otherwise."

Tuffy leaned against the willow, picking at the bark with his thumbnail.

"If I go right up to her and say, 'Nancy, how about me and you hitching up together?' she'll say, 'When, Tuffy?' and I'll say, 'The sooner the better suits me.' Then she'll say, 'Nothing would please me more.' That's all there will be to it, and it'll be all planned and settled. All I'll have to do is get a preacher to marry us, and then me and

Nancy'll be married for a fare-you-well. Getting married wouldn't take long, maybe no longer than tomorrow noon. We'll probably start right in tomorrow some time. That's none too soon for me, and I know it won't be none too soon for Nancy."

Tuffy went over and sat on the woodpile.

"I'll go over there to old Berry Miller's and walk right up to where they're all sitting on the porch and lose no time about it. Berry'll probably want to know what I came for, all dressed up like this in a coat and a new straw hat, and I'll soon tell him, too. 'Well,' I'll say, 'I came to marry Nancy, Berry. How do you like that? Me and her are getting married right off.' He won't scare me a bit, no matter what he says. He might have some little fault to find to begin with, but there's no objection I know about that's good enough to stop me from going ahead and getting married to Nancy. I'll walk right up to where she's sitting on the porch and put my arm around her and show those Millers I mean business and don't mean maybe."

Tuffy picked up a piece of stovewood and began tearing splinters out of it with his fingernails. He piled the splinters in a little stack between his feet.

"If old Berry Miller makes any show of getting his bristles up, I'll reach right down and kiss her in front of all the Millers, and then pick her up and walk off with her without so much as looking back at them even once. That'll show Berry that when I set out to get married, I don't let nothing in the whole wide world stop me. Those Millers can't put the scare into me."

He hurled the stick of stovewood across the yard. It narrowly missed hitting one of his hens asleep in a dust hole under the chinaberry tree. The hen woke up and ran squawking for her life. The other chickens got scared and followed her under the house.

Tuffy took out his handkerchief and wiped the sweatband of his new straw hat. It was a scorching hot day, especially out in the sun at midday, and the heavy wool coat had never felt so tight before.

"If I had thought to get the license yesterday, me and Nancy could have got married today," he said disgustedly, kicking at the ground. "Now, why didn't I think about that yesterday? I'll have to wait till tomorrow before I can go to the courthouse now."

He got up and walked to his car. He had not intended

getting inside, because it was still about half an hour too
soon for him to leave, but he could not wait any longer.
He would have to drive around ten or fifteen miles an
hour, and maybe stop at the creek and wait awhile, but
he was too anxious to be on his way to Nancy's house
to wait around home any longer. He started the car and
drove off, pushing the new straw hat tightly on his head so
the wind could not blow it off.

It was half past twelve o'clock when Tuffy Webb drove
up to the Berry Miller place and stopped his car in the
shade. He had not got there a minute too soon, because
the Millers were at that minute coming out on the porch from
the dinner table. It was getting hotter all the time, and Tuffy
sat in his car for several minutes trying to cool off before
getting out and going up to the house.

Before looking at the Millers on the porch, he took out
his handkerchief and tried to wipe off some of the perspiration that trickled down his cheeks and down the back of his
neck. When he finished, he took off his hat and wiped the
sweatband good and dry.

Old man Berry Miller waved at him from the porch. One
of the Miller boys rose up on his elbow from the porch floor
to see what Tuffy was doing.

Tuffy got out and walked stiff and erect across the yard
to the house. He was uncomfortable all over, and it made
his face flush red when he realized what he was doing there.
The Millers had a way of staring at him that made him forget what he was doing sometimes.

"Come on in on the porch out of that hot sun and have
a slice of watermelon fresh out of the bottom of the well,"
Berry Miller said,. "There's not much left, but what there
is, you're welcome to it. It's only the leavings."

Berry brushed away the flies with his hat. They swarmed
around the porch for a few moments and then settled back
again on the rinds and watermelon seed scattered about on
the floor.

"Well, howdy, folks," Tuffy said.

One of the boys waved his arm at Tuffy, and both the
girls giggled. Berry's wife rocked back and forth in her chair
without saying a thing. A watermelon seed had stuck to her
chin and was drying there. Tuffy wondered why nobody told
her to brush it off.

"Mighty hot day today," he said, flushing red again when
his eyes swept the porch and saw the two girls.

Their white dresses were starched so stiffly that they looked as if corset stays had been sewn into the cloth.

"Sort of," Berry said. "Can't complain, though. Heat's due us."

The boys on the other end of the porch sat up.

"What are you all dressed up for, Tuffy?" Henry asked him. "Going somewhere?"

Tuffy's eyes dropped and he dug the toe of his shoe into the sandy yard.

Nancy, the oldest girl, giggled again.

Tuffy looked up quickly, hoping to see her plain.

"You're dressed up fit to kill, ain't you, Tuffy?" Henry said.

Berry kicked a piece of watermelon rind off the porch.

"That's a mighty fine-looking straw hat you've got on there, Tuffy," Berry said. "You must have bought that at a big store somewhere, and paid a lot of money for it, in the bargain. A pretty all-colored band like that don't come on everyday hats."

Tuffy nodded his head.

The other Miller boy on the porch, Clyde, scraped up a handful of watermelon seed and began shooting them between his fingers. Presently one of the seeds hit Tuffy in the face, making him jump as if somebody had taken a slingshot and hit him in the eye with a hickory nut. Tuffy would not look at Clyde, because he and Clyde never had got along any too well. They had had several fist fights already that summer.

Berry's wife moved to and fro in her rocker, looking disinterestedly at Tuffy. The watermelon seed had dried on her chin and was stuck there for good. He glanced at her, and their eyes met. Whenever she looked at him, it always made Tuffy feel as if she were looking at some object directly behind him. She had never spoken a word to him in all her life.

Nancy smoothed out the skirt of her starched white dress, bending the stiff hem down over her knees. He could still see where her stockings ended on her legs. Nancy's sister looked at Tuffy and giggled.

"I just thought I'd drop by," Tuffy said at last. "I didn't have much else to do today."

"Had any watermelon today so far?" Berry asked him.

"No," Tuffy said.

"If you don't mind eating the leavings," Berry said, waving

his hand at the rind-strewn porch, "you're welcome to have some."

Tuffy looked to see what Nancy was doing, but he could not see the expression on her face when his eyes were watching the black and white garter-line on her legs. She bent the starched hem over again, but when she leaned back, it straightened out again and her legs above the stocking tops were as bold as ever.

"Ain't you staying?" Berry asked.

"I don't care if I do," Tuffy said. "I was just riding around, and I thought I'd stop by."

Clyde picked up a piece of rind and threw it at the tree in the yard.

"It's been quite a while since I last saw you all dressed up like that," Berry said. "If I remember correctly, the last time was at the baptizing over at the church about a month ago. Wasn't you all dressed up that day, Tuffy?"

Nancy giggled and hid her face against her sister's shoulder. Tuffy blushed again.

"I didn't have this new hat then, though," he said.

"So you didn't!" Berry said. "That is right, aint it? That hat looks so natural on your head that I forgot all about it. But you did have on a coat that day, didn't you?"

Tuffy nodded, digging the toe of his shoe into the yard.

"I wish you had come by a little sooner," Berry said. "It's pretty late now to get any of the good part of the melons. The leavings ain't much to offer a body. But of course, now, if you ain't particular, just go ahead and help yourself."

One of the boys kicked a piece of rind across the porch and it fell into the yard near Tuffy's feet. He looked at it, all covered with sand.

"Where you going, Tuffy?" Henry asked him.

"Nowhere much," Tuffy said.

"How about me and you going off a piece?" Henry said, winking. "There's some easy pickings on Sunday afternoons over beyond Hardpan."

Tuffy glanced at Nancy. There was a peculiar look on her face that made him uneasy. The garter-line on her legs wavered in his sight when she rocked slightly in her chair. He dropped his eyes to the ground once more.

"I don't reckon I can right now," he told Henry, blushing red all over.

The two girls began whispering to each other. Every once

in a while Nancy glanced up at Tuffy, and then she quickly looked the other way.

Tuffy took off his hat and fanned his face with it.

"It's about time to do some thinking about a little fox-hunting, ain't it, Tuffy?" Berry said. "These nights now are beginning to have a little nip in them, along about midnight, and the foxes will be running before you know it. Anyway, it don't hurt none to sort of warm up the hounds. They've been laying around here all summer and have got as lazy as can be. I been thinking lately of going out some night pretty soon and giving them a short run."

Tuffy nodded his head, but he did not say anything.

"I been thinking about making a trade of some kind for a couple more hunters," Berry said. "That Blackie is still a little lame from last year, and that Elsie is weighted down with pups. That Rastus looks like he takes to cold-trailing more and more every year, and I'm a little upset. I don't reckon it would do any harm to make a trade of some kind, if I could find exactly what I'm looking for. I've got a mule that's stove-up pretty bad, and I figure I need hunting dogs a lot more now than I do a blamed stiff-legged mule."

Tuffy glanced up at Nancy, looking as if he were bursting with something to say. He looked at her so desperately that she reached over and bent the starched hem and held it down. He could do no more than swallow hard and flush red all over. It made his skin feel prickly under the heavy coat when she looked at him.

Clyde sat up and slid down to the edge of the porch. He sat swinging his legs over the edge and looking at Tuffy. Tuffy was becoming more and more uncomfortable. He had been standing for half an hour in the hot sun, and he caught himself swaying on his feet.

"I sure admire that new straw hat of yours, Tuffy," Berry said. "Especially that all-colored pretty band around it."

Tuffy looked desperately at Nancy, and then glanced at the rest of the family. Everyone, except Nancy, stared right back at him. Nancy hung her head when their eyes met.

Henry crossed the yard between him and the house, taking something out of his pocket. He began pulling on it, making it snap like elastic. When he stopped in front of Tuffy, Tuffy looked to see what Henry was playing with. It was a girl's garter, bound in pink silk, and tied in a bow with a red rosebud sewn into it. Tuffy jumped as if he had been pricked with a pin.

Tuffy backed off, taking short steps towards his car.

"Not going so soon?" Berry said. "Why, it hardly seems like more than a minute ago when you got here."

Tuffy stopped. Henry had kept up with him, snapping the garter. He put one end against Tuffy's arm, pulled the other end back a foot or two, and turned it loose. Tuffy jumped when the elastic stung him.

"Where you going, Tuffy?" Henry asked him.

Tuffy looked at the porch where Nancy was. She had sat upright in the chair, leaning slightly forward, and stopped rocking. The starched flare of her skirt had straightened out once more, and he was glad she wore yellow garters.

He started backing away again. Henry followed him, springing the elastic rosebud-trimmed garter at him.

"Let's me and you ride over beyond Hardpan, Tuffy," Henry urged. "It won't be no trouble at all to find us a couple of girls, and we can make a lot of headway on a Sunday afternoon. How about it, Tuffy, huh?"

Tuffy backed away faster, shaking his head. When he got to the tree where his car was, he turned around and jumped into the front seat.

Nancy ran into the house. She could be heard crying all the way to the back porch.

When Tuffy got his car started, Berry got up and walked out into the yard. He watched the automobile disappear over the hill, trying to turn his ear away from Henry's cursing.

"I hate to see a man rush off like that," Berry said. "I'd have swore he came here for some purpose to begin with."

He stood with his back to the house while Clyde left the porch and crossed the field to get some more watermelons to cool in the bottom of the well.

A Woman in the House

MAX CLOUGH was getting along well until Elam went away over the week end. Max had his winter's wood in, his house was sawdust-banked against the frost, and there was a good supply of pumpkin wine in the cellar. He had settled himself for a good three months' rest and he thought Elam had done the same. Both of them knew that winter was coming, as the ground was frozen every morning, and the sun was already beginning to set in the intervale by two o'clock.

But Elam went away over the week end. He went off without coming to tell Max about it, and he left early Saturday morning before it was light enough for Max to see him go.

Only a few days before, Max had gone across the road and talked for an hour or longer, but Elam had not said a word about going away. He had not even said that he was thinking of taking a short trip. They had talked about how dear money was getting to be, and how much improved the mail delivery was since Cliff Stone had taken over the route through the intervale, and about the prospects for a new State highroad through the town. But Elam had said nothing about his going away over the week end. That was the reason why Max was upset Saturday morning when he went across the road to see Elam a moment, and found that the house was locked and that the shades were drawn.

"When a man gets to be thirty-six years old," Max said, looking sharply at the closed dwelling, "he ought to have sense enough to stay at home, instead of going off for week ends in Lewiston and throwing away dear money for lodging and what-not. Elam might possess a little sense about minor things, but he hasn't got the sense he was born with when it comes to throwing away dear money in Lewiston. Nobody but a plain fool would go to Lewiston and give a woman five-ten dollars for her bed."

He went back across the road and up the slope to his own house, glancing up the intervale and down it, as if he expected to see Elam coming home. But he knew Elam would not come home until Sunday afternoon. He had gone away before like that, and each time he had stayed the two whole days. He knew Elam would not return until the next afternoon.

Max's farm and buildings were on the eastern slope of the intervale, and Elam Stairs' were on the western slope. Between them was the Yorkfield town road. The only advantage Elam had, Max admitted, was longer sunlight in winter. The sun set on Max's house by two o'clock in midwinter, while Elam had an hour's longer sun. But Max was well enough pleased with his place, because he knew that his eastern slope grew better green peas. His land was well watered the year around; in midsummer, Elam's fields became dry.

For the rest of the afternoon and far into the evening, Max could not get off his mind Elam's trip. He did not envy him the week end in Lewiston, because he knew exactly how much it would cost, but he did not wish for Elam to slip off as he did three or four times a year. It upset his carefully planned living. He could do nothing while Elam was absent from home. He had become accustomed to seeing Elam somewhere about his farm at almost any hour of the day when he looked over at the western slope, and when Elam was not there, Max was at a loss to know how to continue doing his work. And, besides that, when Elam was away, there was always the possibility that he would not come back alone. He knew he could never get over Elam's bringing home somebody with him.

They had talked such things over many times. Each time Elam went to Lewiston, he came home talking about the women he had seen on the streets and in the lodginghouses. That was one reason why Max did not like for Elam to go there. Sooner or later, he knew Elam would bring home a woman.

"The women aren't suited to our lives, Elam," Max told him once. "You on your western slope, and me on my eastern slope, live as people ought to live. Just as soon as a man brings home a woman, his house is too small a space for him to live in, eight rooms or twelve rooms. Married, or housekeeper, there's no difference. It's a woman, and there's always trouble under a roof when you mix the two sexes. I wish to stay just as I am. I wish to live peacefully, and my wish is to die the same way."

"Can't somehow always agree with you, Max," Elam said, shaking his head. "You've got a lot of sense; good, sane, horse sense, Max. But God was required to make woman. Why! do you know that before there were any women, the men were fixing to tear the world to pieces unless women were provided?"

"Why?" Max asked.

"Why?" Elam said. "Why! because the men wouldn't stand for it any longer, that's why. They had to have housekeepers, or if they couldn't be had, just wives. There's a world of difference between the two, but at bottom they both are women, and that's what man had to have. Otherwise, us men would have to do all the sewing and cooking."

"Have always got along fairly well doing my own labor," Max said. "Never had a woman to do my work for me. I don't wish to have one in the house to cause trouble."

"Well," Elam said, "they may cause some trouble. I'm willing to grant you that. But taking all in all, their good points pretty well overbalance the bad ones. God was compelled to make them, and I don't aim to disuse anything that is provided. Guess I wish to get all there is in this life to make use of. No sense in letting it go to waste, or to have somebody else take my share, and his too. I wish to have all of everything that's due me."

Max was not convinced then, and he was still firm in his belief that a man could live more happily and peacefully in his house alone. None of the times when Elam tried to make Max admit that women were a necessary part of existence did he succeed. Max was steadfast in his determination to live his life apart from women.

Now that Elam had gone away on another of his quarterly trips to Lewiston, Max was afraid once again that he would bring home a housekeeper. On each occasion before, he had been on edge the whole time Elam was away, and he was never able to calm himself until he could go over and see that Elam had not brought back a housekeeper. He would not even take Elam's word for it. He would first ask Elam if he came home alone, and then he would go from room to room, looking behind doors and into closets, until he was satisfied in his own mind that there was no woman in the house. After that, he would feel better. He could then go back to his own house with a calm mind.

But Elam was away again for the week end, and Max could not sit still. He could not eat his meals, and he could not sleep. He sat beside his window looking across to the western slope, his window raised several inches in case there should be the sound of an automobile in the intervale. He sat by the window all day Saturday, Saturday evening, and Sunday.

Late Sunday afternoon, when Max knew it was time for Elam to come back home, he heard Elam's automobile coming up the intervale. He knew it was Elam's car, and he knew he could not sit there another minute. He jumped up and found his hat and coat and started down the front doorstep.

The road was not within sight of Max's house, as there was a grove of birch trees down there, and he could not see the automobile. He heard Elam drive into his lane, however, and he waited and listened until the sound of the motor stopped abruptly in the barn.

There was something about the abruptness of the sound's stopping that caused him to pause on the doorstep. The motor was shut off the moment the car entered the barn, and then there was complete silence again in the intervale. Not even the rumbling sound of Elam closing the barn doors could be heard. Max wondered if Elam could be in such a hurry to get into his house that he had not waited to close the barn doors. He could not think of any reason to explain that. A man who was in such a great hurry to get into his house would certainly have something of importance coming up. Max thought about that, but he could think of no reason why a man would fail to close the barn doors.

He sat down on the doorstep and waited. He turned his head from side to side, allowing each ear to try to detect some sound in the intervale. Surely, he thought to himself, Elam had not gone and lost his mind. But he could think of no other reason for Elam's failure to close the barn doors. A man who drove his automobile into the barn and then left the doors open would certainly be foolish, and Elam had not been known theretofore as a foolish man. Elam knew better than to leave the barn doors open when evening was coming.

The sun in the intervale was dim and gray. A bank of gray

clouds had risen in the northwest, and before long there
would be no more sunshine. It was after three o'clock then,
and the sun had already set on the western slope. Max had
become accustomed to two o'clock sunsets on the eastern
slope of the intervale, but when it set before three o'clock on
the western slope, he was unprepared for it.

During all the time that he had been sitting on his doorstep, Max had hoped that Elam would come over to see him
and tell him about the trip to Lewiston. Elam had always
done that. Each time Elam had gone away for the week end
in Lewiston, he had come home Sunday afternoon, had
slammed shut the barn doors, and then had walked down the
lane and up the slope and told Max what he had seen and
what he had done in Lewiston. It was long past the time
for him to come, and he had not even closed the barn doors.
Max could not sit still and wait for Elam any longer. He
got up and started down the slope towards the road.

When he reached the road, he stopped a moment and
looked up towards Elam's farm and buildings. The barn door
was wide open, and the automobile stood there exposed to
the weather. There was no one to be seen about the house,
but the shades had been opened, and the entrance door
was ajar. Something was wrong, Max thought. Something had
happened to Elam this time on his trip to Lewiston.

Standing beside Elam's mail box, Max looked up the slope
towards the house. It was only a few hundred yards away,
and he could see everything as plainly as if he had been
standing on the doorstep. The white paint was whiter than
ever in the gray twilight of the intervale, and the green
trim was brighter than the grass in midsummer. Max stood
looking at the place, waiting.

He had been staring at the house for ten minutes without seeing a single sign of Elam, when suddenly Elam appeared at one of the windows. He raised the window with
a single thrust of his arm, and stuck out his head. Immediately another window was raised, on the opposite corner of the
house, and a woman stuck out her head. They looked at
each other for a moment, and then both withdrew their
heads and the windows were lowered so quickly that Max
was certain that the glass had been cracked. For a few
seconds he did not believe what his eyes had seen. He would
not believe that he had actually seen a woman in Elam's
house. But slowly the realization came to him that he had
seen a woman there, a young woman with a full body and

yellow hair, and he stepped backward off Elam's land into the public road.

After what he had seen, Max did not know whether to stand there looking at the house, or whether to turn and go back up the slope to his own place. He knew he would never again set foot on Elam's land, however; he had already made up his mind never to have anything more to do with Elam Stairs. He did not even wish to speak to him again. He could never forgive Elam for having brought home a woman from Lewiston.

While he stood in the road trying to make up his mind about what he was going to do, the woman he had first seen in the window came running around the corner of the house. Max stared unbelievingly. Then a moment later came Elam, running faster than Max thought it possible for anyone to run. He was overtaking the yellow-haired young woman, two strides to her one, and if they had not turned the other corner of the house at that moment, he would have seen Elam grab her. Elam had his coat off, and the woman's dress was open down her back all the way to her waist. The woman was laughing, but Elam was not.

Max waited another five minutes, wishing to be there in case they again ran around the house. Then he turned and walked slowly up the eastern slope of the intervale. The sight of a woman at Elam's house made him wish to go over there and drive her out of the intervale, but he knew he could never do that. Elam would not allow him to run her away. Elam would protect her, and send him back across the road.

By the time that Max had reached his own house, he had definitely made up his mind about what he was going to do. He was going to take a trip himself the following week end. He was going down to Lewiston Saturday morning and stay there until Sunday afternoon. And while he was there he would do the same things that Elam had done.

"Elam Stairs isn't the only man in the intervale who can bring home a woman," he said, taking his seat beside the window and looking over at the western slope where the sun had set. He raised the window several inches so that he might hear any sound that was audible in the intervale. "Will hire me a housekeeper in Lewiston and bring her back here, too. Elam Stairs has an hour's more sunshine because his farm and buildings are on the western slope, and he thinks he can have even more advantage with a housekeeper.

But he shan't. I'll show him that I can go to Lewiston and maybe get a finer-looking housekeeper than he's got."

Max hitched his chair closer to the window.

"Guess I'll chase mine thrice around the house when I bring her here," he said. "And it might be a good plan to wait till she gets right in the middle of changing her clothes to start chasing her, instead of starting after her like Elam did when she only had her dress unfastened down her back. Guess Elam Stairs will see as how I made a pretty smart deal, when he looks out his window some fine day and sees me chasing a naked housekeeper, and gaining on her three strides to her one. He chased his woman once around the house, so I'll chase mine thrice around, with maybe an extra time to show him what I can do when I get good and started."

Max paused to look out across the intervale. While he watched Elam's house, he began going through the motions of washing his hands.

"Don't guess Elam's idea was so bad, after all. Can't think of much to quarrel about with a Lewiston young woman in the house, and not having to pay her five-ten dollars for her bed over the week end."

Soquots

FOR THE PAST four or five years I've made it a practice to go down to Jake Upham's house every Thursday afternoon after work and get some soquots. I'd go down to Jake's and we'd stand around and talk for a while and then I'd pick out as many of them as I wanted. Jake always had plenty on hand, summer and winter alike, because he liked them just as much as I did, and he'd always tell me to help myself to all I could carry. Jake and I had been friendly like that ever since both of us moved to town to work in the stave mill, and if there was something of mine he wanted to use or borrow, I'd always tell him to go ahead and help himself. After I'd picked out the soquots, I'd bring them home and hand them over to my wife, Lorrie, and she'd get busy and fix them for us. I guess she liked them just as much as I did, because she always stood on the front porch and acted real pleased when she saw me bringing them home on Thursday afternoons. Nobody's better than Lorrie when it comes to fixing soquots, and I got so I always looked forward to Thursday nights, because I could count on Lorrie fixing all I wanted. If you've ever had soquots fixed just right, you know how good they can be.

Yesterday morning, though, which was a Thursday, and just when I was getting ready after breakfast to leave the house and go to work at the stave mill, Lorrie's cousin, Oscar Strude, who'd been staying at the house for the past month or longer, said he didn't like soquots and told Lorrie not to fix any more.

That made me mad.

There'd been bad blood building up between Oscar and me ever since he'd come to town and said he thought he'd stay awhile. I don't mind kinfolks visiting one another from time to time, and maybe spending the night if they've come a long way, because there's nothing that'll give you a better inner feeling than sitting around with some kinfolks and speculating about some of the others who're missing. I like to visit kinfolks myself once in a while, but it's stretching kinship 'way too far when somebody moves in like Oscar Strude and just stays and stays and stays.

I was boiling mad in no time at all after Oscar'd said that about the soquots.

"If you don't like it here, why don't you move on some place else?" I said to him. "You've been here longer than kinship calls for, anyhow."

"I didn't say I didn't like it here," Oscar told me. "I like it here better than anywhere else I know. What I said was that I don't like those queer things you bring here to the house every Thursday. Why can't you bring home some chickens or rabbits or fish while you're about it?"

"A man who don't like soquots ought to be taken out and shot," I told him.

"You can't talk like that to my kinfolks," Lorrie spoke up. "That's something I won't stand for, Pete Ellrod. I put up with what you say to me, but I won't stand for that kind of talk about a single one of my kith and kin."

"You wouldn't have to put up with it," I told her, "if he'd pick himself up and get out of the house and stay out. I've been thinking about the way he hangs around here all the time, anyhow. It don't look good to me at all. He might be your second cousin once removed, but I'd say that's stretching kinship 'way too far for any man's peace of mind."

"I'll invite Oscar to stay as long as he wants to," she said right away. "The day will never come when anybody can say that I put one of my kinfolks out of the house."

"If nobody else can say it, I sure can," I told her.

"If Oscar goes," she said right back, "I'm going, too."

"Going where?"

"Going off with him."

That stopped me right up short. I'd never heard Lorrie talk to me like that before in all the seven years we've been married and living together, and I just didn't know what to make of it. I'd come to take it for granted that my ways suited her, and I knew her ways suited me, and in the past when some little something went wrong, we'd have words, but we always made up soon after with no lingering hard feelings. But that was before Oscar Strude came along. Things had been taking a different turn ever since he moved in, and even a blind man could see which way things went. I'd made allowances for Lorrie's turning a man's head now and then, because with all her looks it was to be expected, but I'd never made allowance for a somebody like Oscar Strude. When Lorrie told me in the beginning that he was her second cousin once removed, it sounded a little peculiar to me, because there ought to be a limit somewhere to how far kinship stretches, but I knew how much store she put in kinship, and I just kept quiet about it at the time. Oscar had been off in the army for two or three years, and he said he was just taking his time looking around and getting the feel of things before he settled down somewhere and went to work. If there was one thing I hoped for more than anything else all that time, it was that the army would be sorry it let him go, and would come and get him and send him off to the other side of the world again.

"The trouble with you, Pete," Oscar said to me, "is that you think you can run all of creation the exact way you want it run. It's time you found out that you're not the only human being in this world, and that millions of other people have rights, too. It's people like you who've got to wake up and realize that a man can't live a selfish life in this day and time."

"Now," Lorrie said, nodding her head up and down and showing how much she took up for Oscar, "you can make up your mind here and now, Pete Ellrod. What are you going to do about it?"

I'd never been so baffled before in all my life.

"That's a peculiar way for you to talk, Lorrie," I said to her. "What in the world's got into you, anyhow? First you side with Oscar when he says he don't like soquots, and then you say you'll leave and go off with him if I put him out of the house. Don't I count any more at all?"

"No," she said, shaking her finger at me like she always does when she's set on having her own way. "Not when you say you'll put my kinfolks out of the house. My kinfolks can stay and visit me as long as they please."

"But that one there don't work a lick," I tried to tell her. "He don't do a blessed thing but hang around the house all the time eating up the meals and wearing out the bed. I'm the one who goes to work at the mill every day and earns all the money that's spent. Looks to me like I'd have the right to say who eats and sleeps in my own house. Besides that," I told her, "it don't please me one bit to have him staying here in the house with you all day while I'm off at work in the mill."

"You'd better shake a leg and get to work now," Oscar said, laughing about it, "or you'll be late punching in and they'll hop off some of your pay."

It was getting late, and I knew it. I found my hat and hurried down to the stave mill. I got there just in time to go on the eight-thirty shift.

All morning long I thought about what Lorrie and Oscar had said, and it got me so worried I could hardly do my work. The foreman, Stan Manley, came by in midafternoon and asked what was troubling me. Stan knew I was worried about something, because my lathe kept on getting jammed up and I'd have to pull the switch and clean it out every once in a while. At first I wasn't going to tell him, because everybody knows how private matters, once they are made known, can get gossiped about from one end of the mill to the other, but I knew I had to talk to somebody about my worries, and so I went ahead and told him about Lorrie and Oscar Strude.

"Looks to me like your wife's cousin just don't like soquots," Stan said, laughing a little. "I've heard it said that a lot of people have to learn to like them, just like some folks have to learn to like oysters."

"There's one thing for sure in this world I'm not going to do," I told him, "and that's learning Oscar Strude to like soquots."

"Well, Pete," he said with a serious look, "a simple little thing like that might make all the difference in the world. A man has to do some peculiar things every now and then to please his wife and keep her satisfied. I can see how there'd be people in the world who don't like soquots. When you stop and think about it, there even may be people in the world who've never seen soquots or handled them, much less know what they are or where they come from. If your wife's cousin spent most of his life back up there in those Big Smoky hills, he might never get accustomed to the way we live down here."

"He came from the Big Smoky country," I told Stan, "but there's more to it than that. Any blind man could see that, Stan."

"Maybe you're right, Pete," he admitted, sitting down on the bench and thinking for a while. Presently he looked up at me and nodded. "There could be a heap more to it than that, Pete, just like you said. What cousin does he claim to be to her? First, second, or third?"

"Second cousin once removed."

"That's bad," Stan said, shaking his head.

"Why's it bad?"

"Because it's close enough kin for one thing today, and far enough removed for another thing tomorrow. You'd better punch out and quit work for the day and go home now. That's the wise thing for you to do under the circumstances. I've always found that it's a lot smarter to have a showdown with my wife in the daytime than it is after dark. Somehow it makes a big difference in the outcome."

I left the mill right away and hurried home. Lorrie was sitting in the big chair crying.

"What's the matter, Lorrie?" I asked her.

"Oscar's gone!" she said, crying more.

"Gone where?"

"Gone for good!"

"Well, that's sure taking a little hint in a big hurry," I said, feeling pleased about it. "From the way he talked this morning, I feared he was going to stay forever and a day. What made him leave in such a great hurry?"

"He said I was siding with you."

"How did that come about, Lorrie?"

"He asked me what soquots were, and I told him I didn't know exactly and that he'd have to ask you. That's when he said I was siding with you. Then he packed up and left."

I knew right away that the best thing that ever happened to me was Lorrie's not knowing what soquots were, because if she had known, and had told Oscar, they wouldn't have had that falling-out, and he would still be there eating up meals and wearing out the bed. As it was, now she'd have to quit boasting about Oscar being her second cousin once removed and using that as an excuse. From then on he was going to be her second cousin far removed. I had peace of mind come over me for the first time in more than a month.

I pulled up a chair and gave her a big hug.

"Now, Pete—" she said, wiping away the tears.

I moved closer and kissed her good.

"Lorrie, are you real sure you don't know what soquots are?" I asked her after a while.

"Pete, I never did know what they were, exactly," she said, looking straight at me in a convincing way. "I always meant to ask you, but somehow I just never did."

"Lorrie, do you want me to tell you now what they are?" I asked her.

"No," she said, shaking her head to let me know she meant it. "I don't want to know what they are, Pete. It'll be a big help if anybody ever asks me again."

I sat there in the chair feeling good all over, because I knew if anybody else, kinfolks or no kinfolks, ever came around and asked her what soquots were, I wouldn't have to worry for a single minute. I was satisfied that was going to give me peace of mind for a long time to come.

Yellow Girl

NELL STOOD at the kitchen window packing the basket of eggs. She arranged eleven white eggs carefully, placing the cottonseed hulls between them and under them so that none would be broken. The last one to be put into the basket was large and brown and a little soiled. She dipped into the pan of soap and warm water and wiped it dry with a fresh dish towel. Even then she was not pleased with the way it looked, because it was brown; all the other eggs in the basket were as white as September cotton bolls.

Behind her in the room, Myrtie was scouring the two frying pans with soapy water and a cloth dipped in sand. Nell laid down the brown egg and called Myrtie.

"Here's another of those big brown eggs, Myrtie," she said, pointing at the egg. "Do you have any idea where they come from? Have you seen any strange hens in the yard? There must be a visiting hen laying eggs in the chicken house."

Myrtie laid down the frying pan and came over to the little table by the window. She picked up the large brown egg and looked at it. The egg no longer looked brown. Nell looked at the egg again, wondering why in Myrtie's hands it had apparently changed color.

"Where do these brown eggs come from, Myrtie?" she asked. "There was one last week, and now today there's this. It was in the basket Mr. Willis brought in from the chicken house, but he said he forgot to notice which nest he took it from."

Myrtie turned the egg over in her hands, feeling the weight of it and measuring its enormous circumference with her fingers.

"Don't ask me, Miss Nell," Myrtie said, staring at the egg. "I've never seen a flock of Leghorns yet, though, that didn't lay a few brown eggs, sometime or other. Looks like it just can't be helped."

71

"What do you mean, Myrtie? What on earth are you talking about? Of course Leghorns lay white eggs; this is a brown egg."

"I'm not saying the Leghorns lay them, Miss Nell, and I'm not saying they don't. Those old Buff Orpingtons and Plymouth Rocks and Domineckers lay funny-looking eggs, too, sometimes. I wouldn't take on so much about finding one measly brown egg, though. I've never seen anybody yet, white or colored, who knew how such things happen. But I wouldn't worry about it, Miss Nell. Brown eggs are just as good as white eggs, to my way of tasting."

Nell turned her back on Myrtie and looked out the window until the girl had returned to the other side of the kitchen. Nell disliked to talk to Mytrie, because Myrtie pretended never to know the truth about anything. Even if she did know, she would invariably evade a straightforward answer. Myrtie would begin talking, and talk about everything under the sun from morning to night, but she would never answer a question that she could evade. Nell always forgave her, though; she knew Myrtie was not consciously evading the truth.

While the girl was scouring the pans, Nell picked up the egg again and looked at it closely. Mrs. Farrington had a flock of Dominique chickens, and she gathered in her chicken house eggs of all sizes, shapes, and colors. But that was to be expected, Mrs. Farrington had said, because she had two old roosters that were of no known name or breed. Nell had told Mrs. Farrington that some of her Dominiques were mixed-bred, and consequently they produced eggs of varying sizes, shapes, and colors; but Mrs. Farrington continued to lay all the blame on her two roosters, because, she said, they were a mixture of all breeds.

Once more Nell dipped the brown egg into the pan of water and wiped it with the fresh dish towel, but the egg remained as brown as it was at first. The egg was clean by then, but soap and water would not alter its size or change its color. It was a brown egg, and it would remain brown. Nell gave up, finally; she realized that she could never change it in any way. If she had had another egg to put into the basket in its place, she would have laid it aside and substituted a white one; but she only had a dozen, counting the brown one, and she wished to have enough to make an even exchange with Mrs. Farrington when she went over after some green garden peas.

Before she finally placed the egg in the basket with the others she glanced out the window to see where Willis was. He was sitting in the crib door shelling red seed corn into an old wooden lard pail.

"I'm going over to Mrs. Farrington's now to exchange these eggs for some peas," she told Myrtie. "Keep the fire going good, and put on a pan of water to boil. I'll be back in a little while."

She turned around and looked at Myrtie.

"Suppose you mash the potatoes today, for a change, Myrtie. Mr. Willis likes them that way."

"Are you going to take that big egg, Miss Nell?" Myrtie asked, looking down at it in the basket with the eleven white Leghorns.

"Certainly," she said. "Why?"

"Mrs. Farrington will be surprised to see it in with all those white ones, won't she, Miss Nell?"

"Well, what if she does see it?" Nell asked impatiently.

"Nothing, Miss Nell," Myrtie said. "But she might want to know where it came from. She knows we've got Leghorn hens, and she might think one of her Domineckers laid it."

"I can't help that," Nell said, turning away. "And, besides, she should keep her Dominiques at home if she doesn't want them to lay eggs in somebody else's chicken house."

"That's right, Miss Nell," Myrtie said. "She sure ought to do that. She ought to keep her Domineckers at home."

Nell was annoyed by the girl's comments. It was none of Myrtie's business, anyway. Myrtie was getting to be impertinent, and she was forgetting that she was a hired servant in the house. Nell left the kitchen determined to treat Myrtie more coldly after that. She could not allow a colored cook to tell her what to do and what not to do.

Willis was sitting in the crib door shelling the red seed corn. He glanced up when Nell came down the back steps, and looked at her. He stopped shelling corn for a moment to wipe away the white flakes of husk that clung to his eyes.

"I'm going over to Mrs. Farrington's now and exchange a basket of eggs for some green peas, Willis," she said. "I'll not be gone long."

"Maybe she won't swap with you today," Willis said. He stopped and looked up at her through the thin cloud of flying husk that hovered around him. "How do you know she will want to take eggs for peas today, Nell?"

"Don't be foolish, Willis," she said, smiling at him; "why wouldn't she take eggs in exchange today?"

"She might get to wondering where that big brown egg came from," he said, laughing. "She might think it is an egg one of her hens laid."

Nell stopped, but she did not turn around. She waited, looking towards the house.

"You're as bad as Myrtie, Willis."

"In which way is that?"

The moment he spoke, she turned quickly and looked at him. He was bending over to pick up an ear of seed corn.

"I didn't mean to say that, Willis. Please forget what I said. I didn't mean anything like that."

"Like what?"

"Nothing," she said, relieved. "It wasn't anything; I've even forgotten what it was I said. Good-by."

"Good-by," he said, looking after her, wondering.

Nell turned and walked quickly out of the yard and went around the corner of the house towards the road. The Farrington house was half a mile away, but by taking the path through the cotton field it was two or three hundred yards nearer. She crossed the road and entered the field, walking quickly along the path with the basket of eggs on her arm.

Halfway to the Farringtons' Nell turned around and looked back to see if Willis was still sitting in the crib door shelling seed corn. She did not know why she stopped and looked back, but even though she could not see him there or anywhere else in the yard, she went on towards the Farringtons' without thinking of Willis again.

Mrs. Farrington was sitting on the back porch peeling turnips when Nell turned the corner of the house and walked across the yard. There was a bucket of turnips beside Mrs. Farrington's rocking chair, and long purple peelings were lying scattered on the porch floor around her, twisted into shapes like apple peelings when they were tossed over the shoulder. Nell ran up the steps and picked up the longest peeling she could find; she picked up the peeling even before she spoke to Mrs. Farrington.

"Sakes alive, Nell," Mrs. Farrington said; "why are you throwing turnip peelings over your shoulder? Doesn't that good-for-nothing husband of yours love you any more?"

Nell dropped the turnip peeling, and, picking it up again, tore it into short pieces and threw them into the bucket.

She blushed and sat down in the chair beside Mrs. Farrington.

"Of course, he loves me," Nell said. "I suppose I did that so many times when I was a little girl that I still have the habit."

"You mean it's because you haven't grown up yet, Nell," the woman said, chuckling to herself. "I used to be just like that myself; but, sakes alive, it doesn't last, always, girl."

Both of them laughed, and looked away, one from the other. Over across the cotton field a cloud of white dust hung close to the earth. Mr. Farrington and the colored men were planting cotton, and the earth was so dry it rose up in the air when it was disturbed by the mules' hooves and the cotton planters. There was no wind to carry the dust away, and it hung over the men and mules hiding them from sight.

Presently Mrs. Farrington dropped a peeled turnip into the pan and folded her hands in her lap. She looked at Nell, noting her neatly combed hair and her clean gingham frock and white hands. Mrs. Farrington turned away again after that and gazed once more at the cloud of dust where her husband was at work.

"Maybe you and Willis will always be like that," she said. "Seems like you and Willis are still in love with each other. As long as he stays at home where he belongs and doesn't run off at night, it's a pretty sure sign he isn't getting ready to chase after another woman. Sakes alive, men can't always be depended upon to stay at home at night, though; they go riding off when you are least looking for them to."

Nell sat up, startled by what Mrs. Farrington had said, terrified by the directness of her comments.

"Of course, Willis wouldn't do a thing like that," she said confidently. "I know he wouldn't. Willis wouldn't do a thing like that. That's impossible, Mrs. Farrington."

Mrs. Farrington glanced at Nell, and then once more she looked across the field where the planting was being done. The cloud of white dust followed the men and mules, covering them.

"Seems like men are always saying something about being compelled to go to Macon on business, and even up to Atlanta sometimes," she said, ignoring Nell. "And then there are the times when they say they have to go to town at night. Seems like they are always going off to town at night."

Several Dominique hens came from under the porch and stopped in the yard to scratch on the hard white sand. They scratched listlessly; they went through the motions of scratching as if they knew of nothing else to do. They bent their long necks and looked down at the chicken-scrawls they had made with their claws, and they walked away aimlessly, neither surprised nor angry at not having unearthed a worm to devour. One of them began singing in the heat, drooping her wings until the tips of them dragged on the sand. The other hens paid no attention to her, strolling away without interest in the doleful music.

"You have pretty chickens, Mrs. Farrington," Nell said, watching the Dominiques stroll across the yard and sit down in the shaded dust holes as though they were nests.

"They're nothing but Domineckers," she said; "sakes alive, a body can't call them much of a breed, but they do get around to laying an egg or two once in a while."

Nell glanced down at the basket of eggs in her lap, covering the brown egg with her hand. She looked quickly at Mrs. Farrington to see if she had noticed what she had done.

"How are your Leghorns laying now, Nell?" she asked.

"Very well. Willis gathered sixteen eggs yesterday."

"My Domineckers seem to be taking a spell of resting. I only gathered two eggs yesterday, and that's not enough for a hungry man and a yard full of blacks. Sakes alive, we were saying only last night that we wished you would bring over some eggs in a day or two. And now here you are with them. Half an hour's prayer couldn't have done better."

"I thought you might let me have some green peas for dinner," Nell said, lifting the basket and setting it on the floor. "Willis likes green peas at this time of year, and ours haven't begun to bear yet."

"You're welcome to as many as you want," Mrs. Farrington said. "Just walk into the kitchen, Nell, and look on the big table and you'll find a bushel basket of them. Help yourself to all you think you and Willis will want. We've got more than we can use. Sakes alive, there'll be another bushel ready for picking tomorrow morning, too."

Nell went into the kitchen and placed the eleven Leghorn eggs and the big brown one in a pan. She filled the basket with green peas and came back to the porch, closing the screen noiselessly behind her.

"Sit down, Nell," Mrs. Farrington said, "and tell me what's

been happening. Sakes alive, I sit here all day and never hear a word of what's going on."

"Why, I haven't heard of anything new," Nell said.

"What's Willis doing now?"

"He's getting ready to plant corn. He was shelling the seed when I left home. He should be ready to begin planting this afternoon. The planter broke down yesterday, and he had to send to Macon for a new spoke chain. It should be here in the mail today."

"Myrtie is still there to help you with the house, isn't she?"

"Yes, Myrtie is still there."

The hens laying in the dust holes in the shade of the sycamore tree stood up and flapped their wings violently, beating the dust from their feathers. They stretched, one leg after the other, and flapped their wings a second time. One of them spread her legs, bending her knees as if she were getting ready to squat on the ground, and scratched the hard white sand five or six times in quick succession. The other hens stood and watched her while she stretched her long neck and looked down at the marks she had made; and then, wiping her beak on her leg as one whets a knife blade, she turned and waddled back across the yard and under the porch out of sight. The other hens followed her, singing in the heat.

"Couldn't you find a black woman to help you with the house?" Mrs. Farrington asked.

"A black woman?" Nell said. "Why, Myrtie is colored."

"She's colored all right," Mrs. Farrington said; "but, sakes alive, Nell, she isn't black. Myrtie is yellow."

"Well, that's all right, isn't it?" Nell asked. "Myrtie is yellow, and she is a fairly good cook. I don't know where I could find a better one for the pay."

"I reckon I'd heap rather have a black girl and a poor cook, than to have a yellow girl and the finest cook in the whole country."

Nell glanced quickly at Mrs. Farrington, but her head was turned, and she did not look at Nell.

There was a long silence between them until finally Nell felt that she must know what Mrs. Farrington was talking about.

One of the Dominiques suddenly appeared on the bottom step. She came hopping up to the porch, a step at a time. When she reached the last one, Mrs. Farrington said, "Shoo!" The hen flew to the yard and went back under the porch.

"You don't mean—"

Mrs. Farrington began rocking slowly, backward and forward. She gazed steadily across the field where her husband was planting cotton with the colored men.

"You don't mean Willis and—"

One of the roosters strutted across the yard, his eye first upon the hens under the porch and next upon the two women, and stopped midway in the yard to stand and fix his eye upon Mrs. Farrington and Nell. He stood jerking his head from side to side, his hanging scarlet comb blinding his left eye, while he listened to the squeaking of Mrs. Farrington's chair. After a while he continued across the yard and went out of sight behind the smokehouse.

"Mrs. Farrington, Willis wouldn't do anything like that!" Nell said indignantly.

"Like what?" Mrs. Farrington asked. "Sakes alive, Nell, I didn't say he would do anything."

"I know you didn't say it, Mrs. Farrington, but I thought you said it. I couldn't help thinking that you did say it."

"Well, that's different," she replied, much relieved. "I wouldn't want you to go telling Willis I did say it. Menfolks never understand what a woman means, anyway, and when they are told that a woman says something about them, they sometimes fly off the handle something awful."

Nell got up and stood beside the chair. She wished she could run down the steps and along the path towards home without another second's delay, but she knew she could not jump up and leave Mrs. Farrington like that, after what had been said. She would have to pretend that she was not in such a great hurry to get home.

"You're not going so soon, are you, Nell? Why, sakes alive, it seems like you only got here two or three minutes ago, Nell."

"I know," she said, "but it's getting late, and I've got to go home and get these peas ready for dinner. I'll be back to see you soon."

She walked carelessly down the steps. Mrs. Farrington got up and followed her across the hard yard. When they reached the beginning of the path that led across the field, Mrs. Farrington stopped. She never went any farther than that.

"I'm afraid I must hurry now and hull the peas in time for dinner," Nell said, backing down the path. "I'll be back again in a few days, Mrs. Farrington. Thank you so much for the peas. Willis has wanted some for the past week or longer."

"It's as fair an exchange as I can offer for the Leghorn eggs," she said, laughing. "Because if there's anything I like better than those white Leghorn eggs, I don't know what it is. I get so tired of eating my old Domineckers' brown eggs I sometimes say I hope I may never see another one. Maybe I'll be asking you for a setting of them some day soon."

"Good-by," Nell said, backing farther and farther away. She turned and walked several steps. "I'll bring you another basket soon, Mrs. Farrington."

It seemed as if she would never reach the house, even though it was only half a mile away. She could not run, because Mrs. Farrington was in the yard behind her watching, and she could not walk slowly, because she had to get home as soon as possible. She walked with her eyes on the path in front of her, forcing herself to keep from looking up at the house. She knew that if she did raise her eyes and look at it, she would never be able to keep herself from running. If she did that, Mrs. Farrington would see her.

It was not until she had at last reached the end of the path that she was able to look backward. Mrs. Farrington had left her yard, and Nell ran across the road and around to the back of the house.

Willis was nowhere within sight. She looked first at the crib where she had hoped she would find him, but he was not there, and the crib door was closed and locked. She looked down at the barn, but he was not there, either. When she glanced hastily over the fields, she was still unable to see him anywhere.

She stopped at the bottom step on the back porch. There was no sound within the house that she could hear, and not even the sound of Myrtie's footsteps reached her ears. The place seemed to be entirely deserted, and yet she knew that could not be, because only half an hour before when she left to go to Mrs. Farrington's to exchange eggs, Willis was sitting in the crib door shelling seed corn, and Myrtie was in the kitchen scouring the two frying pans.

Nell's hands went out and searched for the railing that led up the porch steps. Her hands could not find it, and her eyes would not let her see it.

The thought of Mrs. Farrington came back to her again and again. Mrs. Farrington, sitting on her own back porch, talking. Mrs. Farrington, sitting in her rocking chair, looking. Mrs. Farrington, peeling purple-top turnips, talking about yellow girls.

Nell felt deathly sick. She felt as if she had been stricken with an illness that squeezed the core of her body. Deep down within herself, she was deathly ill. A pain that began by piercing her skull struck downward and downward until it became motionless in her stomach. It remained there, gnawing and biting, eating the organs of her body and drinking the flow of her blood. She sank limp and helpless upon the back porch steps. Although she did not know where she was, she could still see Mrs. Farrington. Mrs. Farrington, in her rocking chair, looking. Mrs. Farrington, peeling purple-top turnips, talking about yellow girls.

Nell did not know how much later it was when she opened her eyes. The day was the color of the red seed corn. Willis had been shelling when she last saw him sitting in the crib door, and it swam in a sea so wide that she almost cried out in fear when she saw it. Slowly she remembered how she had come to be where she was. She got to her feet weakly, holding to the railing for support.

Stumbling up the steps and across the porch, she flung open the screen door and went into the kitchen. Myrtie was standing beside the table mashing the boiled Irish potatoes with a long fork that had seven tines. Myrtie looked up when Nell ran in, but she did not have an opportunity to speak. Nell ran headlong through the dining room and on into the front room. Myrtie looked surprised to see her running.

Nell paused a moment in the doorway, looking at Willis, at the room, at the day bed, at the floor, at the rugs, at the open door that led into their room. She stood looking at everything she could see. She looked at the pillows on the day bed, at the rugs on the floor, at the chairs against the wall, at the counterpane on their bed. Remembering, she looked at the carpet in their room. Willis sat in front of her reading the *Macon Telegraph* that had just come in the mail, and he was calmly smoking his pipe. She glanced once more at the day bed, at the pillows arranged upon it, and at the rug in front of it. Running, she went to their room and ran her hands over the counterpane of the bed. She picked up the pillows, feeling them, and laid them down again. She ran back into the other room where Willis was.

Willis looked up at her.

Nell ran and fell on her knees in front of him, forcing her

body between his legs and locking her arms around him. She pressed her feverish face against his cool cheeks and closed her eyes tightly. She forced herself tightly to him, holding him with all her might.

"Did Mrs. Farrington exchange with you?" he asked. "I'll bet a pretty that she had something to say about that big brown egg in a basketful of Leghorns."

Nell felt her body shake convulsively, as if she were shivering with cold. She knew she had no control over herself now.

"Look here," he said, throwing aside the *Telegraph* and lifting her head and looking into her eyes. "I know where that brown egg came from now. I remember all about it. There was one of Mrs. Farrington's old Dominecker hens over here yesterday morning. I saw her scratching in the yard, and she acted like she didn't give a cuss whether she clawed up a worm or not. She would scratch awhile and then walk off without even looking to see if she had turned up a worm."

Nell felt herself shaking again, but she did not attempt to control herself. If she could only lie there close to Willis with her arms around him, she did not care how much she shivered. As long as she was there, she had Willis; when she got up and walked out of the room, she would never again be that certain.

Meddlesome Jack

HOD SHEPPARD was in the kitchen eating breakfast when he heard one of the colored boys yell for him. Before he could get up and look out the window to see what the trouble was, Daisy came running into the room from the garden house in the field looking as if she had been scared out of her wits.

"Hod! Hod!" she screamed at him. "Did you hear it?"

He shook her loose from him and got up from the table. Daisy fell down on the kitchen floor, holding on to his legs with all her might.

"Hear what?" he said. "I heard one of the niggers yelling for me. That's all I heard. What's the matter with you, Daisy?"

Just then Sam, the colored boy, called Hod again louder than ever. Both Hod and Daisy ran to the back door and looked out across the field. The only thing out there they could see was the yellow broom sedge and the dead-leafed blackjack.

"What's all this fuss and racket about, anyway?" Hod said, looking at Daisy.

"I heard something, Hod," she said, trembling.

"Heard what? What did you hear?"

"I don't know what it was, but I heard it."

"What did it sound like—wind, or something?"

"It sounded like—like somebody calling me, Hod."

"Somebody calling you?"

She nodded her head, holding him tightly.

"Who's calling you! If I ever find anybody around here calling you out of the house, I'll butcher him. You'd better not let me see anybody around here after you. I'll kill him so quick—"

Sam came running around the corner of the house, his overall jumper flying out behind, and his crinkly hair jumping like a boxful of little black springs let loose. His eyes were turning white.

"Hey there, you Sam!" Hod yelled at him. "Quit your running around and come back here!"

"Sam heard him, too," Daisy said, standing beside Hod and trembling as if she would fall apart. "Sam's running away from him."

"Heard what—heard who! What's the matter with you, Daisy?"

Daisy held Hod tighter, looking out across the broom sedge. Hod pushed her away and walked out into the backyard. He stood there only a minute before the sound of Sam's pounding feet on the hard white sand grew louder and louder. Sam turned the corner of the house a second later, running even faster than he had before. His eyes were all white by that time, and it looked as if his hair had grown several inches since Hod had last seen him.

Hod reached out and caught Sam's jumper. There was a ripping sound, and Hod looked down to find that he was holding a piece of Sam's overall. Sam was around the house out of sight before Hod could yell at him to stop and come back.

"That nigger is scared of something," Hod said, looking in the doorway at Daisy.

"Sam heard him," Daisy said, trembling.

Hod ran to Daisy and put both hands on her shoulders and shook her violently.

"Heard who!" he yelled at her. "If you don't tell me who it was around here calling you, I'll choke the life out of you. Who was around here calling you? If I catch him, I'll kill him so quick—"

"You're choking me, Hod!" Daisy screamed. "Let me loose! I don't know who it was—honest to God, I don't know who it was, Hod!"

Hod released her and ran out into the yard. Sam had turned and was running down the road towards the lumber mill a mile away. The town of Folger was down there. Two stores, the post office, the lumber mill, and the bank were scorching day after day in an oval of baked clay and sand. Sam was halfway to Folger by then.

"So help me!" Daisy screamed. "There he is, Hod!"

She ran into the kitchen, slamming and bolting the door. Out behind the barn Amos Whittle, Sam's father, was com-

ing through the broom sedge and blackjack with his feet
flying behind him so fast that they looked like the paddles
on a water mill. He had both hands gripped around the
end of a rope, and the rope was being jerked by the biggest,
the ugliest, and the meanest-looking jack that Hod had ever
seen in his whole life. The jack was loping through the broom
sedge like a hoop snake, jerking Amos from side to side
as if he had been the cracker on the end of a rawhide
whip.

"Head him, Mr. Hod!" Amos yelled. "Head him! Please,
sir, head him!"

Hod stood looking at Amos and the jack while they
loped past him. He turned and watched them with mouth
agape while they made a wide circle in the broom sedge and
started back towards the house and barn again.

"Head him, Mr. Hod!" Amos begged. "Please, Mr. Hod,
head him!"

Hod picked up a piece of mule collar and threw it at the
jack's head. The jack stopped dead in his tracks, throwing
out his front feet and dragging his hind feet on the hard
white sand. The animal had stopped so suddenly that Amos
found himself wedged between his two hind legs.

Hod walked towards them and pulled Amos out, but
Amos was up and on his feet before there was any danger
of his being kicked.

"Where'd you get that jack, Amos?" Hod said.

"I don't know where I got him, but I sure wish I'd never
seen him. I been all night trying to hold him, Mr. Hod. I
ain't slept a wink, and my old woman's taken to the tall
bushes. She and the girls heard him, and they must have
thought I don't know exactly what, because they went off
yelling about being scared to hear a sound like that jack
makes."

The jack walked leisurely over to the barn door and began
eating some nubbins that Hod had dropped between the crib
and the stalls. One ear stood straight up, and the other one
lay flat on his neck. He was the meanest-looking jackass that
had ever been in that part of the country. Hod had never
seen anything like him before.

"Get him away from here, Amos," Hod said. "I don't
want no jack around here."

"Mr. Hod," Amos said, "I wish I could get him away
somewhere where I'd never see him again. I sure wish I

could accommodate you, Mr. Hod. He's the troublesomest jack I ever seen."

"Where'd you get him, Amos? What are you doing with him, anyway?"

Amos glanced at Hod, but only for a moment. He kept both eyes on the jack.

"I traded that old dollar watch of mine for him yesterday, Mr. Hod, but that jack ain't worth even four bits to me. I don't know what them things are made for, anyhow."

"I'll give you fifty cents for him," Hod said.

"You will!" Amos shouted. "Lord mercy, Mr. Hod, give it here! I'll sure be glad to get rid of that jack for four bits. He done drove my wife and grown girls crazy, and I don't know what mischief he'll be up to next. If you'll give me fifty cents for him, I'll sure be much obliged to you, Mr. Hod. I don't want to have nothing more to do with that jackass."

"I don't want him around, either," Hod said, turning to look through the kitchen window, "but I figure on making me some money with him. How old is that jack, Amos?"

"The man said he was three years old, but I don't know no way of telling a jack's age, and I don't aim to find out."

"He looks like he might be three or four. I'm going to buy him from you, Amos. I figure on making me a lot of money out of that jack. I don't know any other way to make money these days. I can't seem to get it out of the ground."

"Sure, sure, Mr. Hod. You're welcome to that jack. You're mighty much welcome to him. I don't want to have nothing more to do with no jackass. I wish now I had my watch back, but I reckon it's stopped running by now, anyhow. It was three years old, and it never did keep accurate time for me. I'll sure be tickled to get four bits for that jack, Mr. Hod."

Hod counted out fifty cents in nickels and dimes and handed the money to Amos.

"Now, you've got to help me halter that jack, Amos," Hod said. "Get yourself a good piece of stout rope. Plow lines won't be no good on him."

"I don't know about haltering that jack, Mr. Hod. Looks like to me he's never been halterbroke. If it's all the same to you, Mr. Hod, I'd just as lief go on home now. I've got some stovewood to chop, and I got to—"

"Wait a minute," Hod said. "I'll get the rope to halter him with. You go in the house and wake up Shaw. He's in the bed alseep. You go in there and get him up and tell him to come out here and help us halter the jack. Ain't no sense in him sleeping all morning. I'm damned tired of seeing him do it. When he comes home, he ought to get out and help do some work about the place."

Shaw was Hod's brother who had been at home seven or eight days on leave from the Navy. He was getting ready to go back to his ship in Norfolk in a day or two. Shaw was two years younger than Hod, and only a few years older than Daisy. Daisy was nineteen then.

"I'd sure like to accommodate you, Mr. Hod," Amos said, "but the last time you sent me in to wake up Mr. Shaw, Mr. Shaw he jumped out of bed on top of me and near about twisted my neck off. He said for me never to wake him up again as long as I live. Mr. Hod, you'd better go wake up Mr. Shaw your own self."

Hod reached down and picked up a piece of stovewood. He walked towards Amos swinging the stick in his hand.

"I said go in the house and get him up," Hod told Amos again. "That sailor had better stop coming here to stay in bed half the day and be all the time telling Daisy tales."

Amos opened the kitchen door and went into the house. Hod walked towards the barn where the jack was calmly eating red nubbins by the crib door.

When Hod reached the barnyard gate, the jack lifted his head and looked at him. He had two or three nubbins of red corn in his jaws, and he stopped chewing and crunching the grains and cobs while he looked at Hod. One of the jack's ears lay flat against the top of his head and neck, and the other one stood straight up in the air, as stiff as a cow's horn. The jack's ears were about fourteen or sixteen inches long, and they were as rigid as bones.

Hod tossed the piece of stovewood aside and walked to the opened gate for a piece of rope. He believed he could halter the jack by himself.

He started into the barnyard, but he had gone no farther than a few steps when boards began to fly off the side of the barn. The mare in the stall was kicking like a pump gun. One after the other, the boards flew off, the mare whinnied, and the jack stood listening to the pounding of the mare's hooves against the pine boards.

When Hod saw what was happening to his barn, he ran towards the jack, yelling and waving his arms and trying to get him to the leeward side of the barn.

"Howie! Howie!" he yelled at the jack.

As long as the mare got wind of the jack, nothing could make her stop kicking the boards off the barn from the inside. Hod jumped at the jack, waving his arms and shouting at him.

"Howie! Howie!"

He continued throwing up his arms to scare the jack away, but the jack just turned and looked at Hod with one ear down.

"Howie! You ugly-looking son of a bitch! Howie!"

Hod turned around to look towards the house to see if Shaw and Amos were coming. He turned just in time to see Amos jumping out the window.

"Hey there, Amos!" Hod yelled. "Where's Shaw?"

"Mr. Shaw says he ain't going to get up till he gets ready to. Mr. Shaw cussed pretty bad and made me jump out the window."

The jack began to paw the ground. Hard clods of stable-yard sand and manure flew behind him in all directions. Hod yelled at him again.

"Howie! Howie! You flop-eared bastard!"

The jack stopped and turned his head to look at Amos on the other side of the fence.

"Mr. Hod," Amos said, "if you don't mind, I'd like to have a word with you."

Hod yelled at Amos and at the jack at the same time.

"Mr. Hod," Amos said, "if I don't go home and chop that stovewood, me and my folks won't have no dinner at all."

"Come back here!" Hod shouted at him.

Amos came as far as the gate, but he would not come any farther.

Suddenly the jack lifted his head high in the air and brayed. It sounded as if someone were blowing a trumpet in the ear.

The bray had no more than died out when the mare began pounding the boards with both hind hooves, the boards flying off the side of the barn faster than Hod could count them. He turned and looked to see what Amos was doing, and over his head he saw Daisy at the window. She looked as if she had completely lost her mind.

The jack brayed again, louder than ever, and then he leaped for the open barnyard gate. Hod threw the rope at him, but the rope missed him by six feet. The jack was through the gate and out around the house faster than Hod could yell. Amos stood as if his legs had been fence posts four feet deep in the ground.

The jack stopped at the open bedroom window, turned his head towards the house, and brayed as if he were calling all the mares in the entire county. Daisy ran to the window and looked out, and when she saw the jack no more than arm's length from her, she screamed and fell backward on the floor.

"Head him, Amos!" Hod yelled, running towards the jack.

Amos's feet were more than ever like fence posts. He was shaking like a tumbleweed, but his legs and feet were as stiff as if they had been set in concrete.

"Where in hell is that God-damn sailor!" Hod yelled. "Why in hell don't he get up and help me some around here! If I had the time now, I'd go in there with a piece of cordwood and break every bone in his head. The son of a bitch comes home here on leave once a year and lays up in bed all day and stays out all night running after women. If that seagoing son of a bitch comes here again, I'll kill him!"

"Yonder goes your jack, Mr. Hod," Amos said.

Daisy stuck her head out of the window again. She was looking to see where the jack was, and she did not look at Hod. She was standing there pulling at herself, and getting more wild-eyed every second. She disappeared from sight as quickly as she had first appeared.

"Come on, you black bastard," Hod said; "let's go after him. I ought to pick up a stick and break your neck for bringing that God-damn jack here to raise the devil. He's got the mare kicking down the barn, and Daisy is in there acting crazy as hell."

They started out across the broom sedge after the loping jack. The jack was headed for Folger, a mile away.

"If I ever get my hands on that jack, I'll twist his neck till it looks like a corkscrew," Hod panted, running and leaping over the yellow broom sedge. "Ain't no female safe around a sailor or a jack, and here I am running off after one, and leaving the other in the house."

They lost sight of the jackass in a short while. The beast had begun to circle the town, and he was now headed down the side of the railroad tracks behind the row of Negro cabins. They soon saw him again, though, when the jack slowed down at a pasture where some horses were grazing.

A hundred yards from the cabins they had to run down

into a gully. Just as they were crawling up the other side, a Negro girl suddenly appeared in front of them, springing up from nowhere. She was standing waist-high in the broom sedge, and she was as naked as a pickaninny.

Hod stopped and looked at her.

"Did you see a jack?" he said to her.

"White-folks, I saw that jack, and he brayed right in my face. I just jumped up and started running. I can't sit still when I hear a jackass bray."

Hod started off again, but he stopped and came back to look at the girl.

"Put your clothes back on," he said. "You'll get raped running around in the sedge this close to town like that."

"White-captain," she said, "I ain't hard to rape. I done heard that jackass bray."

Hod turned and looked at Amos for a moment, Amos was walking around in a circle with his hands in his pockets.

"Come on," Hod told him, breaking through the broom sedge. "Let's get that jack, Amos."

They started towards the pasture where the jack had stopped. When the jack saw them coming, he turned and bolted over the railroad tracks and started jogging up the far side of the right-of-way towards Folger. Hod cut across to head him off and Amos was right behind to help.

There were very few men in town at that time of day. Several storekeepers sat on Coca-Cola crates on the sidewalk under the shade of the water-oak trees, and several men were whittling white pine and chewing tobacco. The bank was open, and RB, the cashier, was standing in the door looking out across the railroad tracks and dusty street. Down at the lumber mill, the saws whined hour after hour.

The jack slowed down and ran into the hitching yard behind the brick bank. When Hod saw that the jack had stopped, he stopped running and tried to regain his breath. Both he and Amos were panting and sweating. The August sun shone down on the dry baked clay in the oval where the town was and remained there until sunset.

Hod and Amos sat down in the shade of the depot and fanned themselves with their hats. The jack was standing calmly behind the bank, switching flies with his tail.

"Give me back my fifty cents, Amos," Hod said. "You can have that God-damn jack. I don't want him."

"I couldn't do that, Mr. Hod," Amos pleaded. "We done made the trade, and I can't break it now. You'll just have

to keep that jack. He's yours now. If you want to get shed
of him, go sell him to somebody else. I don't want that jack.
I'd rather have my old dollar watch back again. I wish I'd
never seen that jack in all my life. I can do without him."

Hod said nothing. He looked at the brick bank and saw RB
looking out across the railroad tracks towards the stores
where the men were sitting on upturned Coca-Cola crates
in the water-oak shade.

"Sit here and wait," Hod said, getting up. "I've just thought
of something. You sit here and keep your eyes on that jack
till I come back."

"You won't be gone long, will you, Mr. Hod? I don't mind
watching your animal for you, but I'd sure hate to have to
look at that jack any more than I'm compelled to. He
don't like my looks, and I sure don't like his. That's the
ugliest-looking creature that's ever been in this country."

"Wait here till I get back," Hod said, crossing the tracks
and walking towards the brick bank.

RB saw Hod coming, and he went back inside and stood
behind his cashier's cage.

Hod walked in, took off his hat and leaned his arm on the
little shelf in front of the cage.

"Hello, RB," he said. "It's hot today, ain't it?"

"Do you want to deposit money, or make a loan?"

Hod fanned himself and spat into the cuspidor.

"Miss it?" RB asked, trying to see through the grill.

"Not quite," Hod said.

RB spat into his own cuspidor at his feet.

"What can I do for you?" he said.

"Well, I'll tell you, RB," Hod said. "It's like this. You've
got all this money here in the bank and it ain't doing you
much good where it is. And here I come with all my money
tied up in livestock. There ain't but one answer to that, is
there?"

"When did you get some livestock, Hod?" he asked. "I
didn't know you had anything but that old mare and that
gray mule."

"I made a trade today," Hod said, "and now just when my
money is all tied up in livestock, I find a man who's willing
to let me in on a timber deal. I need fifty dollars to swing
my share. There ain't no use trying to farm these days, RB.
That's why I'm going in for livestock and timber."

"How many head of stock do you own?"

"Well, I've got that mare, Ida, out there at my place, but I ain't counting her. And likewise that old mule."

"How many others do you own?"

"I purchased a high-class stud animal this morning, RB, and I paid out all my ready cash in the deal."

"A bull?"

"No, not exactly a bull, RB."

"What was it then?"

"A jackass, RB."

"A jackass!"

"That's right."

"Who in hell wants to own a jackass, Hod? I can't lend the bank's money on a jackass."

"You're in the moneylending business, RB, and I've got an animal to mortgage. What else do you want? I'm putting up my jack, and you're putting up your money. That's good business."

"Yes, but suppose you force me to foreclose the mortage —I'd have the jack, and then maybe I couldn't find a buyer. Jackass buyers are pretty scarce customers, Hod. I don't recall ever seeing one."

"Anybody would give you a hundred dollars for a good high-class jack, RB. If you knew as much about farming and stock-raising as you do about banking, you'd recognize that without me having to tell you."

"What does a jackass look like?"

"A jack don't look so good to the eye, RB, but that's not a jack's high point. When a jack brays—"

RB came running around from behind his cage and caught Hod by the arm. He was so excited that he was trembling.

"Is that what I heard last night, Hod?"

"What?"

"A jackass braying."

"Wouldn't be surprised if you did. Amos was out exercising him last night, and he said the jack brayed almost all night long."

"Come back here with me," RB said, still shaking. "I'm going to let you have that loan, and take a mortgage on that jack. I want to have a hand in it. If I'll let you have the loan, will you let me take the jack home and keep him at my house for about a week, Hod?"

"You're more than welcome to him, RB. You can keep all the time if you want to. But why do you want to keep a jack at your house? You don't breed mules, do you?"

RB had Hod sign the papers before he replied. He then counted out five ten-dollar bills and put them into Hod's hand.

"This is just between me and you, Hod," he said. "Me and my wife haven't been on speaking terms for more than a month now. She cooks my meals and does her housework, but she's been mad at me about something and she won't say a word or have anything to do with me. But last night, sometime after midnight, we were lying there in the bed, she as far on her side as she could get without falling out, and all at once I heard the damnedest yell I ever heard in all my life. It was that jackass braying. I know now what it was, but I didn't know then. That jack was somewhere out in the sedge, and when he brayed, the first thing I knew, my wife was all over me, she was that scared, or something. That sounds like a lie, after I have told you about her not speaking to me for more than a month, and sleeping as far on her side of the bed as she could get without falling on the floor, but it's the truth if I know what the truth is. That jack brayed just once, and the first thing I knew, my wife was all over me, hugging me and begging me not to leave her. This morning she took up her old ways again, and that's why I want to stable that jack at my house for a week or two. He'll break up that streak of not talking and not having anything to do with me. That Jack is what I am in need of, Hod."

Hod took the money and walked out of the bank towards the depot where Amos was.

"Where's the jack, Hod?" RB said, running after him.

"Out there behind your bank," Hod said. "You can take him home with you tonight when you close up."

Amos got up to meet Hod.

"Come on, Amos," Hod said. "We're going home."

Amos looked back over his shoulder at the jack behind the bank, watching him until he was out of sight. They walked through the broom sedge, circling the big gully, on the way home.

When they reached the front yard, Hod saw Sam sitting under a chinaberry tree. Sam got up and stood leaning against the trunk.

"What are you doing here?" Hod asked him. "What are you hanging around here for? Go on home, Sam."

Sam came forward a step, and stepped backward two.

"Miss Daisy told me to tell you something for her," Sam said, chewing the words.

"She said what?"

"Mr. Hod, Miss Daisy and Mr. Shaw went off down the road while you was chasing that jack. Mr. Shaw said he was taking Miss Daisy with him back to the navy yard, and Miss Daisy said she was going off and never coming back."

Hod went to the front porch and sat down in the shade. His feet hung over the edge of the porch, almost touching the ground.

Amos walked across the yard and sat down on the steps. He looked at Hod for several minutes before he said anything.

"Mr. Hod," he said, chewing the words worse than his son had before him, "I reckon you'd better go back to Folger and get your jack. Looks like that jack has a powerful way of fretting the womenfolks, and you'd better get him to turn one in your direction."

The Medicine Man

THERE WAS NOBODY in Rawley who believed that Effie Henderson would ever find a man to marry her, and Effie herself had just about given up hope. But that was before the traveling herb doctor came to town.

Professor Eaton was a tall gaunt-looking man with permanent, sewn-in creases in his trousers and a high celluloid collar around his neck. He may have been ten years older than Effie, or he may have been ten years younger; it was no more easy to judge his age than it was to determine by the accent of his speech from what section of the country he had originally come.

He drove into Rawley one hot dusty morning in mid-August, selling Indian Root Tonic. Indian Root Tonic was a beady, licorice-tasting cure-all in a fancy green-blown bottle. The bottle was wrapped in a black and white label, on which the most prominent feature was the photographic reproduction of a beefy man exhibiting his expanded chest and muscles and his postage-stamp wrestler's trunks. Professor Eaton declared, and challenged any man alive to deny his statement, that his Indian Root Tonic would cure any ailment known to man, and quite a few known only to women.

Effie Henderson was the first person in town to give him a dollar for a bottle, and the first to come back for the second one.

The stand that Professor Eaton had opened up was the back seat of his mud-spattered touring car. He had paid the mayor ten ragged one-dollar bills for a permit to do business in Rawley, and he had parked his automobile in the middle of the weed-grown vacant lot behind the depot. He sold his medicine over the back seat of his car, lifting the green-blown bottles from a box at his feet as fast as the customers came up and laid down their dollars.

There had been a big crowd standing around in the

94

weed-grown lot the evening before, but there were only a
few people standing around him listening to his talk when
Effie came back in the morning for her second bottle.
Most of the persons there then were Negroes who did not
have a dollar among them, but who had been attracted to
the lot by the alcoholic fumes around the mud-caked auto-
mobile and who were willing to be convinced of Indian Root
Tonic's marvelous curative powers. When Effie came up, the
Negroes stepped aside, and stood at a distance watching
Professor Eaton get ready to make another sale.

Effie walked up to the folded-down top in front of Professor Eaton and laid down a worn dollar bill that was as
limp as a piece of wet cheesecloth.

"I just had to come back this morning for another bottle,"
Effie said, smiling up at Professor Eaton. "The one I took
last night made me feel better than I have ever felt before
in all my life. There's not another medicine in the whole
country like it, and I've tried them all, I reckon."

"Pardon me, madam," Professor Eaton said. "There are
hundreds of preparations on the market today, but there is
only one Indian Root Tonic. You will be doing me a great
favor if you will hereafter refer to my aid-to-human-life by
its true and trade-marked name. Indian Root Tonic is the
name of the one and only cure for ailments of any nature.
It is particularly good for the mature woman, madam."

"You shouldn't call me 'madam,' Professor Eaton," Effie
said, lowering her head. "I'm just a young and foolish girl,
and I'm not married yet, either."

Professor Eaton wiped the perspiration from his upper
lip and looked down at Effie.

"How utterly stupid of me, my dear young lady," he said.
"Anyone can see by looking at your fresh young face that
you are a mere girl. Indian Root Tonic is particularly good
for the young maiden."

Effie turned around to see if any of the Negroes were
close enough to hear what Professor Eaton had said. She
hoped that some of the women who lived on her street
would walk past the corner in time to hear Professor
Eaton talk like that about her.

"I never like to talk about myself, but don't you think I am
too young yet to get married, Professor Eaton?"

"My dear young lady," he continued after having paused
long enough to relight his dead cigar, "Indian Root Tonic is
particularly good for the unmarried girl. It is the greatest

discovery known to medical science since the beginning of mankind. I personally secured the formula for this marvelous medicine from an old Indian chief out in our great and glorious West, and I was compelled to promise him on my bended knee that I would devote the remainder of my life to traveling over this great nation of ours offering Indian Root Tonic to men and women like you who would be helpless invalids without it."

He had to pause for a moment's breath. It was then that he looked down over the folded top and for the first time looked at Effie face to face. The evening before in the glare of the gasoline torch, when the lot was crowded with people pushing and shoving to get to the medicine stand before the special introductory offer was withdrawn, he had not had time to look at everyone who came up to hand him a dollar for a bottle. But now when he looked down and saw Effie, he leaned forward to stare at her.

"Oh, Professor Eaton," Effie said, "you are such a wonderful man! Just to think that you are doing such a great work in the world!"

Professor Eaton continued to stare at Effie. She was as good-looking as the next girl in town, not over thirty, and when she fixed herself up, as she had done for nearly two hours that morning before leaving home, she usually had all the drummers in town for the day staring at her and asking the storekeepers who she was.

After a while Professor Eaton climbed out of the back seat of his car and came around to the rear where she was. He relit his cold cigar, and inspected Effie more closely.

"You know, Professor Eaton, you shouldn't talk like that to me," she said, evading his eyes. "You really don't know me well enough yet to call me 'dear girl.' This is the first time we have been alone together, and—"

"Why! I didn't think that a beautiful young girl like you would seriously object to my honorable admiration," he said, looking her up and down and screwing up his mouth when she plucked at her blouse. "It's so seldom that I have the opportunity of seeing such a charming young girl that I must have lost momentarily all sense of discretion. But, now that we are fully acquainted with each other, I'm sure you won't object to my devoted admiration. Will you?"

"Oh, Professor Eaton," Effie said excitedly, "do you really and truly think I am beautiful? So many men have told me that before, I'm accustomed to hearing it frequently, but you are the first man to say it so thrillingly!"

She tried to step backward, but she was already standing against the rear of the car. Professor Eaton moved another step closer, and there was no way for her to turn. She would not have minded that if she had not been so anxious to have a moment to look down at her blouse. She knew there must be something wrong, surely something had slipped under the waist, because Professor Eaton had not raised his eyes from her bosom since he got out of the car and came down beside her. She wondered then if she should not have confined herself when she dressed that morning, putting on all the undergarments she wore to church on Sunday morning.

"My dear girl, there is not the slightest doubt in my mind concerning your beauty. In fact, I think you are the most charming young girl it has been my good fortune to encounter during my many travels over this great country of ours—from coast to coast, from the Lakes to the Gulf."

"You make me feel so young and foolish, Professor Eaton!" Effie said, smoothing her shirtwaist over her bosom. "You make me feel like—"

Professor Eaton turned abruptly and reached into the back seat for a bottle of Indian Root Tonic. He closed his teeth over the cork stopper and popped it out, and, with no further loss of time, handed it to Effie.

"Have this one on me, my dear girl," he said. "Just drink it down, and then see if it doesn't make you feel even better still."

Effie took the green-blown bottle, looking at the picture of the strong young man in wrestler's trunks.

"I drank the whole bottle I bought last night," she said. "I drank it just before going to bed, and it made me feel so good I just couldn't lie still. I had to get up and sit on the back porch and sing awhile."

"There was never a more beneficial—"

"What particular ailment is the medicine good for, Professor Eaton?"

"Indian Root Tonic is good for whatever ails you. In fact, merely as a general conditioner it is supreme in its field. And then on the other hand, there is no complaint known to medical science that it has yet failed to allevi——to help."

Effie turned up the bottle and drank down the beady,

licorice-tasting fluid, all eight ounces of it. The Negroes standing around the car looked on wistfully while the alcoholic fumes from the opened bottle drifted over the lot. Effie handed the empty bottle to Professor Eaton, after taking one last look at the picture on the label.

"Oh, Professor Eaton," she said, coming closer, "it makes me feel better already. I feel just like I was going to rise off the ground and fly away somewhere."

"Perhaps you would allow me—"

"To do what, Professor Eaton? What?"

He flicked the ashes from his cigar with the tip of his little finger.

"Perhaps you would allow me to escort you to your home," he said. "Now, it's almost dinnertime, and I was just getting ready to close up my stand until the afternoon, so if you will permit me, I'll be very glad to drive you home in my automobile. Just tell me how to get there, and we'll start right away."

"You talk so romantic, Professor Eaton," Effie said, touching his arm with her hand. "You make me feel just like a foolish young girl around you."

"Then you will permit me to see you home?"

"Of course, I will."

"Step this way, please," he said, holding open the door and taking her arm firmly in his grasp.

After they had settled themselves in the front seat, Effie turned around and looked at Professor Eaton.

"I'll bet you have had just lots and lots of love affairs with young girls like me all over the country."

"On the contrary," he said, starting the motor, "this is the first time I have ever given my serious consideration to one of your sex. You see, I apply myself faithfully to the promotion, distribution, and sale of Indian Root Tonic. But this occasion, of course, draws me willingly from the cares of business. In fact, I consider your presence in my car a great honor. I have often wished that I might—"

"And am I the first young girl—the first woman you ever courted?"

"Absolutely," he said. "Absolutely."

Professor Eaton drove out of the vacant weed-grown lot and turned the car up the street toward Effie's house. She lived only two blocks away, and during the time it took them to drive that distance neither of them spoke. Effie was busy looking out to see if people were watching her ride with Professor Eaton in his automobile, and he was busily engaged in steering through the deep white sand in the street. When they got there, Effie told him to park the machine in front of the gate where they could step out and walk directly into the house.

They got out and Effie led the way through the front door and into the parlor. She raised one of the shades a few inches and dusted off the sofa.

Professor Eaton stood near the middle of the room, looking uneasily through the small opening under the shade, and listening intently for sounds elsewhere in the house.

"Just sit down here on the sofa beside me," Effie said. "I know I am perfectly safe alone with you, Professor Eaton."

Effie closed her eyes and allowed herself the pleasure of feeling scared to death of Professor Eaton. It was an even nicer feeling than the one she had had the night before when she drank the first bottle of Indian Root Tonic and got into bed.

"And this is the ancestral home?" he asked.

"Don't let's talk about anything but you—and me," Effie said. "Wouldn't you just like to talk about us?"

Professor Eaton began to feel more at ease, now that it was evident that they were alone in the house.

"Perhaps," Professor Eaton said, sitting closer to Effie and looking down once more at her blouse, "perhaps you will permit me to diagnose your complaint. You see, I am well versed in the medical science, and I can tell you how many bottles of Indian Root Tonic you should use in your particular case. Naturally, some people require a greater number of bottles than others do."

Effie glanced out the window for a second, and then she turned to Professor Eaton.

"I won't have to—"

"Oh, no," he said, "that won't be at all necessary, though you may do as you like about it. I can just—"

"Are you sure it's perfectly all right, Professor Eaton?"

"Absolutely," he said. "Absolutely."

Effie smoothed her shirtwaist with her hands and pushed her shoulders forward. Professor Eaton bent towards her, reaching for her hand.

He held her hand for a few seconds, feeling her pulse, and then dropped it to press his ear against her bosom to listen to her heartbeat. While he listened, Effie tucked up a few loose strands of hair that had fallen over her temples.

"Perhaps," he said, raising his head momentarily, "perhaps if you will merely—"

"Of course, Professor Eaton," Effie said excitedly.

He bent closer after she had fumbled nervously with the blouse and pressed his head against her breasts. Her heartbeat jarred his eardrum.

After a while Professor Eaton sat up and loosened the knot in his necktie and wiped the perspiration from his upper lip with the back of his hand. It was warm in the room, and there was no ventilation with the door closed.

"Perhaps I have already told you—"

"Oh, no! You haven't told me!" she said eagerly, holding her hands tightly clasped and looking down at herself with bated breath. "Please go ahead and tell me, Professor Eaton!"

"Perhaps," he said, fingering the open needlework in her blouse, "perhaps you would like to know that Indian Root Tonic is the only complete aid for general health on the market today. And in addition to its general curative properties, Indian Root Tonic possesses the virtues most women find themselves in need of during the middle and later stages of life. In other words, it imparts a vital force to the glands that are in most need of new vitality. I am sure that once you discover for yourself the marvelous power of rejuvenation that Indian Root Tonic possesses, you will never again be alone in the house without it. In fact, I can say without fear of successful contradiction that—"

Effie laid her blouse aside.

"Do you want me to take—"

"Oh, yes; by all means," he replied hastily. "Now, as I was saying—"

"And this, too, Professor Eaton? This, too?"

Professor Eaton reached over and pinched her lightly. Effie giggled and passed her hands over her bosom as though she were smoothing her shirtwaist.

"I don't suppose you happen to have another bottle of that tonic in your pocket, do you, Professor Eaton?"

"I'm afraid I haven't," he said, "but just outside in my car there are several cases full. If you'll let me, I'll step out and—"

"Oh, no!" Effie cried, clutching at his arms and pulling him back beside her. "Oh, Professor Eaton, don't leave me now!"

"Very well," he said, sitting down beside her once more.

"And now as I was saying, Indian Root Tonic's supernatural powers of re——"

"Professor Eaton, do you want me to take off all of this—like this?"

"Absolutely," he said. "And Indian Root Tonic has never been known to fail, whereas in so many—"

"You don't want me to leave anything—"

"Of course not. Being a doctor of the medical science, in addition to my many other activities, I need absolute freedom. Now, if you feel that you cannot place yourself entirely in my hands, perhaps it would be better if I—"

"Oh, please don't go!" Effie cried, pulling him back to the sofa beside her. "You know I have complete confidence in your abilities, Professor Eaton. I know you wouldn't—"

"Wouldn't do what?" he asked, looking down at her again.

"Oh, Professor Eaton! I'm just a young girl!"

"Well," he said, "if you are ready to place yourself entirely in my hands, I can proceed with my diagnosis. Otherwise—"

"I was only teasing you, Professor Eaton!" Effie said, squeezing his hand. "Of course I trust you. You are such a strong man, and I know you wouldn't take advantage of a weak young girl like me. If you didn't take care of me, I'd more than likely run away with myself."

"Absolutely," he said. "Now, if you will continue removing the—"

"There is only this left, Professor Eaton," Effie said. "Are you sure it will be all right?"

"Absolutely."

"But I feel so—so bare, Professor Eaton."

"'Tis only natural to feel like that," he said, comforting her. "A young girl who has never before experienced the—"

"Experienced the what?"

"Well—as I was saying—"

"You make me feel so funny, Professor Eaton. And are you sure—"

"Absolutely," he said. "Absolutely."

"I've never felt like this before. It feels like—"

"Just place yourself completely in my hands, my dear young girl, and I promise nothing will—"

Without warning the parlor door was thrown open and Effie's brother, Burke, came in. Burke was the town marshal.

"Is dinner ready, Effie?" Burke asked, standing in the doorway and trying to accustom his eyes to the near-darkness of the parlor. "It's a quarter after twelve and——"

Burke stopped in the midst of what he was saying and stared at Effie and Professor Eaton. Effie screamed and pushed Professor Eaton away from her. He got up and stood beside Effie and the sofa, looking first at Burke and then at Effie. He did not know what to do. Effie reached for the things she had thrown aside. Professor Eaton bent down and picked up something and threw it at her.

The room suddenly appeared to Professor Eaton to be as bright as day.

"Well, I'll be damned!" Burke said, coming slowly across the floor. His holster hung from his right hip, and it swung heavily as he swayed from step to step. "I'll be damned!"

Professor Eaton stood first on one foot and then on the other. He was between Effie and her brother, and he knew of no way by which he could change his position in the room. He wished to get as far away from Effie as he possibly could. Until she had dressed herself, he hoped he would not be forced to look at her.

Burke stepped forward and pushed Professor Eaton aside. He looked at Effie and at the herb doctor, but he gave no indication of what he intended doing.

Professor Eaton shifted the weight of his body to his other foot, and Burke's hand dropped to the top of the holster, his fingers feeling for the pearl handle that protruded from it.

Effie snapped a safety pin and ran between Burke and Professor Eaton. She was still not completely dressed, but she was fully covered.

"What are you going to do, Burke?" she cried.

"That all depends on what the Professor is going to do," Burke said, still fingering the pearl handle on the pistol. "What is the Professor going to do?"

"Why, Professor Eaton and I are going to be married, Burke," she said. "Aren't we, Professor Eaton?"

"I had not intended making known the announcement of our engagement and forthcoming marriage at this time," he said, "but since we are to be married very shortly, Effie's brother should by all means be the first to know of our intentions."

"Thanks for telling me, Professor," Burke said. "It had better by a damn sight be forthcoming."

Effie ran to Professor Eaton and locked her arms around his neck.

"Oh, do you really mean it, Professor Eaton? I'm so happy

I don't know what to do! But why didn't you tell me sooner that you really wanted to marry me? Do you really and truly mean it, Professor Eaton?"

"Sure," Burke said; "he means it."

"I'm the happiest girl in the whole town of Rawley," Effie cried, pressing her face against Professor Eaton's celluloid collar. "It was all so unexpected! I had never dreamed of it happening to me so soon!"

Burke backed across the room, one hand still around the pearl handle that protruded from the cowhide holster. He backed across the room and reached for the telephone receiver on the wall. He rang the central office and took the receiver from the hook.

"Hello, Janie," he said into the mouthpiece. "Ring up Reverend Edwards for me, will you, right away."

Burke leaned against the wall, looking at Effie and Professor Eaton while Janie at the central office was ringing the Reverend Edwards's number.

"Just to think that I'm going to marry a traveling herb doctor!" Effie said. "Why! all the girls in town will be so envious of me they won't speak for a month!"

"Absolutely," Professor Eaton said, pulling tight the loosened knot in his tie and adjusting it in the opening of his celluloid collar. "Absolutely. Indian Root Tonic has unlimited powers. It is undoubtedly the medical and scientific marvel of the age. Indian Root Tonic has been known to produce the most astounding results in the annals of medical history."

Effie pinned up a strand of hair that had fallen over her forehead and looked proudly upon Professor Eaton.

Clyde Bickle and Dora

FOLLOWING a morning-long drizzle from the dismal sky, there had been a pelting summer shower in late afternoon, and when Clyde put away the leaf rakes and grass clippers and got ready to go home, the air was cool and breezy and the sun was beaming brightly over the western horizon. After leaving the tool shed, first having made certain that the door was securely locked and then putting the key into his pocket, Clyde shaved himself and parted his hair precisely down the middle of his head as he always did on such occasions. Then, watchful of the time, he put on clean clothes and shined his shoes.

It was another Saturday afternoon, and it made him feel good to know that he was going to spend the night with Dora. Even though he and Dora had been married for eleven years, each time he got ready to go to see her on Saturday night, which he had been able to do regularly every week for the past six months, he always felt as if he were courting her all over again.

Although neither of them took particular notice of it, a change had come over Clyde and Dora during those past eleven years. The passing of time, and circumstances, had been responsible for the change. Dora, who was now in her early forties, had grown stout and broad-backed, and through the years her bright blond hair had gradually turned to a lusterless brown. Having always been proud of her appearance, however, and particularly during the past year when she had been a day waitress in the café at the bus depot, Dora had made it a habit to go to the beauty parlor once a week and have her hair shampooed and set in tight ringlets of curls. Clyde, who was in his middle forties, had grown thinner year by year since they were married and his shoulders were slightly stooped by that time. His hair had remained coal-black even though it was no longer thick and bushy, but there was still enough of it left for him to part it in the middle the way he liked.

Walking briskly into the office at the front of the building, Clyde looked up at the big round face of the clock on the wall just as the hands pointed to six o'clock. The round face of the clock reminded him not only of Dora, but also of the fact that it was the time when she got off from work at the café in the bus depot, and he hurriedly found his record card in the rack, jotted down the date and time, and signed his name. Fred Holmes, one of the clerks, looked up from the desk where he was making out the daily reports.

"There you go, off again for another Saturday-night romp," Fred remarked with a wistful expression.

"Sure am," Clyde said, grinning. "The only trouble is that Saturday nights are too far apart to suit me."

"Tell me something, Clyde," Fred said, leaning forward on his desk. "Do you always have yourself a big romp every Saturday night?"

"Haven't failed yet," Clyde assured him. "Don't see why I should start failing now."

Fred took a deep breath and shook his head. "You don't know what a lucky son of a bitch you are, Clyde. There're times when I wish I could trade places with you. Like right now. Just look at me. I've got to go home to my old woman tonight and hand over my pay check." He laughed expressionlessly. "And what do you think I'm going to get for it, Clyde?"

With an understanding nod, but making no reply, Clyde left the big stone building and crossed the street. Instead of going southward past the courthouse and through the business section of town, which was the quickest and most direct way home, he went through the city park, passing the water fountain and the lily pond, and went straight westward toward the Gulf Coast and Western Railroad tracks. It took him about ten minutes to reach the tracks, and when he got there, he started walking on the crossties, counting them familiarly one by one until he had counted exactly a hundred and thirty-seven. Then he ran down the railroad embankment and followed the path through the weeds toward the tin roof gleaming in the late-afternoon sun.

He did not mind the longer time it took him to get there, because he knew it pleased Dora, and he always liked to find her happy and uncomplaining when he got home on

Saturday night. Dora had begged him not to come straight through town, saying it would be embarrassing to her to have people see him walking along the main street, and he had been taking the longer way home during those past six months.

It was still nearly half an hour before seven o'clock when Clyde opened the front gate and walked around the side of the house to the back porch. That was another thing Dora had begged him to do, because, she had said, it was embarrassing to have him walk up to the front door where all the neighbors could see him.

As he had hoped she would be, Dora was sitting on the back porch when he came around the corner of the house. She had got home from the bus depot only a few minutes before that, and, still dressed in the blue-trimmed white uniform that she wore during working hours in the café, she was fanning herself with a piece of newspaper. Clyde stopped at the bottom step and waited for a smile of greeting from Dora, at the same time watching her inquiringly as he always did when he came home on Saturday night. Moment after moment passed while they gazed at each other as though neither intended to be the first to speak.

Presently, even though not a word had passed between them, Clyde came cautiously up the steps and went to the chair where Dora was sitting. Then, standing behind her, he patted her lightly on her broad back. She fanned herself faster and faster.

"Well, Dora," he said after that, "it sure is good to see you again. Every time I come back, it always seems to me a heap longer than a week since I saw you the last time."

Quickly turning in her chair, Dora looked at him with a darting glance. A moment later she got up and went to the door. There was a deep frown on her round face.

"If you want to know the real truth, Clyde Bickle," she spoke out in a sharp tone of voice, "I'll tell you what I think about it."

"What's that, Dora?" he asked, surprised.

Reaching behind her, she opened the screened door.

"Maybe it seems longer to you every time," she told him harshly, "But it's never long enough to suit me."

Before he had a chance to say another word to her, Dora had turned and gone into the house, loudly slamming the screened door behind her. Clyde listened to the sound of her walking down the hall to the bedroom, and after that he sat down in one of the chairs, put his feet on the porch railing, and filled his pipe.

He was not worried about Dora's remark. She was always saying something like that when he first got there, and then later, as time went on and darkness settled down, she became her real self again. Toward morning, at dawn, just before he had to get out of bed and leave, she had always cried a little and hugged him desperately in her strong arms and told him that she was sorry about all the mean things she had said. And after that, without fail, she had always told him that she would be waiting for him when he came back the following Saturday night.

Clyde had finished smoking the first pipeful of tobacco and was refilling the bowl when Dora came back to the porch. The sun had set and twilight was falling, but even in the shadow of the porch he could see that she had taken off the blue-trimmed white uniform and was wearing a summery pink house dress. Clyde waited until she had sat down. By that time he was aware that the frown on her round face had become deeper and darker.

"Now, Dora—" he began.

"Don't you 'Now, Dora' me!" she said in a loud voice, frantically striking the sides of the chair with her hands. "I just can't stand this any longer! I just can't!"

"Can't stand what, Dora?" he asked, puzzled.

"You know good and well what I'm talking about, Clyde Bickle," she said at once. "The way you come here like this every Saturday night and get me so upset I don't sleep a wink till you go away again Sunday morning. I don't know why in the world I've put up with it as long as I have. Any other woman would've put a stop to it a long time ago."

"But I don't come through the main part of town," he reminded her. "You know I always take the long way around, down by the railroad tracks, just exactly like you said you wanted me to. Besides that, I always come around to the back porch instead of coming in the front door."

"I know, I know," she said, closing her eyes and tossing her head from side to side in a helpless gesture. "You did do that for me. I'll have to give you credit for sparing my feelings that way. But even that doesn't help any more—"

"Then what's the trouble exactly about, Dora?" he asked helpfully.

"It's those awful clothes you wear, that's what. Why can't you wear different clothes when you're here, instead of being dressed in those mortifying things?"

"But I do take them off when I go to bed, Dora," he reminded her. "And every time I do that, and hang them on the chair for the night, you always say it makes you feel——"

"That's different," she said quickly. "That's not what I'm talking about." She picked up the piece of newspaper and fanned herself with nervous motions of her hands. "Right now you're sitting there with them on like you're proud of it —while I have to sit here and worry myself sick for fear some of the neighbors might drop in for a visit. If that happened, I'd be mortified to death. All I ask is that you take off those awful things and wear something else when you're sitting out here on the porch."

"I couldn't do that, Dora," he told her, shaking his head determinedly. "That wouldn't be fair, I promised Mr. Ed Johnson I'd wear these clothes every minute of the time from Saturday night to Sunday morning, just like I do the rest of the week—excepting when I'm in bed. He said himself it wouldn't make sense to go to bed dressed up like that. We talked it over, and I know Mr. Ed Johnson trusts me, and I sure wouldn't go back on my word for anything in the world. Besides, if I did go back on my word, he'd take me off the trusty roll, and then I'd never be able to come home on Saturday nights again. And if that happened, it'd be the worst calamity I can think of."

"You could get transferred, Clyde," she said, lowering her voice and leaning closer. "Don't you see? If you got transferred from the county jail to the city jail, you wouldn't have to wear those awful striped jumpers and pants when you came home on Saturday nights. Everybody in the city jails wears ordinary clothes, don't they, Clyde? Now, you'd do that for my sake, wouldn't you?"

Clyde shook his head time after time. He was leaning over the porch railing and knocking the ash from his pipe.

"It's true that the people in the city jail don't wear stripes, but the city jail don't have trusties, neither," he told her. "No, sir!" He banged his pipe on the railing. "I wouldn't want to swap places for anything in the world. I'm too proud to swap places, anyhow, because it'd be like getting demoted. The people in the county jail are a higher class of folks than those in the city jail. That's filled up with drunks and wife beaters and pickpockets and other no-accounts.

All of us at the county jail have bigger reasons for being there. That's why Mr. Ed Johnson can have trusties like me coming and going without lock and key the way we do. He knows we ain't ordinary crooks by nature. Besides, I've worked hard to get to be a trusty, and that's something to be proud of. Nobody in the county jail can work himself up higher than that."

Dora was crying by that time, and, before he could go to her and pat her back and comfort her, she left the porch and ran into the house. Clyde followed her through the hall and sat down beside her on the bed. For a long time he patted her broad back the way he always did when she had one of her crying spells. After a while he took off his jumper and pants and hung them carefully over the back of a chair the way he was in the habit of doing when he went to bed on Saturday nights. When he came back to the bed, he could see Dora watching him while tears streamed down her round face. He was sitting there wondering what he could do to make her feel better when she reached over the side of the bed and smoothed a wrinkle in his striped pants.

"Clyde, I made the biggest mistake in my whole life when I had you arrested for nonsupport," she said, her voice quavering with regret. "I had to go to work myself after that, anyway, waiting on tables in that café at the bus depot, so I could support myself and pay house rent and buy clothes. While I was doing that, you got yourself made a trusty at the county jail so you could come and go as you pleased, and not have to worry about making a single dime for rent and food and clothes. If I was doing it all over again, Clyde, I wouldn't have you arrested for non-support. I know now that it just won't work in my favor at all."

He moved closer to her and stroked her broad back.

"I sure appreciate what you said, Dora," he told her. "It was mighty nice of you to say it. But the truth is, I'm sort of pleased about the way things turned out, after all, and I wouldn't want to change a single thing now. I've got so I like being a trusty and working in the sheriff's vegetable garden and taking care of lawns and shrubs for some of the deputies, besides being able to spend Saturday nights at home the way I do. Right now I couldn't think of a better way to live, when you stop and think about the way other folks on the outside have to groan and sweat at a job so they can get enough money to pay rent and grocery bills, and it'd make me awfully sad to have to give up what I've got. Just as I was leaving the county jail this afternoon, Fred Holmes, one of the clerks in the sheriff's office, was saying to me that he—"

Wiping the tears from her face, Dora sat up beside him. He felt her warm arms tighten around his neck.

"Clyde," he heard her say after that, "Clyde, I'm going to undo all the harm I've caused. I've made up my mind to undo it even if it's the last deed I do on this earth. The first thing Monday morning I'm going straight to the courthouse and tell the judge I've changed my mind and don't want you charged with nonsupport. I'm going to tell him to let you out of the county jail so you can stay at home all the time. I'll tell him about the good job I've got waiting on tables in the café at the bus depot and how I make all the money we need for rent and clothes and things like that. If the judge won't listen to me at first, I'll get down on my knees and stay there till he does pay attention to me. Nobody is going to keep me from undoing the harm I've done."

"But, Dora, I don't want a thing changed now," he protested. "I've got used to things the way they are, and I—"

"Now, you stop worrying, Clyde," she said, tightening her arms around him and hugging him with all her might. "From now on I'm going to see to it that every night is Saturday night. All I want you to do is ask the sheriff if you can bring home an old pair of those striped jumpers and pants for us to keep. I don't know what it is, but there's something about them that makes me feel all cozy and loving every time I see them hanging on the back of the chair like that. You'll bring a pair home to keep, won't you, Clyde?"

He took a long, deep breath before answering her.

"I'll ask Mr. Ed Johnson about that and see what he says," he promised her at last.

Sighing happily, Dora leaned forward and tenderly stroked the striped pants on the back of the chair.

Midsummer Passion

MIDDLE-AGED BEN HACKETT and the team, Cromwell and Julia, were haying to beat hell when the thunderstorm broke on the east ridge. Ben knew it was coming, because all morning the thunder had rumbled up and down the river; but Ben did not want the storm to break until he had drawn the hay to the barn, and when the deluge was over he felt like killing somebody. Ben had been sweating-hot before the storm came and now he was mad. The rain water cooled him and took some of the anger out of him. But he still swore at the thunderstorm for ruining his first-crop hay.

The storm had passed over and the sun came out again as hot as ever, but just the same he had to throw off the load of hay he had on the rack. Swearing and sweating, Ben unloaded and drove Cromwell and Julia across the hayfield into the lane. Ben filled his pipe and climbed up on the hayrack. Clucking like a hen with a new brood of chicks, Ben urged the team toward the highroad half a mile away. The sun was out, and it was hot again. But the hay was wet. Damn it all!

"If God knows all about making hay in this kind of weather, He ought to come down and get it in Himself, by Jesus," Ben told Cromwell and Julia.

Cromwell swished his horsehairs in Ben's face and Julia snorted some thistledown out of her nose.

Glaring up at the sky and sucking on his pipe, Ben was almost thrown to the ground between the team when Cromwell and Julia suddenly came to a standstill.

"Get along there, Cromwell!" Ben growled at the horse. "What's ailing you, Julia!"

The horse and mare moved a pace and again halted. Ben stood up, balancing himself on the hayrack.

"By Jesus!" He grunted, staring down the lane.

An automobile, unoccupied, blocked the narrow trail.

Ben climbed down, swearing to Cromwell and Julia. He

paced around the automobile uncertainly, inspecting it belligerently. No person was in sight.

"Damn a man who'd stand his auto ablocking the lane," Ben grumbled, glancing at Cromwell and Julia for confirmation. "I guess I'll have to push the thing out of the way myself. By Jesus, if whoever left it here was here I'd tell him something he wouldn't forget soon. Not by a damn sight!"

But Ben could not move the car. It creaked and groaned when he pushed and when he pulled, but it would not budge a single inch. Knocking out his pipe and wiping his face, Ben led the team around the automobile through the undergrowth. When he got back into the lane, he stopped the horses and went back to the car. He glanced inside for the first time.

"By Jesus!" Ben exclaimed high-pitched.

Hastily glancing up the lane and down, he opened the door and pulled out a pair of silk stockings.

Ben was too excited to say anything, or to do anything. Still fingering the stockings, he presently looked in the driver's seat, and there, to his surprise, under the steering wheel sat a gallon jug of cider almost empty. Ben immediately pulled the cork to smell if it was hard. It was. He jabbed his thumb through the handle hole and threw the jug in his elbow. It was hard all right, but there was very little of it left.

"Cromwell," he announced, smacking his lips with satisfaction, "that's pretty good cider, for a windfall."

As he carefully replaced the jug under the steering wheel, Ben saw a garment lying on the floor. It was entangled with the do-funnys that operated the car. Carefully he pulled the garment out and held it before his eyes. He could not figure out just what it was, yet he knew it was something women wore. It was pinkish and it was silkish and it looked pretty. And there was very little of it. Ben stared open-mouthed and wild-eyed.

"By Jesus, Cromwell," Ben licked his mustache lip, "what do you know about that!"

Cromwell and the mare nibbled at the road grass, unconcerned.

Ben fingered the drawers a little more intimately. He turned them slowly around.

"It's a female thing, all right, Cromwell." Ben danced excitedly. "It's a female thing, all right!"

Holding the garment high in his hands, Ben climbed on the hayrack and drove down the lane into the highroad. The garment was nice and soft in his hands, and it smelled good, too.

He rode down the road thinking about the drawers. They filled him with the urge to do something out of the ordinary but he didn't know what he could do. When he reached Fred Williams's place, he drew up the team. Fred's wife was stooping over in the garden. Ben pushed the garment carefully into his pants pocket.

"Nice day, today, Mrs. Williams," he called airily, his voice breaking foolishly. "Where's Fred?"

"Fred's gone to the village," she answered, looking around bent over her knees.

Ben's hand stole into the pocket feeling the garment. Even in his pocket out of sight it made him feel different today.

Hitching the team to the horse rack, Ben went into the garden with Fred's wife. She was picking peas for supper. She wasn't bad-looking. Not by a damn sight!

Watching her while she pulled the peas from the vines, Ben strode around her in a circle, putting his hand into the pocket where the pink drawers were. The woman did not say much, and Ben said nothing at all. He was getting so now he could feel the drawers without even touching them with his hands.

Suddenly Ben threw his arms around her waist and squeezed her excitedly.

"Help!" she yelled at the top of her voice, diving forward. "Help!" she cried. "Help!"

When she dived forward, both of them fell on the pea vines, tearing them and uprooting them. She yelled and scratched, but Ben was determined, and he held her with all his strength. They rolled in the dirt and on the pea vines. Ben jerked out the pink drawers. They rolled over and over tearing up more of the pea vines. Ben struggled to pull the drawers over her feet. He got one foot through one drawers leg. They rolled down to the end of the row tearing up all the pea vines. Fred would raise hell about his pea vines when he came home.

Ben was panting and blowing like a horse at a horse-pulling, but he could not get the other drawers leg over the other foot. They rolled up against the fence and Fred's wife stopped struggling. She sat up, looking down at Ben in the dirt. Both of them were brown with the garden soil and Ben was sweating through his mask.

"Ben Hackett, what are you trying to do?" she sputtered through the earth on her face.

Ben released her legs and looked up at her. He did not say anything. She stood up, putting her foot in the empty leg, pulling the drawers up under her skirt. That was where he had been trying all this time to put them. Damn it!

Ben got up dusting his clothes. He followed her across the garden into the front yard.

"Wait here," she told him.

When she returned, she carried a basin of water and a towel.

"Wash the dirt off your face and hands, Ben Hackett," she directed, standing over him, wearing the pink drawers.

Ben did as he was told to do. When he finished washing his face and hands, he slapped some of the dirt out of his pants.

"It was mighty nice of you to bring the towel and water," he thanked her.

"You are halfway fit to go home now," she approved, pinning up her hair.

"Good day," Ben said.

"Good day," said Fred's wife.

Handsome Brown's Day Off

MA WENT UP THE STREET to the next corner after breakfast to talk to Mrs. Howard about the Sycamore Ladies' Im-
provement Society meeting, and the last thing she said before she left was for Handsome Brown to have the dishes
washed and dried and the dishcloths rinsed and hung out to
dry in the sun before she got back. It was Handsome's
day off, although he had never had a day off, even though
he had worked for us ever since he was eleven years old,
because something always seemed to happen that kept him
from going away somewhere and loafing for a whole day.
Handsome always liked to take his time doing the dishes, no
matter whether it was just a regular day like all the others,
or whether it was really his day off, because he knew every
day always turned out in the end to be the same as any
other, anyway; and he generally managed to find a good excuse for not doing the dishes any sooner than he had to.
That morning after Ma had gone up to Mrs. Howard's, he
said he was hungry; he went into the kitchen and cooked
himself a skilletful of hog-liver scrapple.

My old man was sprawled on the back porch steps dozing
in the sun, just as he did every morning after breakfast
when he had the chance, because he said a nap after breakfast always made him feel a lot better for the remainder of
the day. Handsome took a long time to eat the scrapple, as
he knew he had the dishes to do when he finished, and he
was still sitting in a chair hunched over the cookstove eating
out of the skillet when somebody knocked on our front
door. Since both Pa and Handsome were busy, I went around
to the side of the house to find out who it was.

When I got to the front yard, I saw a strange-looking
girl, about eighteen or twenty years old, standing at the door
with her face pressed against the screen trying to see in-

side. She was carrying a square tan bag made like a small suitcase, and she was bareheaded with long brown hair curled on the ends. I knew right away I'd never seen her anywhere before, and I thought she was a stranger trying to find the house of somebody in town she had come to visit. I watched her until she put her hand on the latch and tried to open the screen door.

"Who do you want to see?" I asked her, going as far as the bottom step and stopping.

She turned around as quick as a flash.

"Hello, sonny," she said, coming to the edge of the porch. "Is your father at home?"

"Pa's taking a nap on the back porch," I told her. "I'll go tell him."

"Wait a second!" she said excitedly, running down the steps and grabbing me by the arm. "You show me where he is. That'll be a lot better."

"What do you want to see him about?" I asked, wondering who she was if she really knew my old man. "Are you looking for somebody's house?"

"Never mind, sonny," she smiled. "You take me to him."

We walked around the side of the house and went through the gate into the back yard. Every time the girl took a step a big wave of perfume blew off of her and her stockings began sagging under her knees. My old man was sound asleep with his mouth hanging open and the back of his head resting on the top step. He always sprawled out that way when he was sleeping in the sun, because he said it was the only way he could feel comfortable while he dozed. I could see Handsome standing in the kitchen and looking out at us through the screen door while he ate the scrapple from the skillet.

The girl put down her suitcase, pulled her stockings up under her garters, and tiptoed to where my old man was sprawled over the steps. Then she got down beside him and put both hands over his eyes. I could see Handsome stop eating just when he had raised a spoonful of scrapple half-way to his mouth.

"Guess who!" the girl cried.

My old man jumped sort of sidewise, the way he generally did when Ma woke him up when he wasn't expecting it. He didn't leap clear off the steps though, because almost as soon as he sat up, the girl pushed his head back and kept him from seeing anything at all. I could see his nose flare open and shut like a hound sniffling a coon up a tree when he got a whiff of the perfume.

"Guess who!" she said again, laughing out loud.

"I'll bet it ain't Martha," Pa said, feeling her arms all the way up to her elbows.

"Guess again!" she said, teasing him.

My old man flung her hands away and sat up wild-eyed.

"Well, I'll be dogged!" my old man said. "Who in the world are you?"

The girl got up from the steps, still laughing, and went for her suitcase. While all three of us watched to see what she was going to do, she opened the lid and took out an armful of brand-new neckties. She had more ties than a store.

Pa rubbed the sleep out of his eyes and took a good look at the girl while she was bending over the suitcase.

"This would look wonderful on you," she said, picking out a tie made of bright green and yellow cloth. She went over to where he sat and looped it around his neck. "It was made for you!"

"For me?" Pa said, looking up and sniffing the perfume that floated all around her.

"Of course," she said, turning her head sideways and taking a good look at Pa and the tie. "It couldn't suit you better."

"Lady," Pa told her, "I don't know what you're up to, but whatever it is, you're wasting your time at it. I ain't got no more use for a necktie than a pig has with a sidesaddle."

"But it's such a beautiful tie," she said, dropping the armful of ties into her suitcase and coming up closer to my old man. "It just suits your complexion."

She sat down close beside him on the step and began tying a knot in the tie. They sat there beside each other until my old man's face turned red all over. The perfume had drifted all over the place by that time.

"Well, what do you know about that!" Pa said, looking as though he didn't know what he was saying. "Who'd have ever thought a necktie would've suited my complexion!"

"Let's see you in a mirror," she told him, patting the tie against his chest. "When you look at yourself in a mirror, you'll know you can't get along without that tie. Why, it's perfect on you!"

My old man cut his eyes around and glanced up the street towards Mrs. Howard's house on the corner.

"There's a mirror inside," he said, talking in a low voice as though he didn't want anybody else to hear him.

"Come on, then," the girl said, pulling him by the arm.

She picked up her suitcase and went inside with my old man right behind her. After they were inside Handsome came out of the kitchen and we hurried to the far side of the house where we could look through one of the windows.

"What did I tell you?" the girl said. "Didn't I tell you it was a beauty? I'll bet you never had a tie like that in all your life before."

"I reckon you're right, at that," Pa said. "It's sure a beauty, all right. It sort of sets me off, don't it?"

"Of course," she said, standing behind my old man and looking over his shoulder into the mirror. "Here, let me tie a better knot in it for you."

She went around in front of my old man and drew the knot tighter under his chin. Then she just stood there with her hands on his shoulders and smiled up at him. My old man stopped looking at himself in the mirror and looked at her. Handsome began getting fidgety.

"Mis' Martha'll be coming home almost any minute now," he said. "Your Pa ought to take care. There's liable to be a big fuss if Mis' Martha comes home while he's standing in there like that fooling around with that necktie. I wish I had them dishes all done so I could go and take my day off before Mis' Martha gets back."

My old man leaned over and smelled the air over the girl's head and put his arms around her waist.

"How much do you get for it?" he asked her.

"Fifty cents," she told him.

Pa shook his head from side to side.

"I ain't got fifty cents to my name," he said sadly.

"Oh, now, come on and loosen up," she said, shaking him hard. "Fifty cents isn't anything at all."

"But I just ain't got it," he told her, getting a tighter grip around her waist. "I just ain't, that's all."

"Don't you know where you can get it?"

"Not exactly."

Handsome groaned.

"I wish your Pa would stop messing around over that old necktie like that," he said. "I just know ain't nothing good's going to come out of it. I feel in my bones that something bad's going to come along, and it looks like I'm always the one who gets in trouble when something like that happens.

I declare, I wish my day off had started long before that girl came here with them neckties."

The girl put her arms around my old man's neck and squeezed herself up against him. They stood that way for a long time.

"I think maybe I could get me a half-a-dollar somewheres," my old man told her. "I've just been thinking about it. I feel maybe I can, after all."

"All right," she said, taking her arms down and backing away. "Hurry and get it."

"Will you wait right here til I come back?" he asked.

"Of course. But don't stay away too long."

My old man started backing towards the door.

"You wait right here where you are," he told her. "Don't budge a single inch from this room. I'll be back before you know it."

In barely any time at all he came running out on the back porch.

"Handsome!" he shouted. "Handsome Brown!"

Handsome groaned as if he were getting ready to die.

"What you want with me on my day off, Mr. Morris?" he said, sticking his head around the corner of the house.

"Never mind what I want," Pa told him, hurrying down the steps. "You come on with me like I tell you. Hurry up, now!"

"What we aiming to do, Mr. Morris?" Handsome said. "Mis' Martha told me to be sure and do them dishes in the kitchen before she got back. I can't do nothing else but that when she done told me to do it."

"The dishes can wait," my old man said. "They'll get dirty after we eat off them the next time, anyway." He grabbed Handsome by the sleeve and pulled him towards the street. "Get a hustle on and do like I tell you."

We went down the street with Handsome trotting to keep up. When we got to Mr. Tom Owens' house, we turned into the yard. Mr. Owens was hoeing witch grass out of his garden.

"Tom," Pa shouted over the fence, "I've decided to let Handsome work for you a day like you wanted. He's ready to start in right away!"

He pushed Handsome inside Mr. Owens' garden and made him hurry up between the rows of cabbages and turnips to where Mr. Owens was.

"Give Handsome the hoe, Tom," Pa said, taking it away from Mr. Owens and shoving it at Handsome.

"But, Mr. Morris, ain't you clear forgot about this being my day off?" Handsome said. "I declare, I just naturally don't want to hoe that old witch grass, anyway."

"Shut up, Handsome," Pa said, turning and shaking him hard by the shoulder. "Mind your own business."

"But I is minding my own business, Mr. Morris," Handsome said. "Ain't it my business when I have a day off coming to me?"

"You've got a whole lifetime ahead of you to take a day off in," Pa told him. "Now, start grubbing out that witch grass like I told you."

Handsome raised the hoe and let the blade fall on a bunch of witch grass. The growth was so wiry and tough that the hoe blade bounced a foot off the ground when it struck it.

"Now, Tom," Pa said, turning around, "give me the fifty cents."

"I ain't going to pay him till he does a day's work," Mr. Owens said, shaking his head. "Suppose he don't do a half-a-dollar's worth of work? I'd be cheating myself if I went and paid out the money and then found out he wasn't worth it."

"You don't have to worry about that part of it," Pa said. "I'll see to it that you get your money's worth out of Handsome. I'll be back here ever so often just to stand over him and see to it that he's doing the work like he ought to for the pay he's getting."

"Mr. Morris, please, sir?" Handsome said, looking at Pa.

"What is it, Handsome?" he asked.

"I don't want to have to hoe this old witch grass, please, sir. I want my day off."

Pa gave Handsome a hard look and pointed at the hoe with his foot.

"Now, just give me the fifty cents, Tom," he said.

"What makes you in such a big hurry to collect the pay before the work's done?"

"I've got something that has got to be settled right away. Now, if you'll just hand me the money, Tom—"

Mr. Owens watched Handsome hitting the witch grass with the blade for a while, and then he put his hand into his overalls pocket and took out a handful of nails, screws, and small change. He hunted through the pile until he had picked out half-a-dollar in nickels and dimes.

"This'll be the last time I'll ever hire that colored boy to do anything for me if he don't do a good hard day's work," he told Pa.

"You won't regret hiring Handsome," Pa said. "Handsome Brown's one of the hardest workers I ever seen anywhere."

Mr. Owens handed Pa the money and put the rest of the pile back into his pocket. As soon as my old man had the money, he started for the gate.

"Mr. Morris, please, sir?" Handsome said.

"What do you want now, Handsome?" Pa shouted back at him. "Don't you see how busy I am?"

"Could I get off sort of early this afternoon and have a little bit of my day off?"

"No!" Pa shouted back. "I don't want to hear no more talk about taking a day off, anyway. You don't never see me taking a day off, do you?"

My old man was in such a hurry by that time that he didn't wait to say anything more even to Mr. Owens. He hurried back up the street and ran into the house. He latched the screen door on the way in.

The girl was sitting on the bed folding neckties one by one and laying them in her suitcase. She looked up when Pa ran into the room.

"Here's the money, just like I said!" he told her. He sat down on the bed beside her and dropped the nickels and dimes into her hand. "It didn't take me no time at all to collect it."

The girl put the money in her purse, folded some more ties, and pulled her stockings up around her knees.

"Here's your tie," she said, picking the bright green and yellow one up from the bed and putting it into Pa's hand. The tie fell on the floor at his feet.

"But, ain't you going——" he said, surprised, looking at her hard.

"Ain't I going to do what?" she said right back.

My old man stared at her with his mouth hanging open. She bent over and folded the rest of the ties and put them into the suitcase.

"Well, I thought maybe you'd put it around my neck and tie it again like you did just a little while ago," he said slowly.

"Listen," she said. "I made the sale, didn't I? What else do you want for fifty cents? I've got this whole town to cover between now and night. How many sales do you think I'd make if I spent all my time tying neckties around people's necks after I'd already made me a sale?"

"But—but—I thought—" my old man stammered.

"You thought what?"

"Well, I kind of thought maybe you'd—I thought maybe you'd want to tie it around my neck again—"

"Oh, yeah?" she laughed.

She got up and slammed the cover on her suitcase. My old man sat where he was, watching her while she picked it up and walked out of the room. The front door slammed and we could hear her running down the steps. In no time at all she was all the way down the street in front of Mr. Owens' house and was turning into his yard.

My old man sat on the bed for a long time looking at the green and yellow necktie on the floor. After a while he stood up and kicked it with all his might across the room, and then he went out on the back porch and sat down on the steps where he could stretch out in the sun again.

A Small Day

GOVERNOR GIL was standing astride the path, knocking heads off the weeds, when Walter Lane came up the hill from the spring. A wide circle of wilted weeds lay on the ground around him, and his walking stick was still swinging. It looked as if he had been waiting there for half an hour or longer.

"It's been mighty hot today," Walter said, stopping and lowering the two pails of water to the ground.

"It's a small day when the sun don't shine," Governor Gil said. "Where's the rest of your family, and the girl?"

"My wife and the young ones went over to visit her folks this afternoon," Walter told him. "They'll be coming home some time tonight after supper." He turned around and looked down the path behind. "Daisy's coming up the path any minute now. She's down at the spring filling a bucket."

Governor Gil looked down the path, but Daisy was not within sight. It was almost a hundred yards from the crown of the slope down to the bottom of the hill, where the spring was.

"I reckon I can wait here," he said, taking a new grip on his walking stick and bending forward to reach the weeds farthest away. "It's a small day when I can't afford to spend a little time waiting."

Walter watched the heads tumble off the stalks of weeds. Governor Gil went about it as if he were determined not to let a weed in the whole county go to seed that year. Every once in a while he shifted his position a little, stamping down the wilted weeds and reaching for new ones to whack at. Sometimes he started out in the morning, after breakfast, on horseback to see how his cotton and cane crops were growing, but before he got out of sight of home he always got off his horse and started whacking away at the weeds with his walking stick. He hated weeds worse than he did boll weevils or screwworms. However, for some reason or other, he never paid any attention to the weeds that grew in the yard around his house; they were so rank there that sometimes his hunting dogs got lost in the growth and had to backtrack their way out.

"Did you want to see me, Governor Gil, or was it Daisy you asked about?" Walter said, wondering.

Instead of answering, Governor Gil stopped a moment and glanced down the path. He nodded his head in that direction, and returned to swinging his stick at the weeds.

Governor Gil Counts had once, for a term, been governor of the state, about twenty-five or thirty years before, and the title suited him so well that nobody ever thought of calling him anything else. He ran his farm with the help of Walter Lane and several other tenants, and never left it. He had not been out of the county since the day he came home from the governor's office, and he had said he would never leave home again. He lived a quarter of a mile up the road in a big three-story mansion, from which the white paint had peeled while he was serving his term in office. The once-white, three-story columns rising from the front porch were now as dark and rough as the bark on a pine tree.

"There's no sense in standing out here in the sun," Walter said. "Come on to my house and take a seat in the porch shade, Governor Gil. Daisy'll be along to the house just about as soon as she'll get here."

"This'll do," he said, stopping and looking down the path. "I haven't got time to sit down now."

He went past Walter and started down the path toward the spring. Walter left his pails and followed behind. Heads of weeds tumbled to the right and left of them.

At the crown of the slope they saw Daisy coming up. She was carrying a pail of water in one hand and fanning herself with a willow branch.

"I may as well tell you now, Walter," Governor Gil said, stopping. "It's time for your girl to marry. It's dangerous business to put it off after they get a certain age."

Walter took half a dozen steps around Governor Gil and stopped where he could see his face.

"Who ought she to marry?" Walter said.

Governor Gil let go at some pigweeds around his knees, whacking his stick at them just under the seed pods. The heads flew in all directions.

"I've arranged for that," he said. "I sent my lawyer a letter today telling him to get a license. It'll be here in a few days."

Walter looked again at Governor Gil, and then down the path. Daisy had come over the crown of the slope.

"That might be all right," Walter said, "But I don't know if she'll be tamed. Right now she's just about as wild as they come. Of course, now, I'm not raising any serious objections. I'm just going over in my mind the drawbacks a man might run into."

"A year from now there might be plenty of drawbacks," Governor Gil said. "Right this minute drawbacks don't count, because she's reached the marrying age, and nothing else matters. If I had a daughter, Walter, I'd want to do the right thing by her. I'd want her to marry before drawbacks had a chance to spoil her. I'm ready to marry her without an argument."

"You damned old fool," Daisy said, dropping her pail, "what put that into your head?"

Governor Gil had drawn back to let go at a clump of weeds swaying in the breeze beside the path, but he never finished the stroke. His stick fell back against his knees and the clump of weeds continued to sway in the wind.

"Now, that's what I was thinking about," Walter said. "I had an idea she wouldn't be willing to be tamed just yet."

"Why, I've been counting on this for a pretty long time," Governor Gil said excitedly. "I've just been biding my time all this while when you were growing up, Daisy. I've had my eyes on you for about three years now, just waiting for you to grow up."

"You damned old fool," Daisy said, stooping down for her pail and starting around them in the path.

Walter did not try to stop her. He looked at Governor Gil to see what he had to say now.

They watched her for a moment.

"She'll tame," Governor Gil said, nodding his head at Walter and following her up the path to the house.

When they got to the back door, Daisy put the pail on the shelf and sat down on the doorstep. She sat and looked at them with her knees drawn up under her elbows and her chin cupped in her hands.

"Maybe if you could just wait—" Walter began. He was waved aside by a sweep of the walking stick.

"I'm going to have the handseling tonight," Governor Gil said, nodding his head at Daisy and flourishing the stick in the air. "The marrying can wait, but the handseling can't.

The license will be along from my lawyer in a day or two, and that's just a matter of formality, anyway."

Walter looked at Daisy, but she only stared most sullenly at them.

"I reckon we ought to wait till my wife gets back from visiting her folks," Walter said. "She ought to have a little say-so. For one thing, she'll have to make Daisy some clothes first, because Daisy hasn't got much to wear except what she's got on, and that's so little it wouldn't be decent if we weren't homefolks. Just about all she's got to her name is that little slimsy gingham jumper she's wearing. My wife will want to make her a petticoat, if nothing else. It would be a sin and a shame for her to get married like she is now. If she had something to wear under what she's got on, it might be different, but I won't be in favor of sending her out to get married in just a slimsy jumper between her and the outside world."

Governor Gil shook his walking stick in the air as if to wave away any possible objection Walter might mention.

"That's all right for the marriage," he said, "but that won't be for a few days yet. Your wife will have plenty of time to make up a petticoat for her if she wants to. But she won't even have to do that, because I'll buy her whatever she'll need after the marriage. And what she'll need for the handseling won't be worth mentioning."

He stopped and turned around to look at the sun. It was already setting behind the pine grove in the west.

"Had your supper yet?" he asked, looking at Walter and nodding at Daisy.

"Not yet," Walter said. "We didn't stop work in the cotton until about half an hour ago, and the first thing that needed doing was carrying up the water from the spring. Daisy, you go in the kitchen and start getting something ready to eat. Maybe Governor Gil will stay and eat with us tonight."

"No," he said, waving his stick at Daisy, "don't do that, Daisy. You just come up to my house and get your meal there tonight. There's no sense in you getting all worn out over a hot stove now. There's plenty to eat up there."

He turned to Walter.

"If your wife won't be home until late tonight, you just come up to my house and go around to the kitchen, and the help will set you out a good meal, Walter."

He started walking across the yard toward the road. When he got to the corner of the house, he stopped and found that neither Daisy nor her father had made a move to follow him.

"What's the matter?" he said impatiently.

"Well, now," Walter said, "I can make Daisy go up to your house, Governor Gil, but I can't be held responsible for what she does after she gets there. I wish you would wait till my wife came back tonight before you took Daisy off, but if your mind is made up not to wait, then all I can say is you'll have to charge her yourself after she gets there."

"She won't need any charging," Governor Gil said. "I've yet to know the wildest one of them that wouldn't tame when the time comes to handsel."

He turned around and started walking toward the road that led to his house, a quarter of a mile away.

Walter looked down at the doorstep, where Daisy still sat sullen and motionless.

"You ought to be tickled to death to have the chance to marry Governor Gil," he told her. "Who else is there in the county who'll treat you nice and give you all you want? I'll bet there's many a girl who'd jump at the chance to marry him."

"The damned old fool," Daisy said.

"Well, you'd better," he told her. "I'll bet your mother will make you, if I can't. She's no fool, either. She knows how well off you'll be, not having to go hungry for something to eat, and having enough clothes to cover your nakedness, neither one of which you've got now, or ever will have, if you don't go on up there like you ought to."

Walter sat down on the bottom step and waited for Daisy to say something. The sun had set, and it would be getting dark soon. If she did not go right away, Governor Gil might get mad and change his mind.

Presently he turned around and looked at her.

"What's the matter with you, Daisy? You won't even say anything. What's got into you, anyway?"

"What does he want me to go up there tonight for?" she asked. "He said the license wouldn't be here for two or three days."

"That's just Governor Gil's way, Daisy. He makes up his mind to do something, and nothing stops him once it's made up. He wants to marry you, and he wants to right now. There's no sense in putting it off, anyway. The best thing for you to do is to start right in before he changes his mind. If you don't, you'll live to be sorry, because tomorrow you'll have to go right back to the field again—tomorrow and every day as long as cotton grows."

Daisy got up without saying anything and went into the house. She was in her room for ten or fifteen minutes, and when she came to the door it was dark outside. She could barely see her father sitting on the steps at her feet.

"Now, that's what I call sense," Walter said. "I thought you'd change your mind after you got to thinking about all these hot days in the sun out there in the cotton."

She went down the steps past him and crossed the yard without a word. She started up the road in the direction of Governor Gil's mansion.

After Daisy had gone, Walter began to wonder what his wife would say when she came home. He was certain she would be glad to hear that Governor Gil wanted to marry Daisy, but he was not so sure of what she would say when he told her that the marriage license would not come for another two or three days. He decided it would be best not to say anything about that part to her. Just as long as she knew Governor Gil had come to the house to ask Daisy to marry him, she would be satisfied.

It was pitch-dark when he got up and went into the kitchen, made a light, and looked around for something to eat. He found some bread left over from dinner, and he did not have to build a fire in the cookstove after all. He sat down at the kitchen table and ate his fill of bread and sorghum.

After he had finished, he blew out the light and went to the front porch to sit and wait for his wife to come home.

Up the road he could see lights in Governor Gil's house. There was a light in the kitchen, as usual, and one in the front part of the house too. Upstairs, two or three rooms were lighted for the first time since he could remember.

Just when he was expecting his wife and children to get there any moment, he heard somebody running down the road. He got up and listened as the sound came closer. It was somebody running fast, because the sound came closer every second.

He ran out to the road to see who it was. At first he thought it might be Daisy, but he soon knew it wasn't, because a boy called out to him.

"Mr. Walter! Mr. Walter!"

"Who's that?" he shouted back.

A Negro houseboy stopped, panting, in the road beside him.

"What's the matter, Lawson?"

"Mr. Walter, Governor said to tell you if you ever raise another hellcat like Miss Daisy, he'll chop your head off. Now, Mr. Walter, I didn't say it! Please, sir, don't think I said it! It was Governor who told me to tell you that! You know I wouldn't say that myself, don't you, Mr. Walter?"

"What's the matter up there, Lawson?" Walter asked the boy.

"I don't know exactly, Mr. Walter, except that Governor started yelling upstairs a while ago, and he hasn't stopped yet. He told me to telephone for the doctor and the lawyer to come in a hurry. He hardly stopped yelling long enough to tell me, either. Soon as I telephoned for them, he told me to run down here as fast as I could and tell you what I told you."

"Was Miss Daisy up there then?" Walter asked.

"I reckon it was Miss Daisy who made him yell," Lawson said hesitatingly.

"Why?"

"I don't know if Governor wants me to tell you," Lawson said. "He only told me to tell you what I already told you, Mr. Walter."

"You'd better tell me, Lawson. What was it?"

"Miss Daisy flew into him and pretty near bit the daylights out of him. Governor was yelling and nursing his hurt so much, he didn't have time to say much else."

Walter started back to the porch to sit down and wait for his wife to come home. He could not keep from laughing a little, but he tried to hold himself back so he could laugh all the more with his wife when she got there.

Lawson was still standing outside the yard. He turned around to tell the boy to go on back.

"What else did Governor Gil say, Lawson?" he asked him.

"I didn't hear him say much else, except Governor said it'll be a mighty small day when he tries to handsel a hellcat like Miss Daisy again."

Walter went to the porch and sat down. He leaned back and started to laugh. He could not wait for his wife any longer. He leaned back and laughed until he slid out of the chair.

The Growing Season

THE HEAT was enough to drive anybody crazy.

The wire grass was growing faster than Jesse English could keep it chopped down and covered up. He had been going over the twelve acres of cotton for five days already, and he was just about ready to give up.

At noon when his wife called him to dinner, Jesse unhitched the mule from the scraper and turned him loose. The mule walked unsteadily towards the barn, stumbling over the rows as if he had blind staggers. Jesse's eyes were bloodshot by the heat, and he was afraid he was going to get a sunstroke. He got to the house, but he could not eat anything. He stretched out on the porch, his straw hat over his face to shut out the glare of the sun, feeling as if he could never get up again as long as he lived.

Lizzie came to the door and told him to get up and eat the meal she had cooked. Jesse did not answer her, and after a while she went back inside out of sight.

The rattling of the trace chain in the yard woke Jesse up. He raised himself on his elbow and looked out under the chinaberry tree at Fiddler. Fiddler crawled around the tree, winding the chain around the trunk of the chinaberry. When Fiddler had wound the chain as far as he could, he lay down again.

Jesse stared at Fiddler with his bloodshot eyes burning into his head until he could not stand it any longer. He dug his knuckles into his eye sockets until the pain had left for a while.

Fiddler got up and made as if to stand. Instead, he pitched forward like a drunken man, falling into a mass. Jesse felt a new rush of blood in his head each time Fiddler rattled the chain. While watching him, he began to wonder what was going to happen to his crop of cotton. It had rained for a solid week just when the cotton was ready to hoe, and before he could catch up with it, the

130

wire grass had got ahead of him. Lizzie had had a sunstroke the year before, and every time she stayed in the sun fifteen or twenty minutes she fainted. She could not help him hoe; there was nobody to help him. There was not even a Negro on the place.

When he looked out over the field, he realized how little he had accomplished since sunup that morning. He did not see how he would ever be able to clear out the grass before the cotton plants got choked out.

The trace chain rattled again. Jesse pushed himself on his hands and feet to the edge of the porch and sat there staring at Fiddler. Lizzie came to the door once more and told him to come and eat his dinner, but he did not hear her.

Fiddler turned over on the ground and lay with his head up against the trunk of the chinaberry tree.

Sitting on the edge of the porch with his feet swinging back and forth, Jesse rubbed his eyes with his knuckles and tried to reason clearly. The heat, even in the shade of the porch roof, was blinding him. His eyes burned like hot chestnuts in his head. When he heard Fiddler rattle the chain again, he tried to stare at him through the heat, but Fiddler was by then no more than a blue patch in the yard.

The crop was going to ruin because there was nobody to help him get the grass out before the cotton plants were choked to death by the wire grass.

Jesse eased himself off the edge of the porch and climbed the steps and went into the hall. His shotgun was standing in the corner behind the door. It was kept loaded all the time, and he did not stop to see if there were any shells in the barrels.

"Your dinner's getting spoiled, Jesse," his wife said somewhere in the house.

He did not answer her.

Outside in the sun and heat once more, Jesse could see the wire grass choking the life out of his crop of cotton. He ran to the far end of the yard and out into the field and began kicking the cotton plants and grass with his feet. Even then the wire grass sprang back like coils in a bedspring. The cotton plants he had kicked from their roots began slowly to wilt in the noonday heat. By the time he had turned away, the plants had shriveled up and died.

He went back into the yard and kicked the trace chain. One end was fastened to the chinaberry tree, and the other end was clamped around Fiddler's neck. He stood the shotgun against the tree and began fumbling with the clamp. While he was stooped over, Lizzie came to the porch again.

"What are you aiming to do with that shotgun, Jesse?" she asked, shading her eyes with her hands.

When he did not answer her, she ran down the steps and raced across the yard to the chinaberry.

The clamp was unfastened then. Jesse grabbed the gun and jerked the chain. He jerked the chain harder the next time, and Fiddler rolled to his feet and went wobbling across the yard like a drunken man trying to walk.

Lizzie tried to jerk the chain out of Jesse's hand. He pushed her aside.

"Jesse!" she screamed at him. "Jesse, what you going to do with Fiddler!"

He pushed her behind him. Fiddler wobbled on his undeveloped legs and Jesse poked him upright with the gunstock each time he looked as if he would fall. Lizzie came screaming after them and fell around her husband's legs. Jesse got away from her before she could lock her arms around his knees.

Fiddler had started running towards the barn. Jesse ran behind, holding the gun ahead so he could prod Fiddler in the direction he wanted him to go.

The crop was ruined. But he had forgotten all about the wire grass choking out the tender cotton plants. The grass had got ahead of him before he could stop it. If Lizzie had not been sunstruck, or if he had had anybody else to help him, he could have saved his cotton. The wire grass on twelve acres was too much for one man, once he fell behind.

His eyes were so bloodshot he could not see Fiddler very well. The heat and the throbbing in his head made him forget everything except that he had to get Fiddler out behind the barn where the gully was. He threw a corncob at the mule to get him out of Fiddler's way. The mule went into the barn.

Fiddler ran off in another direction, but Jesse headed him back to the gully with the butt end of the shotgun. He hit Fiddler again with the stock to keep him from going in the wrong direction.

Lizzie was screaming in the front yard. She did not have her sunbonnet on, and she had already got a touch of heat.

When they got to the gully, Jesse shoved Fiddler down

into it. Fiddler lay on the bottom on the wash, digging at the sides and trying to get out.

Jesse raised his gun to sight down the barrels, and all he could see was a wiggling gray mass against the red clay gully-bank. He pulled the trigger anyway, and waited a moment. Without lowering the gun, he fired the second shell at Fiddler.

Fiddler was making more noise than he had ever made before. Jesse sat down on the side of the gully and rubbed his eyes with his knuckles. He felt the dried earth give way under his knees, and he moved back a little to keep from sliding down into the gully where Fiddler was floundering like a fish that had been tossed upon dry land.

"Stop that kicking and squealing, and die, damn you!" Jesse shouted. "Die! Damn you, die!"

He could not sit there any longer. He had waited as long as he could wait for Fiddler to stop thrashing around in the gully. The birdshot in the shells was strong enough to kill a mule at short range, but they had not been strong enough to kill Fiddler.

Lizzie screaming under the chinaberry tree and the heat and the blazing sun overhead sent Jesse running to the woodpile at the back of the house. He grabbed up the ax and came running back to the gully. Fiddler was still thrashing around on the bottom like a chicken with its head cut off. Jesse jumped down the bank and struck at Fiddler three or four times. When he stopped, blood was all over the ax handle and blade, and the bottoms of his overall legs were soaked with it.

After a while Fiddler lay still, and Jesse walked down to the lower end of the gully where the banks were not so steep and climbed to the top. On the way back to the house he could see Lizzie lying on the ground under the chinaberry tree where Fiddler had been kept chained.

He carried the ax to the woodpile and swung the blade into a hickory log. After that he sat down on the woodpile and wiped his face with his hands and tried to stop the burning of his eyeballs by digging at them with his knuckles.

From somewhere a breeze came up, and the wind against his hot face made him feel better all over. He ran his thumb under one overall strap and threw it off. The breeze blowing against his wet shirt and skin felt like a gentle rain.

One of the hounds that had been sleeping under the house got up and walked out to the woodpile and began licking the ax handle. Jesse watched him until he had finished. When the dog started licking his overall legs, Jesse kicked him with all his might. The hound tumbled to his feet and ran yelping back under the house.

Jesse wiped his face with his hands again, and got up. He found the hoe leaning against the side of the house. He carried it to the porch and pulled the rat-tailed file out of the weatherboarding where it had been stuck since the last time he used it.

He thought he heard his wife stumbling through the hall of the house.

Propping the hoe against the porch, Jesse began filing the blade until it was as keen as a corn knife. After that was done, he jabbed the file back into the weatherboarding and walked towards the cotton field, bareheaded in the hot sun, carrying the hoe over his shoulder.

Jesse was not certain, but he felt he might be able to save his crop. The wire grass could not stand up under a sharp hoe blade, and he could go back and file his hoe with the rat-tailed file whenever it wanted sharpening.

Kneel to the Rising Sun

A SHIVER went through Lonnie. He drew his hand away from his sharp chin, remembering what Clem had said. It made him feel now as if he were committing a crime by standing in Arch Gunnard's presence and allowing his face to be seen.

He and Clem had been walking up the road together that afternoon on their way to the filling station when he told Clem how much he needed rations. Clem stopped a moment to kick a rock out of the road, and said that if you worked for Arch Gunnard long enough, your face would be sharp enough to split the boards for your own coffin.

As Lonnie turned away to sit down on an empty box beside the gasoline pump, he could not help wishing that he could be as unafraid of Arch Gunnard as Clem was. Even if Clem was a Negro, he never hesitated to ask for rations when he needed something to eat; and when he and his family did not get enough, Clem came right out and told Arch so. Arch stood for that, but he swore that he was going to run Clem out of the country the first chance he got.

Lonnie knew without turning around that Clem was standing at the corner of the filling station with two or three other Negroes and looking at him, but for some reason he was unable to meet Clem's eyes.

Arch Gunnard was sitting in the sun, honing his jackknife blade on his boot top. He glanced once or twice at Lonnie's hound, Nancy, who was lying in the middle of the road waiting for Lonnie to go home.

"That your dog, Lonnie?"

Jumping with fear, Lonnie's hand went to his chin to hide the lean face that would accuse Arch of short-rationing.

Arch snapped his fingers and the hound stood up, wagging her tail. She waited to be called.

"Mr. Arch, I—"

Arch called the dog. She began crawling towards them

135

on her belly, wagging her tail a little faster each time Arch's fingers snapped. When she was several feet away, she turned over on her back and lay on the ground with her four paws in the air.

Dudley Smith and Jim Weaver, who were lounging around the filling station, laughed. They had been leaning against the side of the building, but they straightened up to see what Arch was up to.

Arch spat some more tobacco juice on his boot top and whetted the jackknife blade some more.

"What kind of a hound dog is that, anyway, Lonnie?" Arch said. "Looks like to me it might be a ketch hound."

Lonnie could feel Clem Henry's eyes boring into the back of his head. He wondered what Clem would do if it had been his dog Arch Gunnard was snapping his fingers at and calling like that.

"His tail's way too long for a coon hound or a bird dog, ain't it, Arch?" somebody behind Lonnie said, laughing out loud.

Everybody laughed then, including Arch. They looked at Lonnie, waiting to hear what he was going to say to Arch.

"Is he a ketch hound, Lonnie?" Arch said, snapping his finger again.

"Mr. Arch, I—"

"Don't be ashamed of him, Lonnie, if he don't show signs of turning out to be a bird dog or a foxhound. Everybody needs a hound around the house that can go out and catch pigs and rabbits when you are in a hurry for them. A ketch hound is a mighty respectable animal. I've known the time when I was mighty proud to own one."

Everybody laughed.

Arch Gunnard was getting ready to grab Nancy by the tail. Lonnie sat up, twisting his neck until he caught a glimpse of Clem Henry at the other corner of the filling station. Clem was staring at him with unmistakable meaning, with the same look in his eyes he had had that afternoon when he said that nobody who worked for Arch Gunnard ought to stand for short-rationing. Lonnie lowered his eyes. He could not figure out how a Negro could be braver than he was. There were a lot of times like that when he would have given anything he had to be able to jump into Clem's shoes and change places with him.

"The trouble with this hound of yours, Lonnie, is that he's too heavy on his feet. Don't you reckon it would be a pretty slick little trick to lighten the load some, being as how he's a ketch hound to begin with?"

Lonnie remembered then what Clem Henry had said he would do if Arch Gunnard ever tried to cut off his dog's tail. Lonnie knew, and Clem knew, and everybody else knew, that that would give Arch the chance he was waiting for. All Arch asked, he had said, was for Clem Henry to overstep his place just one little half inch, or to talk back to him with just one little short word, and he would do the rest. Everybody knew what Arch meant by that, especially if Clem did not turn and run. And Clem had not been known to run from anybody, after fifteen years in the country.

Arch reached down and grabbed Nancy's tail while Lonnie was wondering about Clem. Nancy acted as if she thought Arch were playing some kind of a game with her. She turned her head around until she could reach Arch's hand to lick it. He cracked her on the bridge of the nose with the end of the jackknife.

"He's a mighty playful dog, Lonnie," Arch said, catching up a shorter grip on the tail, "but his wagpole is way too long for a dog his size, especially when he wants to be a ketch hound."

Lonnie swallowed hard.

"Mr. Arch, she's a mighty fine rabbit tracker. I—"

"Shucks, Lonnie," Arch said, whetting the knife blade on the dog's tail, "I ain't ever seen a hound in all my life that needed a tail that long to hunt rabbits with. It's way too long for just a common, ordinary, everyday ketch hound."

Lonnie looked up hopefully at Dudley Smith and the others. None of them offered any help. It was useless for him to try to stop Arch, because Arch Gunnard would let nothing stand in his way when once he had set his head on what he wished to do. Lonnie knew that if he should let himself show any anger or resentment, Arch would drive him off the farm before sundown that night. Clem Henry was the only person there who would help him, but Clem . . .

The white men and the Negroes at both corners of the filling station waited to see what Lonnie was going to do about it. All of them hoped he would put up a fight for his hound. If anyone ever had the nerve to stop Arch Gunnard from cutting off a dog's tail, it might put an end to it. It was plain, though, that Lonnie, who was one of Arch's sharecroppers, was afraid to speak up. Clem Henry might; Clem was the only one who might try to stop Arch, even if

it meant trouble. And all of them knew that Arch would in-
sist on running Clem out of the country, or filling him full of
lead.

"I reckon it's all right with you, ain't it, Lonnie?" Arch
said. "I don't seem to hear no objections."

Clem Henry stepped forward several paces, and stopped.

Arch laughed, watching Lonnie's face, and jerked Nancy
to her feet. The hound cried out in pain and surprise, but
Arch made her be quiet by kicking her in the belly.

Lonnie winced. He could hardly bear to see anybody kick
his dog like that.

"Mr. Arch, I . . ."

A contraction in his throat almost choked him for several
moments, and he had to open his mouth wide and fight for
breath. The other white men around him were silent. Nobody liked to see a dog kicked in the belly like that.

Lonnie could see the other end of the filling station from
the corner of his eye. He saw a couple of Negroes go up
behind Clem and grasp his overalls. Clem spat on the
ground, between outspread feet, but he did not try to
break away from them.

"Being as how I don't hear no objections, I reckon it's
all right to go ahead and cut it off," Arch said, spitting.

Lonnie's head went forward and all he could see of Nancy
was her hind feet. He had come to ask for a slab of sowbelly and some molasses, or something. Now he did not
know if he could ever bring himself to ask for rations, no
matter how much hungrier they became at home.

"I always make it a habit of asking a man first," Arch
said. "I wouldn't want to go ahead and cut off a tail if a
man had any objections. That wouldn't be right. No, sir, it
just wouldn't be fair and square."

Arch caught a shorter grip on the hound's tail and placed
the knife blade on it two or three inches from the rump. It
looked to those who were watching as if his mouth were
watering, because tobacco juice began to trickle down the
corners of his lips. He brought up the back of his hand and
wiped his mouth.

A noisy automobile came plowing down the road through
the deep red dust. Everyone looked up as it passed in order
to see who was in it.

Lonnie glanced at it, but he could not keep his eyes raised.
His head fell downward once more until he could feel his

sharp chin cutting into his chest. He wondered then if Arch had noticed how lean his face was.

"I keep two or three ketch hounds around my place," Arch said, honing the blade on the tail of the dog as if it were a razor strop until his actions brought smiles to the faces of the men grouped around him, "but I never could see the sense of a ketch hound having a long tail. It only gets in their way when I send them out to catch a pig or a rabbit for my supper."

Pulling with his left hand and pushing with his right, Arch Gunnard docked the hound's tail as quickly and as easily as if he were cutting a willow switch in the pasture to drive the cows home with. The dog sprang forward with the release of her tail until she was far beyond Arch's reach, and began howling so loud she could be heard half a mile away. Nancy stopped once and looked back at Arch, and then she sprang to the middle of the road and began leaping and twisting in circles. All that time she was yelping and biting at the bleeding stub of her tail.

Arch leaned backward and twirled the severed tail in one hand while he wiped the jackknife blade on his boot sole. He watched Lonnie's dog chasing herself around in circles in the red dust.

Nobody had anything to say then. Lonnie tried not to watch his dog's agony, and he forced himself to keep from looking at Clem Henry. Then, with his eyes shut, he wondered why he had remained on Arch Gunnard's plantation all those past years, sharecropping for a mere living on short rations, and becoming leaner and leaner all the time. He knew then how true it was what Clem had said about Arch's sharecroppers' faces becoming sharp enough to hew their own coffins. His hands went to his chin before he knew what he was doing. His hand dropped when he had felt the bones of jaw and the exposed tendons of his cheeks.

As hungry as he was, he knew that even if Arch did give him some rations then, there would not be nearly enough for them to eat for the following week. Hatty, his wife, was already broken down from hunger and work in the fields, and his father, Mark Newsome, stone-deaf for the past twenty years, was always asking him why there was never enough food in the house for them to have a solid meal. Lonnie's head fell forward a little more, and he could feel his eyes becoming damp.

The pressure of his sharp chin against his chest made him so uncomfortable that he had to raise his head at last in order to ease the pain of it.

The first thing he saw when he looked up was Arch Gunnard twirling Nancy's tail in his left hand. Arch Gunnard had a trunk full of dogs' tails at home. He had been cutting off tails ever since anyone could remember, and during all those years he had accumulated a collection of which he was so proud that he kept the trunk locked and the key tied around his neck on a string. On Sunday afternoons when the preacher came to visit, or when a crowd was there to loll on the front porch and swap stories, Arch showed them off, naming each tail from memory just as well as if he had had a tag on it.

Clem Henry had left the filling station and was walking alone down the road towards the plantation. Clem Henry's house was in a cluster of Negro cabins below Arch's big house, and he had to pass Lonnie's house to get there. Lonnie was on the verge of getting up and leaving when he saw Arch looking at him. He did not know whether Arch was looking at his lean face, or whether he was watching to see if he were going to get up and go down the road with Clem.

The thought of leaving reminded him of his reason for being there. He had to have some rations before suppertime that night, no matter how short they were.

"Mr. Arch, I . . ."

Arch stared at him for a moment, appearing as if he had turned to listen to some strange sound unheard of before that moment.

Lonnie bit his lips, wondering if Arch was going to say anything about how lean and hungry he looked. But Arch was thinking about something else. He slapped his hand on his leg and laughed out loud.

"I sometimes wish niggers had tails," Arch said, coiling Nancy's tail into a ball and putting it into his pocket. "I'd a heap rather cut off nigger tails than dog tails. There'd be more to cut, for one thing."

Dudley Smith and somebody else behind them laughed for a brief moment. The laughter died out almost as suddenly as it had risen.

The Negroes who had heard Arch shuffled their feet in the dust and moved backwards. It was only a few minutes until not one was left at the filling station. They went up the road behind the red wooden building until they were out of sight.

Arch got up and stretched. The sun was getting low, and it was no longer comfortable in the October air. "Well, I reckon I'll be getting on home to get me some supper," he said.

He walked slowly to the middle of the road and stopped to look at Nancy retreating along the ditch.

"Nobody going my way?" he asked. "What's wrong with you, Lonnie? Going home to supper, ain't you?"

"Mr. Arch, I . . ."

Lonnie found himself jumping to his feet. His first thought was to ask for the sowbelly and molasses, and maybe some corn meal; but when he opened his mouth, the words refused to come out. He took several steps forward and shook his head. He did not know what Arch might say or do if he said "No."

"Hatty'll be looking for you," Arch said, turning his back and walking off.

He reached into his hip pocket and took out Nancy's tail. He began twirling it as he walked down the road towards the big house in the distance.

Dudley Smith went inside the filling station, and the others walked away.

After Arch had gone several hundred yards, Lonnie sat down heavily on the box beside the gas pump from which he had got up when Arch spoke to him. He sat down heavily, his shoulders drooping, his arms falling between his outspread legs.

Lonnie did not know how long his eyes had been closed, but when he opened them, he saw Nancy lying between his feet, licking the docked tail. While he watched her, he felt the sharp point of his chin cutting into his chest again. Presently the door behind him was slammed shut, and a minute later he could hear Dudley Smith walking away from the filling station on his way home.

II

Lonnie had been sleeping fitfully for several hours when he suddenly found himself wide awake. Hatty shook him again. He raised himself on his elbow and tried to see into the darkness of the room. Without knowing what time it was, he was able to determine that it was still nearly two hours until sunrise.

"Lonnie," Hatty said again, trembling in the cold night air, "Lonnie, your pa ain't in the house."

Lonnie sat upright in bed.

"How do you know he ain't?" he said.

"I've been lying here wide awake ever since I got in bed, and I heard him when he went out. He's been gone all that time."

"Maybe he just stepped out for a while," Lonnie said, turning and trying to see through the bedroom window.

"I know what I'm saying, Lonnie," Hatty insisted. "Your pa's been gone a heap too long."

Both of them sat without a sound for several minutes while they listened for Mark Newsome.

Lonnie got up and lit a lamp. He shivered while he was putting on his shirt, overalls, and shoes. He tied his shoe-laces in hard knots because he couldn't see in the faint light. Outside the window it was almost pitch-dark, and Lonnie could feel the damp October air blowing against his face.

"I'll go help look," Hatty said, throwing the covers off and starting to get up.

Lonnie went to the bed and drew the covers back over her and pushed her back into place.

"You try to get some sleep, Hatty," he said; "you can't stay awake the whole night. I'll go bring Pa back."

He left Hatty, blowing out the lamp, and stumbled through the dark hall, feeling his way to the front porch by touching the wall with his hands. When he got to the porch, he could still barely see any distance ahead, but his eyes were becoming more accustomed to the darkness. He waited a minute, listening.

Feeling his way down the steps into the yard, he walked around the corner of the house and stopped to listen again before calling his father.

"Oh, Pa!" he said loudly. "Oh, Pa!"

He stopped under the bedroom window when he realized what he had been doing.

"Now that's a fool thing for me to be out here doing," he said, scolding himself. "Pa couldn't hear it thunder."

He heard a rustling of the bed.

"He's been gone long enough to get clear to the cross-roads, or more," Hatty said, calling through the window.

"Now you lay down and try to get a little sleep, Hatty," Lonnie told her. "I'll bring him back in no time."

He could hear Nancy scratching fleas under the house, but he knew she was in no condition to help look for Mark. It would be several days before she recovered from the shock of losing her tail.

"He's been gone a long time," Hatty said, unable to keep still.

"That don't make no difference," Lonnie said. "I'll find him sooner or later. Now you go on to sleep like I told you, Hatty."

Lonnie walked towards the barn, listening for some sound. Over at the big house he could hear the hogs grunting and squealing, and he wished they would be quiet so he could hear other sounds. Arch Gunnard's dogs were howling occasionally, but they were not making any more noise than they usually did at night, and he was accustomed to their howling.

Lonnie went to the barn, looking inside and out. After walking around the barn, he went into the field as far as the cotton shed. He knew it was useless, but he could not keep from calling his father time after time.

"Oh, Pa!" he said, trying to penetrate the darkness.

He went farther into the field.

"Now, what in the world could have become of Pa?" he said, stopping and wondering where to look next.

After he had gone back to the front yard, he began to feel uneasy for the first time. Mark had not acted any more strangely during the past week than he ordinarily did, but Lonnie knew he was upset over the way Arch Gunnard was giving out short rations. Mark had even said that, at the rate they were being fed, all of them would starve to death inside another three months.

Lonnie left the yard and went down the road towards the Negro cabins. When he got to Clem's house, he turned in and walked up the path to the door. He knocked several times and waited. There was no answer, and he rapped louder.

"Who's that?" he heard Clem say from bed.

"It's me," Lonnie said. "I've got to see you a minute, Clem. I'm out in the front yard."

He sat down and waited for Clem to dress and come outside. While he waited, he strained his ears to catch any sound that might be in the air. Over the fields towards the big house he could hear the fattening hogs grunt and squeal.

n came out and shut the door. He stood on the door-
a moment speaking to his wife in bed, telling her he
would be back and not to worry.

"Who's that?" Clem said, coming down into the yard.

Lonnie got up and met Clem halfway.

"What's the trouble?" Clem asked then, buttoning up his
overall jumper.

"Pa's not in his bed," Lonnie said, "and Hatty says he's
been gone from the house most all night. I went out in the
field, and all around the barn, but I couldn't find a trace
of him anywhere."

Clem then finished buttoning his jumper and began rolling a cigarette. He walked slowly down the path to the
road. It was still dark, and it would be at least an hour
before dawn made it any lighter.

"Maybe he was too hungry to stay in bed any longer,"
Clem said. "When I saw him yesterday, he said he was so
shrunk up and weak he didn't know if he could last much
longer. He looked like his skin and bones couldn't shrivel
much more."

"I asked Arch last night after suppertime for some rations—just a little piece of sowbelly and some molasses. He
said he'd get around to letting me have some the first thing
this morning."

"Why don't you tell him to give you full rations or none?"
Clem said. "If you knew you wasn't going to get none at
all, you could move away and find a better man to sharecrop
for, couldn't you?"

"I've been loyal to Arch Gunnard for a long time now,"
Lonnie said. "I'd hate to haul off and leave him like that."

Clem looked at Lonnie, but he did not say anything more
just then. They turned up the road towards the driveway
that led up to the big house. The fattening hogs were still
grunting and squealing in the pen, and one of Arch's hounds
came down a cotton row beside the driveway to smell their
shoes.

"Them fattening hogs always get enough to eat," Clem
said. "There's not a one of them that don't weigh seven
hundred pounds right now, and they're getting bigger every
day. Besides taking all that's thrown to them, they make a
lot of meals off the chickens that get in there to peck
around."

Lonnie listened to the grunting of the hogs as they walked
up the driveway towards the big house.

"Reckon we'd better get Arch up to help look for Pa?" Lonnie said. "I'd hate to wake him up, but I'm scared Pa might stray off into the swamp and get lost for good. He couldn't hear it thunder, even. I never could find him back there in all that tangle if he got into it."

Clem said something under his breath and went on towards the barn and hog pen. He reached the pen before Lonnie got there.

"You'd better come here quick," Clem said, turning around to see where Lonnie was.

Lonnie ran to the hog pen. He stopped and climbed half-way up the wooden-and-wire sides of the fence. At first he could see nothing, but gradually he was able to see the moving mass of black fattening hogs on the other side of the pen. They were biting and snarling at each other like a pack of hungry hounds turned loose on a dead rabbit.

Lonnie scrambled to the top of the fence, but Clem caught him and pulled him back.

"Don't go in that hog pen that way," he said. "Them hogs will tear you to pieces, they're that wild. They're fighting over something."

Both of them ran around the corner of the pen and got to the side where the hogs were. Down under their feet on the ground Lonnie caught a glimpse of a dark mass splotched with white. He was able to see it for a moment only, because one of the hogs trampled over it.

Clem opened and closed his mouth several times before he was able to say anything at all. He clutched at Lonnie's arm, shaking him.

"That looks like it might be your pa," he said. "I swear before goodness, Lonnie, it does look like it."

Lonnie still could not believe it. He climbed to the top of the fence and began kicking his feet at the hogs, trying to drive them away. They paid no attention to him.

While Lonnie was perched there, Clem had gone to the wagon shed, and he ran back with two singletrees he had somehow managed to find there in the dark. He handed one to Lonnie, poking it at him until Lonnie's attention was drawn from the hogs long enough to take it.

Clem leaped over the fence and began swinging the single-tree at the hogs. Lonnie slid down beside him, yelling at them. One hog turned on Lonnie and snapped at him, and Clem struck it over the back of the neck with enough force to drive it off momentarily.

By then Lonnie was able to realize what had happened. He ran to the mass of hogs, kicking them with his heavy stiff shoes and striking them on their heads with the iron-tipped singletree. Once he felt a stinging sensation, and looked down to see one of the hogs biting the calf of his leg. He had just enough time to hit the hog and drive it away before his leg was torn. He knew most of his overall leg had been ripped away, because he could feel the night air on his bare wet calf.

Clem had gone ahead and had driven the hogs back. There was no other way to do anything. They were in a snarling circle around them, and both of them had to keep the singletrees swinging back and forth all the time to keep the hogs off. Finally Lonnie reached down and got a grip on Mark's leg. With Clem helping, Lonnie carried his father to the fence and lifted him over to the other side.

They were too much out of breath for a while to say anything, or to do anything else. The snarling, fattening hogs were at the fence, biting the wood and wire, and making more noise than ever.

While Lonnie was searching in his pockets for a match, Clem struck one. He held the flame close to Mark New-some's head.

They both stared unbelievingly, and then Clem blew out the match. There was nothing said as they stared at each other in the darkness.

Clem walked several steps away, and turned and came back beside Lonnie.

"It's him, though," Clem said, sitting down on the ground. "It's him, all right."

"I reckon so," Lonnie said. He could think of nothing else to say then.

They sat on the ground, one on each side of Mark, looking at the body. There had been no sign of life in the body beside them since they had first touched it. The face, throat, and stomach had been completely devoured.

"You'd better go wake up Arch Gunnard," Clem said after awhile.

"What for?" Lonnie said. "He can't help none now. It's too late for help."

"Makes no difference," Clem insisted. "You'd better go wake him up and let him see what there is to see. If you wait till morning, he might take it into his head to say the hogs didn't do it. Right now is the time to get him up so he can see what his hogs did."

Clem turned around and looked at the big house. The dark outline against the dark sky made him hesitate.

"A man who short-rations tenants ought to have to sit and look at that till it's buried."

Lonnie looked at Clem fearfully. He knew Clem was right, but he was scared to hear a Negro say anything like that about a white man.

"You oughtn't talk like that about Arch," Lonnie said. "He's in bed asleep. He didn't have a thing to do with it. He didn't have no more to do with it than I did."

Clem laughed a little, and threw the singletree on the ground between his feet. After letting it lie there a little while, he picked it up and began beating the ground with it.

Lonnie got to his feet alowly. He had never seen Clem act like that before, and he did not know what to think about it. He left without saying anything and walked stiffly to the house in the darkness to wake up Arch Gunnard.

III

Arch was hard to wake up. And even after he was awake, he was in no hurry to get up. Lonnie was standing outside the bedroom window, and Arch was lying in bed six or eight feet away. Lonnie could hear him toss and grumble.

"Who told you to come and wake me up in the middle of the night?" Arch said.

"Well, Clem Henry's out here, and he said maybe you'd like to know about it."

Arch tossed around on the bed, flailing the pillow with his fists.

"You tell Clem Henry I said that one of these days he's going to find himself turned inside out, like a coat sleeve."

Lonnie waited doggedly. He knew Clem was right in insisting that Arch ought to wake up and come out there to see what had happened. Lonnie was afraid to go back to the barnyard and tell Clem that Arch was not coming. He did not know, but he had a feeling that Clem might go into the bedroom and drag Arch out of bed. He did not like to think of anything like that taking place.

"Are you still out there, Lonnie?" Arch shouted.

"I'm right here, Mr. Arch. I—"

"If I wasn't so sleepy, I'd come out there and take a stick and—I don't know what I wouldn't do!"

Lonnie met Arch at the back step. On the way out to the hog pen Arch did not speak to him. Arch walked heavily ahead, not even waiting to see if Lonnie was coming. The lantern that Arch was carrying cast long flat beams of yellow light over the ground; and when they got to where Clem was waiting beside Mark's body, the Negro's face shone in the night like a highly polished plowshare.

"What was Mark doing in my hog pen at night, anyway?" Arch said, shouting at them both.

Neither Clem nor Lonnie replied. Arch glared at them for not answering. But no matter how many times he looked at them, his eyes returned each time to stare at the torn body of Mark Newsome on the ground at his feet.

"There's nothing to be done now," Arch said finally. "We'll just have to wait till daylight and send for the undertaker." He walked a few steps away. "Looks like you could have waited till morning in the first place. There wasn't no sense in getting me up."

He turned his back and looked sideways at Clem. Clem stood up and looked him straight in the eyes.

"What do you want, Clem Henry?" he said. "Who told you to be coming around my house in the middle of the night? I don't want niggers coming here except when I send for them."

"I couldn't stand to see anybody eaten up by the hogs, and not do anything about it," Clem said.

"You mind your own business," Arch told him. "And when you talk to me, take off your hat, or you'll be sorry for it. It wouldn't take much to make me do you up the way you belong."

Lonnie backed away. There was a feeling of uneasiness around them. That was how trouble between Clem and Arch always began. He had seen it start that way dozens of times before. As long as Clem turned and went away, nothing happened, but sometimes he stayed right where he was and talked up to Arch just as if he had been a white man, too.

Lonnie hoped it would not happen this time. Arch was already mad enough about being waked up in the middle of the night, and Lonnie knew there was no limit to what Arch would do when he got good and mad at a Negro. No-

body had ever seen him kill a Negro, but he had said
he had, and he told people that he was not scared to do it
again.

"I reckon you know how he came to get eaten up by the
hogs like that," Clem said, looking straight at Arch.

Arch whirled around.

"Are you talking to me . . . ?"

"I asked you that," Clem stated.

"God damn you, yellow-blooded . . ." Arch yelled.

He swung the lantern at Clem's head. Clem dodged, but
the bottom of it hit his shoulder, and it was smashed to
pieces. The oil splattered on the ground, igniting in the air
from the flaming wick. Clem was lucky not to have it splash
on his face and overalls.

"Now, look here . . ." Clem said.

"You yellow-blooded nigger," Arch said, rushing at him.
"I'll teach you to talk back to me. You've got too big for
your place for the last time. I've been taking too much
from you, but I ain't doing it no more."

"Mr. Arch, I . . ." Lonnie said, stepping forward partly
between them. No one heard him.

Arch stood back and watched the kerosene flicker out on
the ground.

"You know good and well why he got eaten up by the
fattening hogs," Clem said, standing his ground. "He was so
hungry he had to get up out of bed in the middle of the
night and come up here in the dark trying to find something
to eat. Maybe he was trying to find the smokehouse. It makes
no difference, either way. He's been on short rations like
everybody else working on your place, and he was so old he
didn't know where else to look for food except in your
smokehouse. You know good and well that's how he got lost
up here in the dark and fell in the hog pen."

The kerosene had died out completely. In the last faint
flare, Arch had reached down and grabbed up the singletree
that had been lying on the ground where Lonnie had dropped
it.

Arch raised the singletree over his head and struck with
all his might at Clem. Clem dodged, but Arch drew back
again quickly and landed a blow on his arm just above the
elbow before Clem could dodge it. Clem's arm dropped to
his side, dangling lifelessly.

"You God-damn yellow-blooded nigger!" Arch shouted.

"Now's your time, you black bastard! I've been waiting for the chance to teach you your lesson. And this's going to be one you won't never forget."

Clem felt the ground with his feet until he had located the other singletree. He stooped down and got it. Raising it, he did not try to hit Arch, but held it in front of him so he could ward off Arch's blows at his head. He continued to stand his ground, not giving Arch an inch.

"Drop that singletree," Arch said.

"I won't stand here and let you beat me like that," Clem protested.

"By God, that's all I want to hear," Arch said, his mouth curling. "Nigger, your time has come, by God!"

He swung once more at Clem, but Clem turned and ran towards the barn. Arch went after him a few steps and stopped. He threw aside the singletree and turned and ran back to the house.

Lonnie went to the fence and tried to think what was best for him to do. He knew he could not take sides with a Negro, in the open, even if Clem had helped him, and especially after Clem had talked to Arch in the way he wished he could himself. He was a white man, and to save his life he could not stand to think of turning against Arch, no matter what happened.

Presently a light burst through one of the windows of the house, and he heard Arch shouting at his wife to wake her up.

When he saw Arch's wife go to the telephone, Lonnie realized what was going to happen. She was calling up the neighbors and Arch's friends. They would not mind getting up in the night when they found out what was going to take place.

Out behind the barn he could hear Clem calling him. Leaving the yard, Lonnie felt his way out there in the dark.

"What's the trouble, Clem?" he said.

"I reckon my time has come," Clem said. "Arch Gunnard talks that way when he's good and mad. He talked just like he did that time he carried Jim Moffin off to the swamp —and Jim never came back."

"Arch wouldn't do anything like that to you, Clem," Lonnie said excitedly, but he knew better.

Clem said nothing.

"Maybe you'd better strike out for the swamps till he

changes his mind and cools off some," Lonnie said. "You might be right, Clem."

Lonnie could feel Clem's eyes burning into him.

"Wouldn't be no sense in that, if you'd help me," Clem said. "Wouldn't you stand by me?"

Lonnie trembled as the meaning of Clem's suggestion became clear to him. His back was to the side of the barn, and he leaned against it while sheets of black and white passed before his eyes.

"Wouldn't you stand by me?" Clem asked again.

"I don't know what Arch would say to that," Lonnie told him haltingly.

Clem walked away several paces. He stood with his back to Lonnie while he looked across the field towards the quarter where his home was.

"I could go in that little patch of woods out there and stay till they get tired of looking for me," Clem said, turning around to see Lonnie.

"You'd better go somewhere," Lonnie said uneasily. "I know Arch Gunnard. He's hard to handle when he makes up his mind to do something he wants to do. I couldn't stop him an inch. Maybe you'd better get clear out of the country, Clem."

"I couldn't do that, and leave my family down there across the field," Clem said.

"He's going to get you if you don't."

"If you'd only sort of help me out a little, he wouldn't. I would only have to go and hide out in that little patch of woods over there a while. Looks like you could do that for me, being as how I helped you find your pa when he was in the hog pen."

Lonnie nodded, listening for sounds from the big house. He continued to nod at Clem while Clem was waiting to be assured.

"If you're going to stand up for me," Clem said, "I can just go over there in the woods and wait till they get it off their minds. You won't be telling them where I'm at, and you could say I struck out for the swamp. They wouldn't ever find me without bloodhounds."

"That's right," Lonnie said, listening for sounds of Arch's coming out of the house. He did not wish to be found back there behind the barn where Arch could accuse him of talking to Clem.

The moment Lonnie replied, Clem turned and ran off into the night. Lonnie went after him a few steps, as if he had suddenly changed his mind about helping him, but Clem was lost in the darkness by then.

Lonnie waited for a few minutes, listening to Clem crashing through the underbrush in the patch of woods a quarter of a mile away. When he could hear Clem no longer, he went around the barn to meet Arch.

Arch came out of the house carrying his double-barreled shotgun and the lantern he had picked up in the house. His pockets were bulging with shells.

"Where is that damn nigger, Lonnie?" Arch asked him. "Where'd he go to?"

Lonnie opened his mouth, but no words came out.

"You know which way he went, don't you?"

Lonnie again tried to say something, but there were no sounds. He jumped when he found himself nodding his head to Arch.

"Mr. Arch, I—"

"That's all right, then," Arch said. "That's all I need to know now. Dudley Smith and Tom Hawkins and Frank and Dave Howard and the rest will be here in a minute, and you can stay right here so you can show us where he's hiding out."

Frantically Lonnie tried to say something. Then he reached for Arch's sleeve to stop him, but Arch had gone.

Arch ran around the house to the front yard. Soon a car came racing down the road, its headlights lighting up the whole place, hog pen and all. Lonnie knew it was probably Dudley Smith, because his was the first house in that direction, only half a mile away. While he was turning into the driveway, several other automobiles came into sight, both up the road and down it.

Lonnie trembled. He was afraid Arch was going to tell him to point out where Clem had gone to hide. Then he knew Arch would tell him. He had promised Clem he would not do that. But try as he might, he could not make himself believe that Arch Gunnard would do anything more than whip Clem.

Clem had not done anything that called for lynching. He had not raped a white woman, he had not shot at a white man; he had only talked back to Arch, with his hat on. But Arch was mad enough to do anything; he was mad enough at Clem not to stop at anything short of lynching.

The whole crowd of men was swarming around him before he realized it. And there was Arch clutching his arm and shouting into his face.

"Mr. Arch, I—"

Lonnie recognized every man in the feeble dawn. They were excited, and they looked like men on the last lap of an all-night fox-hunting party. Their shotguns and pistols were held at their waist, ready for the kill.

"What's the matter with you, Lonnie?" Arch said, shouting into his ear. "Wake up and say where Clem Henry went to hide out. We're ready to go get him."

Lonnie remembered looking up and seeing Frank Howard dropping yellow twelve-gauge shells into the breech of his gun. Frank bent forward so he could hear Lonnie tell Arch where Clem was hiding.

"You ain't going to kill Clem this time, are you, Mr. Arch?" Lonnie asked.

"Kill him?" Dudley Smith repeated. "What do you reckon I've been waiting all this time for if it wasn't for a chance to get Clem. That nigger has had it coming to him ever since he came to this county. He's a bad nigger, and it's coming to him."

"It wasn't exactly Clem's fault," Lonnie said. "If Pa hadn't come up here and fell in the hog pen, Clem wouldn't have had a thing to do with it. He was helping me, that's all."

"Shut up, Lonnie," somebody shouted at him. "You're so excited you don't know what you're saying. You're taking up for a nigger when you talk like that."

People were crowding around him so tightly he felt as if he were being squeezed to death. He had to get some air, get his breath, get out of the crowd.

"That's right," Lonnie said.

He heard himself speak, but he did not know what he was saying.

"But Clem helped me find Pa when he got lost looking around for something to eat."

"Shut up, Lonnie," somebody said again. "You damn fool, shut up!"

Arch grabbed his shoulder and shook him until his teeth rattled. Then Lonnie realized what he had been saying.

"Now, look here, Lonnie," Arch shouted. "You must be out of your head, because you know good and well you wouldn't talk like a nigger-lover in your right mind."

"That's right," Lonnie said, trembling all over. "I sure wouldn't want to talk like that."

He could still feel the grip on his shoulder where Arch's strong fingers had hurt him.

"Did Clem go to the swamp, Lonnie?" Dudley Smith said. "Is that right, Lonnie?"

Lonnie tried to shake his head; he tried to nod his head. Then Arch's fingers squeezed his thin neck. Lonnie looked at the men wild-eyed.

"Where's Clem hiding, Lonnie?" Arch demanded, squeezing.

Lonnie went three or four steps towards the barn. When he stopped, the men behind him pushed forward again. He found himself being rushed behind the barn and beyond it.

"All right, Lonnie," Arch said. "Now which way?"

Lonnie pointed towards the patch of woods where the creek was. The swamp was in the other direction.

"He said he was going to hide out in that little patch of woods along the creek over there, Mr. Arch," Lonnie said. "I reckon he's over there now."

Lonnie felt himself being swept forward, and he stumbled over the rough ground trying to keep from being knocked down and trampled upon. Nobody was talking, and everyone seemed to be walking on tiptoes. The gray light of early dawn was increasing enough both to hide them and to show the way ahead.

Just before they reached the fringe of the woods, the men separated, and Lonnie found himself a part of the circle that was closing in on Clem.

Lonnie was alone, and there was nobody to stop him, but he was unable to move forward or backward. It began to be clear to him what he had done.

Clem was probably up a tree somewhere in the woods ahead, but by that time he had been surrounded on all sides. If he should attempt to break and run, he would be shot down like a rabbit.

Lonnie sat down on a log and tried to think what to do. The sun would be up in a few more minutes, and as soon as it came up, the men would close in on the creek and Clem. He would have no chance at all among all those shotguns and pistols.

Once or twice he saw the flare of a match through the underbrush where some of the men were lying in wait. A whiff of cigarette smoke struck his nostrils, and he found himself wondering if Clem could smell it wherever he was in the woods.

There was still no sound anywhere around him, and he knew that Arch Gunnard and the rest of the men were waiting for the sun, which would in a few minutes come up behind him in the east.

It was light enough by that time to see plainly the rough ground and the tangled underbrush and the curling bark on the pine trees.

The men had already begun to creep forward, guns raised as if stalking a deer. The woods were not large, and the circle of men would be able to cover it in a few minutes at the rate they were going forward. There was still a chance that Clem had slipped through the circle before dawn broke, but Lonnie felt that he was still there. He began to feel then that Clem was there because he himself had placed him there for the men to find easily.

Lonnie found himself moving forward, drawn into the narrowing circle. Presently he could see the men all around him in dim outline. Their eyes were searching the heavy green pine tops as they went forward from tree to tree.

"Oh, Pa!" he said in a hoarse whisper. "Oh, Pa!"

He went forward a few steps, looking into the bushes and up into the treetops. When he saw the other men again, he realized that it was not Mark Newsome being sought. He did not know what had made him forget like that.

The creeping forward began to work into the movement of Lonnie's body. He found himself springing forward on his toes, and his body was leaning in that direction. It was like creeping up on a rabbit when you did not have a gun to hunt with.

He forgot again what he was doing there. The springing motion in his legs seemed to be growing stronger with each step. He bent forward so far he could almost touch the ground with his fingertips. He could not stop now. He was keeping up with the circle of men.

The fifteen men were drawing closer and closer together. The dawn had broken enough to show the time on the face of a watch. The sun was beginning to color the sky above.

Lonnie was far in advance of anyone else by then. He could not hold himself back. The strength in his legs was more than he could hold in check.

He had for so long been unable to buy shells for his gun that he had forgotten how much he liked to hunt.

The sound of the men's steady creeping had become a rhythm in his ears.

"Here's the bastard!" somebody shouted, and there was a concerted crashing through the dry underbrush. Lonnie dashed forward, reaching the tree almost as quickly as anyone else.

He could see everybody with guns raised, and far into the sky above the sharply outlined face of Clem Henry gleamed in the rising sun. His body was hugging the slender top of the pine.

Lonnie did not know who was the first to fire, but the rest of the men did not hesitate. There was a deafening roar as the shotguns and revolvers flared and smoked around the trunk of the tree.

He closed his eyes; he was afraid to look again at the face above. The firing continued without break. Clem hugged the tree with all his might, and then, with the faraway sound of splintering wood, the top of the tree and Clem came crashing through the lower limbs to the ground. The body, sprawling and torn, landed on the ground with a thud that stopped Lonnie's heart for a moment.

He turned, clutching for the support of a tree, as the firing began once more. The crumpled body was tossed time after time, like a sackful of kittens being killed with an automatic shotgun, as charges of lead were fired into it from all sides. A cloud of dust rose from the ground and drifted overhead with the choking odor of burned powder.

Lonnie did not remember how long the shooting lasted. He found himself running from tree to tree, clutching at the rough pine bark, stumbling wildly towards the cleared ground. The sky had turned from gray to red when he emerged in the open, and as he ran, falling over the hard clods in the plowed field, he tried to keep his eyes on the house ahead.

Once he fell and found it almost impossible to rise again to his feet. He struggled to his knees, facing the round red sun. The warmth gave him the strength to rise to his feet, and he muttered unintelligibly to himself. He tried to say things he had never thought to say before.

When he got home, Hatty was waiting for him in the yard. She had heard the shots in the woods, and she had seen him stumbling over the hard clods in the field, and she had seen him kneeling there looking straight into the face of the sun. Hatty was trembling as she ran to Lonnie to find out what the matter was.

Once in his own yard, Lonnie turned and looked for a second over his shoulder. He saw the men climbing over the fence at Arch Gunnard's. Arch's wife was standing on the back porch, and she was speaking to them.

"Where's your pa, Lonnie?" Hatty said. "And what in the world was all that shooting in the woods for?" Lonnie stumbled forward until he had reached the front porch. He fell upon the steps.

"Lonnie, Lonnie!" Hatty was saying. "Wake up and tell me what in the world is the matter. I've never seen the like of all that's going on."

"Nothing," Lonnie said. "Nothing."

"Well, if there's nothing the matter, can't you go up to the big house and ask for a little piece of streak-of-lean? We ain't got a thing to cook for breakfast. Your pa's going to be hungrier than ever after being up walking around all night."

"What?" Lonnie said, his voice rising to a shout as he jumped to his feet.

"Why, I only said go up to the big house and get a little piece of streak-of-lean, Lonnie. That's all I said."

He grabbed his wife about the shoulders.

"Meat?" he yelled, shaking her roughly.

"Yes," she said, pulling away from him in surprise. "Couldn't you go ask Arch Gunnard for a little bit of steak-of-lean?"

Lonnie slumped down again on the steps, his hands falling between his outspread legs and his chin falling on his chest.

"No," he said almost inaudibly. "No. I ain't hungry."

Country Full of Swedes

THERE I WAS, standing in the middle of the chamber, trembling like I was coming down with the flu, and still not knowing what God-awful something had happened. In all my days in the Back Kingdom, I never heard such noises so early in the forenoon.

It was about half an hour after sunrise, and a gun went off like a cofferdam breaking up under ice at twenty below, and I'd swear it sounded like it wasn't any farther away than my feet are from my head. That gun shot off, pitching me six-seven inches off the bed, and, before I could come down out of the air, there was another roar like somebody coughing through a megaphone, with a two-weeks cold, right in my ear. God-helping, I hope I never get waked up like that again until I can get myself home to the Back Kingdom where I rightfully belong to stay.

I must have stood there ten-fifteen minutes shivering in my nightshirt, my heart pounding inside of me like a ramrod working on a plugged-up bore, and listening for that gun again, if it was going to shoot some more. A man never knows what's going to happen next in the State of Maine; that's why I wish sometimes I'd never left the Back Kingdom to begin with. I was making sixty a month, with the best of bed and board, back there in the intervale; but like a God-damn fool I had to jerk loose and came down here near the Bay. I'm going back where I came from, God-helping; I've never had a purely calm and peaceful day since I got here three-four years ago. This is the damnedest country for the unexpected raising of all kinds of unlooked-for hell a man is apt to run across in a lifetime of traveling. If a man's born and raised in the Back Kingdom, he ought to stay there where he belongs; that's what I'd done if I'd had the sense to stay out of this down-country near the Bay, where you don't ever know, God-helping, what's going to happen next, where, or when.

But there I was, standing in the middle of the upstairs chamber, shaking like a ragweed in an August windstorm, and not knowing what minute, maybe right at me, that gun was going to shoot off again, for all I knew. Just then, though. I heard Jim and Mrs. Frost trip-trapping around downstairs in their bare feet. Even if I didn't know what God-awful something had happened, I knew things around the place weren't calm and peaceful, like they generally were of a Sunday morning in May, because it took a stiff mixture of heaven and hell to get Jim and Mrs. Frost up and out of a warm bed before six of a forenoon, any of the days of the week.

I ran to the window and stuck my head out as far as I could get it, to hear what the trouble was. Everything out there was as quiet and peaceful as midnight on a back road in middlemost winter. But I knew something was up, because Jim and Mrs. Frost didn't make a practice of getting up and out of a warm bed that time of forenoon in the chillish Maytime.

There wasn't any sense in me standing there in the cold air shivering in my nightshirt, so I put on my clothes, whistling all the time through my teeth to drive away the chill, and trying to figure out what God-damn fool was around so early shooting off a gun of a Sunday morning. Just then I heard the downstairs door open, and up the steps, two at a time, came Jim in his breeches and his shirttail flying out behind him.

He wasn't long in coming up the stairs, for a man sixty-seven, but before he reached the door to my room, that gun went off again: BOOM! Just like that; and the echo came rolling back through the open window from the hills: BOOM! BOOM! Like fireworks going off with your eyes shut. Jim had busted through the door already, but when he heard that BOOM! sound he sort of spun around, like a cockeyed weathervane, five-six times, and ran out of the door again like he had been shot in the hind parts with a moose gun. That BOOM! so early in the afternoon was enough to scare the daylights out of any man, and Jim wasn't any different from me or anybody else in the town of East Joloppi. He just turned around and jumped through the door to the first tread on the stairway like his mind was made up to go somewhere else in a hurry, and no fooling around at the start.

I'd been hired to Jim and Mrs. Frost for all of three-

four years, and I was near about as much of a Frost, excepting name, as Jim himself was. Jim and me got along
first-rate together, doing chores and haying and farm work
in general, because neither one of us was ever trying to make
the other do more of the work. We were hitched to make a
fine team, and I never had a kick coming, and Jim said he
didn't either. Jim had the name of Frost, to be sure, but I
wouldn't ever hold that against a man.

The echo of that gunshot was still rolling around in the
hills and coming in through the window, when all at once
that God-awful coughlike whoop through a megaphone
sounded again right there in the room and everywhere else,
like it might have been, in the whole town of East Joloppi.
The man or beast or whatever animal he was who hollered
like that ought to be locked up to keep him from scaring all
the women and children to death, and it wasn't any stomach-
comforting sound for a grown man who's used to the peaceful calm of the Back Kingdom all his life to hear so early
of a Sunday forenoon, either.

I jumped to the door where Jim, just a minute before,
leaped through. He didn't stop till he got clear to the bottom of the stairs. He stood there, looking up at me like a
wild-eyed cow moose surprised in the sheriff's corn field.

"Who fired that God-awful shot, Jim?" I yelled at him,
leaping down the stairs quicker than a man of my years
ought to let himself do.

"Good God!" Jim said, his voice hoarse, and falling all
to pieces like a stump of punkwood. "The Swedes! The
Swedes are shooting, Stan!"

"What Swedes, Jim—those Swedes who own the farm and
buildings across the road over there?" I said, trying to find
the buttonholes in my shirt. "Have they come back here to
live on that farm?"

"Good God, yes!" he said, his voice croaking deep down in
his throat, like he had swallowed too much water. "The
Swedes are all over the place. They're everywhere you can
see, there's that many of them."

"What's their name, Jim?" I asked him. "You and Mrs.
Frost never told me what their name is."

"Good God, I don't know. I never heard them called
anything but Swedes, and that's what it is, I guess. It ought
to be that, if it ain't."

I ran across the hall to look out a window, but it was
on the wrong side of the house, and I couldn't see a thing.

Mrs. Frost was stepping around in the downstairs chamber, locking things up in the drawers and closet and forgetting where she was hiding the keys. I could see her through the open door, and she was more scared-looking than Jim was. She was so scared of the Swedes she didn't know what she was doing, none of the time.

"What made those Swedes come back for, Jim?" I said to him. "I thought you said they were gone for good, this time."

"Good God, Stan," he said, "I don't know what they came back for. I guess hard times are bringing everybody back to the land, and the Swedes are always in the front rush of everything. I don't know what brought them back, but they're all over the place, shooting and yelling and raising hell. There are thirty-forty of them, looks like to me, counting everything with heads."

"What are they doing now, Jim, except yelling and shooting?"

"Good God," Jim said, looking behind him to see what Mrs. Frost was doing with his things in the downstairs chamber. "I don't know what they're not doing. But I can hear them, Stan! You hurry out right now and lock up all the tools in the barn and bring in the cows and tie them up in the stalls. I've got to hurry out now and bring in all of those new 'cedar fence posts across the front of the yard before they start pulling them up and carrying them off. Good God, Stan, the Swedes are everywhere you look outdoors! We've got to make haste, Stan!"

Jim ran to the side door and out the back of the house, but I took my time about going. I wasn't scared of the Swedes, like Jim and Mrs. Frost were, and I didn't aim to have Jim putting me to doing tasks and chores, or anything else, before breakfast and the proper time. I wasn't any more scared of the Swedes than I was of the Finns and Portuguese, anyway. It's a God-awful shame for Americans to let Swedes and Finns and the Portuguese scare the daylights out of them. God-helping, they are no different than us, and you never see a Finn or a Swede scared of an American. But people like Jim and Mrs. Frost are scared to death of Swedes and other people from the old countries; Jim and Mrs. Frost and people like that never stop to think that all of us Americans came over from the old countries, one time or another, to begin with.

But there wasn't any sense in trying to argue with Jim and

Mrs. Frost right then, when the Swedes, like a fired nest of yellow-headed bumblebees, were swarming all over the place as far as the eye could see, and when Mrs. Frost was scared to death that they were coming into the house and carry out all of her and Jim's furniture and household goods. So while Mrs. Frost was tying her and Jim's shoes in pillowcases and putting them out of sight in closets and behind beds, I went to the kitchen window and looked out to see what was going on around that tall yellow house across the road.

Jim and Mrs. Frost both were right about there being Swedes all over the place. God-helping, there were Swedes all over the country, near about all over the whole town of East Joloppi, for what I could see out of the window. They were as thick around the barn and pump and the woodpile as if they had been a nest of yellow-headed bumblebees strewn over the countryside. There were Swedes everywhere a man could see, and the ones that couldn't be seen could be heard yelling their heads off inside the yellow clapboarded house across the road. There wasn't any mistake about there being Swedes there, either; because I've never yet seen a man who mistakes a Swede or a Finn for an American. Once you see a Finn or a Swede you know, God-helping, that he is a Swede or a Finn, and not a Portugee or an American.

There was a Swede everywhere a man could look. Some of them were little Swedes; and women Swedes, to be sure; but little Swedes, in the end, and women Swedes too, near about, grow up as big as any of them. When you come right down to it, there's no sense in counting out the little Swedes and the women Swedes.

Out in the road in front of their house were seven-eight autos and trucks loaded down with furniture and household goods. All around, everything was Swedes. The Swedes were yelling and shouting at one another, the little Swedes and the women Swedes just as loud as the big Swedes, and it looked like none of them knew what all the shouting and yelling was for, and when they found out, they didn't give a damn about it. That was because all of them were Swedes. It didn't make any difference what a Swede was yelling about; just as long as he had leave to open his mouth, he was tickled to death about it.

I have never seen the like of so much yelling and shouting anywhere else before; but down here in the State of

Maine, in the down-country on the Bay, there's no sense in being taken back at the sights to be seen, because anything on God's green earth is likely and liable to happen between day and night, and the other way around, too.

Now, you take the Finns; there's any God's number of them around in the woods, where you least expect to see them, logging and such. When a Finn crew breaks a woods camp, it looks like there's a Finn for every tree in the whole State, but you don't see them going around making the noise that Swedes do, with all their yelling and shouting and shooting off guns. Finns are quiet about their hell-raising. The Portuguese are quiet, too; you see them tramping around, minding their own business, and working hard on a river dam or something, but you never hear them shouting and yelling and shooting off guns at five-six of a Sunday morning. There's no known likeness to the noise that a houseful of Swedes can make when they get to yelling and shouting at one another early in the forenoon.

I was standing there all that time, looking out the window at the Swedes across the road, when Jim came into the kitchen with an armful of wood and threw it into the wood box behind the range.

"Good God, Stan," Jim said, "the Swedes are everywhere you can look outdoors. They're not going to get that armful of wood, anyway, though."

Mrs. Frost came to the door and stood looking like she didn't know it was her business to cook breakfast for Jim and me. I made a fire in the range and put on a pan of water to boil for the coffee. Jim kept running to the window to look out, and there wasn't much use in expecting Mrs. Frost to start cooking unless somebody set her to it, in the shape she was in, with all the Swedes around the place. She was so upset, it was a downright pity to look at her. But Jim and me had to eat, and I went and took her by the arm and brought her to the range and left her standing there so close she would get burned if she didn't stir around and make breakfast.

"Good God, Stan," Jim said, "those Swedes are into everything. They're in the barn, and in the pasture running the cows, and I don't know what else they've been into since I looked last. They'll take the tools and the horses and cows, and the cedar posts, too, if we don't get out there and put everything under lock and key."

"Now, hold on, Jim," I said, looking out the window.

"Them you see are little Swedes out there, and they're not going to make off with anything of yours and Mrs. Frost's. The big Swedes are busy carrying in furniture and household goods. Those Swedes aren't going to tamper with anything of yours and Mrs. Frost's. They're people just like us. They don't go around stealing everything in sight. Now, let's just sit here by the window and watch them while Mrs. Frost is getting breakfast ready."

"Good God, Stan, they're Swedes," Jim said, "and they're moving into the house across the road. I've got to put everything under lock and key before—"

"Hold on, Jim," I told him. "It's their house they're moving into. God-helping, they're not moving into your and Jim's house, are they, Mrs. Frost?"

"Jim," Mrs. Frost said, shaking her finger at him and looking at me wild-eyed and sort of flustered-like, "Jim, don't you sit there and let Stanley stop you from saving the stock and tools. Stanley doesn't know the Swedes like we do. Stanley came down here from the Back Kingdom, and he doesn't know anything about Swedes."

Mrs. Frost was partly right, because I've never seen the things in my whole life that I've seen down here near the Bay; but there wasn't any sense in Americans like Jim and Mrs. Frost being scared of Swedes. I've seen enough Finns and Portuguese in my time in the Back Kingdom, up in the intervale, to know that Americans are no different from the others.

"Now, you hold on a while, Jim," I said. "Swedes are no different than Finns. Finns don't go around stealing another man's stock and tools. Up in the Back Kingdom the Finns are the finest kind of neighbors."

"That may be so up in the Back Kingdom, Stan," Jim said, "but Swedes down here near the Bay are nothing like anything that's ever been before or since. Those Swedes over there across the road work in a pulp mill over to Waterville three-four years, and when they've got enough money saved up, or when they lose it all, as the case may be, they all move back here to East Joloppi on this farm of theirs for two-three years at a time. That's what they do. And they've been doing it for the past thirty-forty years, ever since I can remember, and they haven't changed none in all that time. I can recall the first time they came to East Joloppi; they built that house across the road then, and if you've ever seen a sight like Swedes building a house in a hurry, you haven't got much else to live for. Why! Stan, those Swedes built that house in four-five days—just like that! I've never seen the equal of it. Of course now, Stan, it's the damnedest-looking house a man ever saw, because it's not a farmhouse, and it's not a city house, and it's no kind of a house an American would erect. Why! Those Swedes threw that house together in four-five days—just like that! But whoever saw a house like that before, with three stories to it, and only six rooms in the whole building! And painted yellow, too; good God, Stan, white is the only color to paint a house, and those Swedes went and painted it yellow. Then on top of that, they went and painted the barn red. And of all of the shouting and yelling, at all times of the day and night, a man never saw or heard before. Those Swedes acted like they were purely crazy for the whole of four-five days, and they were, and they still are. But what gets me is the painting of it yellow, and the making of it three stories high, with only six rooms in the whole building. Nobody but Swedes would go and do a think like that; an American would have built a farmhouse, here in the country, resting square on the ground, with one story, maybe a story and a half, and then painted it lead-white. But good God, Stan, those fool Swedes had to put up three stories, to hold six rooms, and then went and painted the building yellow."

"Swedes are a little queer, sometimes," I said. "But Finns and Portuguese are too, Jim. And Americans sometimes—"

"A little queer!" Jim said. "Why! good God, Stan, the Swedes are the queerest people on the earth, if that's the right word for them. You don't know Swedes, Stan. This is the first time you've ever seen those Swedes across the road, and that's why you don't know what they're like after being shut up in a pulpwood mill over to Waterville for four-five years. They're purely wild, I tell you, Stan. They don't stop for anything they set their heads on. If you was to walk out there now and tell them to move their autos and trucks off of the town road so the travelers could get past without having to drive around through the brush, they'd tear you apart, they're that wild, after being shut up in the pulp mill over to Waterville these three-four, maybe four-five, years."

"Finns get that way, too," I tried to tell Jim. "After Finns have been shut up in a woods camp all winter, they make a lot of noise when they get out. Everybody who has to stay close to the job for three-four years likes to act free when he gets out from under the job. Now, Jim, you take the Portuguese—"

"Don't you sit there, Jim, and let Stanley keep you from putting the tools away," Mrs. Frost said. "Stanley doesn't know the Swedes like we do. He's lived up in the Back Kingdom most of his life, tucked away in the intervale, and he's never seen Swedes—"

"Good God, Stan," Jim said, standing up, he was that nervous and upset, "the Swedes are overrunning the whole country. I'll bet there are more Swedes in the town of East Joloppi than there are in the rest of the country. Everybody knows there's more Swedes in the State of Maine than there are in the old country. Why Jim, they take to this state like potato bugs take to—"

"Don't you sit there and let Stanley keep you back, Jim," Mrs. Frost put in again. "Stanley doesn't know the Swedes like we do. Stanley's lived up there in the Back Kingdom most of his life."

Just then one of the big Swedes started yelling at some of the little Swedes and women Swedes. I'll swear, those big Swedes sounded like a pastureful of hoarse bulls, near the end of May, mad about the black flies. God-helping, they yelled like they were fixing to kill all the little Swedes and women Swedes they could get their hands on. It didn't amount to anything, though; because the little Swedes and the women Swedes yelled right back at them just like they had been big Swedes too. The little Swedes and women Swedes couldn't yell hoarse bull bass, but it was close enough to it to make a man who's lived most of his life up in the Back Kingdom, in the intervale, think that the whole town of East Joloppi was full of big Swedes.

Jim was all for getting out after the tools and stock right away, but I pulled him back to the table. I wasn't going to let Jim and Mrs. Frost set me to doing tasks and chores before breakfast and the regular time. Forty dollars a month isn't much to pay a man for ten-eleven hours' work a day, including Sundays, when the stock has to be attended to like any other day, and I set myself that I wasn't going to work twelve-thirteen hours a day by them, even if I was practically one of the Frosts myself, except in name, by that time.

"Now, hold on awhile, Jim," I said. "Let's just sit here by the window and watch them carry their furniture and household goods inside while Mrs. Frost's getting the cooking ready to eat. If they start taking off any of you and Mrs. Frost's things, we can see them just as good from here by the window as we could out there in the yard and road."

"Now, Jim, I'm telling you," Mrs. Frost said, shaking all over, and not even trying to cook us a meal, "don't you sit there and let Stanley keep you from saving the stock and tools. Stanley doesn't know the Swedes like we do. He thinks they're like everybody else."

Jim wasn't for staying in the house when all of his tools were lying around in the yard, and while his cows were in the pasture unprotected, but he saw how it would be better to wait where we could hurry up Mrs. Frost with the cooking, if we were ever going to eat breakfast that forenoon. She was so excited and nervous about the Swedes moving back to East Joloppi from the pulp mill in Waterville that she hadn't got the beans and brown bread fully heated from the night before, and we had to sit and eat them cold.

We were sitting there by the window eating the cold beans and brown bread, and watching the Swedes, when two of the little Swedes started running across Jim and Mrs. Frost's lawn. They were chasing one of their big yellow tomcats they had brought with them from Waterville. The yellow tom was as large as an eight-months collie puppy, and he ran like he was on fire and didn't know how to put it out. His great big bushy tail stuck straight up in the air behind him, like a flag, and he was leaping over the lawn like a devilish calf, newborn.

Jim and Mrs. Frost saw the little Swedes and big yellow tomcat at the same time I did.

"Good God," Jim shouted, raising himself part out of the chair. "Here they come now!"

"Hold on now, Jim," I said, pulling him back to the table. "They're only chasing one of their tomcats. They're not after taking anything that belongs to you and Mrs. Frost. Let's just sit here and finish eating the beans, and watch them out the window."

"My crown in heaven!" Mrs. Frost cried out, running to the window and looking through. "Those Swedes are going to kill every plant on the place. They'll dig up all the bulbs and pull up all the vines in the flower bed."

"Now you just sit and calm yourself, Mrs. Frost," I told her. "Those little Swedes are just chasing a tomcat. They're not after doing hurt to your flowers."

The big Swedes were unloading the autos and trucks and

carrying the furniture and household goods into their three-story yellow clapboarded house. None of them was paying any attention to the little Swedes chasing the yellow tom over Jim and Mrs. Frost's lawn.

Just then the kitchen door burst open, and the two little Swedes stood there looking at us, panting and blowing their heads off.

Mrs. Frost took one look at them, and then she let out a yell, but the kids didn't notice her at all.

"Hey," one of them shouted, "come out here and help us get the cat. He climbed up in one of your trees."

By that time, Mrs. Frost was all for slamming the door in their faces, but I pushed in front of her and went out into the yard with them. Jim came right behind me, after he had finished calming Mrs. Frost, and telling her we wouldn't let the Swedes come and carry out her furniture and household goods.

The yellow tom was all the way up in one of Jim's young maple shade trees. The maple wasn't strong enough to support even the smallest of the little Swedes, if he should take it into his head to climb to the top after the cat, and neither Jim nor me was hurting ourselves trying to think of a way to get the feline down. We were all for letting the cat stay where he was, till he got ready to come down of his own free will, but the little Swedes couldn't wait for anything. They wanted the tom right away, then and there, and no wasting of time in getting him.

"You boys go home and wait for the cat to come down," Jim told them. "There's no way to make him come down now, till he gets ready to come down of his own mind."

But no, those two boys were little Swedes. They weren't thinking of going back home till they got the yellow tom down from the maple. One of them ran to the tree, before Jim or me could head him off, and started shinnying up it like a popeyed squirrel. In no time, it seemed to me like, he was up amongst the limbs, jumping around up there from one limb to another like he had been brought up in just such a tree.

"Good God, Stan," Jim said, "can't you keep them out of the trees?"

There was no answer for that, and Jim knew there wasn't. There's no way of stopping a Swede from doing what he has set his head on doing.

The boy got almost to the top branch, where the yellow

tom was clinging and spitting, when the tree began to bend towards the house. I knew what was coming, if something wasn't done about it pretty quick, and so did Jim. Jim saw his young maple shade tree begin to bend, and he almost had a fit looking at it. He ran to the lumber stack and came back dragging two lengths of two-by-fours. He got them set up against the tree before it had time to do any splitting, and then we stood there, like two damn fools, shoring up the tree and yelling at the little Swede to come down out of there before we broke his neck for being up in it.

The big Swedes across the road heard the fuss we were making, and they came running out of that three-story, six-room house like it had been on fire inside.

"Good God, Stan," Jim shouted at me, "here comes the Swedes!"

"Don't turn and run off, Jim," I cautioned him, yanking him back by his coattail. "They're not wild beasts; we're not scared of them. Hold on where you are, Jim."

I could see Mrs. Frost's head almost breaking through the window glass in the kitchen. She was all for coming out and driving the Swedes off her lawn and out of her flowers, but she was too scared to unlock the kitchen door and open it.

Jim was getting ready to run again, when he saw the Swedes coming towards us like a nest of yellow-headed bumblebees, but I wasn't scared of them, and I held on to Jim's coattail and told him I wasn't. Jim and me were shoring up the young maple, and I knew if one of us let go, the tree would bend to the ground right away and split wide open right up the middle. There was no sense in ruining a young maple shade tree like that, and I told Jim there wasn't.

"Hey," one of the big Swedes shouted at the little Swede up in the top of the maple, "come down out of that tree and go home to your mother."

"Aw, to hell with the Old Lady," the little Swede shouted down. "I'm getting the cat by the tail."

The big Swede looked at Jim and me. Jim was almost ready to run again by that time, but I wasn't, and I held him and told him I wasn't. There was no sense in letting the Swedes scare the daylights out of us.

"What in hell can you do with kids when they get that age?" he asked Jim and me.

Jim was all for telling him to make the boy come down out of the maple before it bent over and split wide open, but I knew there was no sense in trying to make him come down out of there until he got good and ready to come, or else got the yellow tom by the tail.

Just then another big Swede came running out of that three-story, six-room house across the road, holding a double-bladed ax out in front of him, like it was a red-hot poker, and yelling for all he was worth at the other Swedes.

"Good God, Stan," Jim said, "don't let those Swedes cut down my young maple!"

I had lots better sense than to try to make the Swedes stop doing what they had set their heads on doing. A man would be purely a fool to try to stop it from raining from above when it got ready to, even if he was trying to get his corn crop planted.

I looked around again, and there was Mrs. Frost all but popping through the window glass. I could see what she was thinking, but I couldn't hear a word she was saying. It was good and plenty though, whatever it was.

"Come down out of that tree!" the Swede yelled at the boy up in Jim's maple.

Instead of starting to climb down, the little Swede reached up for the big yellow tom cat's tail. The tom reached out a big fat paw and harried the boy five-six times, just like that, quicker than the eye could follow. The kid let out a yell and a shout that must have been heard all the way to the other side of town, sounding like a whole houseful of Swedes up in the maple.

The big Swede covered the distance to the tree in one stride, pushing everything behind him.

"Good God, Stan," Jim shouted at me, "we've got to do something!"

There wasn't anything a man could do, unless he was either a Swede himself, or a man of prayer. Americans like Jim and me had no business getting in a Swede's way, especially when he was swinging a big double-bladed ax, and he just out of a pulp mill after being shut up making paper four-five years.

The big Swede grabbed the ax and let go at the trunk of the maple with it. There was no stopping him then, because he had the ax going, and it was whipping around his shoulders like a cow's tail in a swarm of black flies. The little maple shook all over every time the ax blade struck it, like wind blowing a cornstalk, and then it began to bend on the other side from Jim and me where we were shoring it up with the two-by-fours. Chips as big as dinner plates were flying across the lawn and pelting the house like a gang of boys stoning telephone insulators. One of those big dinner-plate chips crashed through the window where Mrs. Frost was, about that time. Both Jim and me thought at first she had fallen through the window, but when we looked again, we could see that she was still on the inside, and madder than ever at the Swedes.

The two-by-fours weren't any good any longer, because it was too late to get to the other side of the maple in time to keep it from bending in that direction. The Swede with the doubled-bladed ax took one more swing, and the tree began to bend towards the ground.

The tree came down, the little Swede came down, and the big yellow tom came down on top of everything, holding for all he was worth to the top of the little Swede's head. Long before the tree and the boy struck the ground, the big yellow tom had sprung what looked like thirty feet, and landed in the middle of Mrs. Frost's flowers and bulbs. The little Swede let out a yell and a whoop when he hit the ground that brought out six-seven more Swedes from that three-story, six-room house, piling out into the road like it was the first time they had ever heard a kid bawl. The women Swedes and the little Swedes and the big Swedes piled out on Jim and Mrs. Frost's front lawn like they had been dropped out of a dump truck and didn't know which was straight up from straight down.

I thought Mrs. Frost was going to have a fit right then and there in the kitchen window. When she saw that swarm of Swedes coming across her lawn, and the big yellow tom-cat in her flower bed among the tender plants and bulbs, digging up the things she had planted, and the Swedes with their No. 12 heels squashing the green shoots she had been nursing along—well, I guess she just sort of caved in, and fell out of sight for the time being. I didn't have time to run to see what was wrong with her, because Jim and me had to tear out behind the tom and the Swedes to try to save as much as we could.

"Good God, Stan," Jim shouted at me, "go run in the house and ring up all the neighbors on the line, and tell them to hurry over here and help up before the Swedes wreck my farm and buildings. There's no telling what they'll do next. They'll be setting fire to the house and barn the next thing, maybe. Hurry, Stan!"

I didn't have time to waste talking to the neighbors on the telephone line. I was right behind Jim and the Swedes to see what they were going to do next.

"I pay you good pay, Stan," Jim said, "and I want my money's worth. Now, you go ring up the neighbors and tell them to hurry."

The big yellow tom made one more spring when he hit the flower bed, and that leap landed him over the stone wall. He struck out for the deep woods with every Swede on the place behind him. When Jim and me got to the stone wall, I pulled up short and held Jim back.

"Well, Jim," I said, "if you want me to, I'll go down in the woods and raise hell with every Swede on the place for cutting down your young maple and tearing up Mrs. Frost's flower bed."

We turned around and there was Mrs. Frost, right behind us. There was no knowing how she got there so quick after the Swedes had left for the woods.

"My crown in heaven," Mrs. Frost said, running up to Jim and holding on to him. "Jim, don't let Stanley make the Swedes mad. This is the only place we have got to live in, and they'll be here a year now this time, maybe two-three, if the hard times don't get better soon."

"That's right, Stan," he said. "You don't know the Swedes like we do. You would have to be a Swede yourself to know what to tell them. Don't go over there doing anything like that."

"God-helping, Jim," I said, "you and Mrs. Frost ain't scared of the Swedes, are you?"

"God God, no," he said, his eyes popping out; "but don't go making them mad."

The Negro in the Well

JULE ROBINSON was lying in bed snoring when his fox-hounds struck a live trail a mile away and their baying woke him up with a start. He jumped to the floor, jerked on his shoes, and ran out into the front yard. It was about an hour before dawn.

Holding his hat to the side of his head like a swollen hand, he listened to the trailing on the ridge above the house. With his hat to deflect the sound into his ear, he could hear the dogs treading in the dry underbrush as plainly as his own breathing. It had taken him only a few seconds to determine that the hounds were not cold-trailing, and he put his hat back on his head and stooped over to lace his shoes.

"Papa," a frightened voice said, "please don't go off again now—wait till daybreak, anyway."

Jule turned around and saw the dim outline of his two girls. They were huddled together in the window of their bedroom. Jessie and Clara were old enough to take care of themselves, he thought, but that did not stop them from getting in his way when he wanted to go fox hunting.

"Go on back to bed and sleep, Jessie—you and Clara," he said gruffly. "Those hounds are just up on the ridge. They can't take me much out of hollering distance before sunup."

"We're scared, Papa," Clara said.

"Scared of what?" Jule asked impatiently. "There ain't a thing for two big girls like you and Jessie to be scared of. What's there to be scared of in this big country, anyway?"

The hounds stopped trailing for a moment, and Jule straightened up to listen in the silence. All at once they began again, and he bent down to finish tying his shoes.

Off in the distance he could hear several other packs of trailing hounds, and by looking closely at the horizon he could see the twinkle of campfires where bands of fox hunters had stopped to warm their hands and feet.

"Are you going, anyway, Papa?" Clara asked.

"I'm going, anyway," he answered.

The two girls ran back to bed and pulled the covers over their heads. There was no way to argue with Jule Robinson when he had set his head on following his fox-hounds.

The craze must have started anew sometime during the holidays, because by the end of the first week in January it looked and sounded as if everybody in Georgia were trading foxhounds by day and bellowing "Whoo-way-oh!" by night. From the time the sun went down until the next morning when it came up, the woods, fields, pastures, and swamps were crawling with beggar-liced men and yelping hound-dogs. Nobody would have thought of riding horseback after the hounds in a country where there was a barb-wire fence every few hundred yards.

Automobiles roared and rattled over the rough country roads all night long. The fox hunters had to travel fast in order to keep up with the pack.

It was not safe for any living thing with four legs to be out after sundown, because the hounds had the hunting fever too, and packs of those rangy half-starved dogs were running down and devouring calves, hogs, and even yellow-furred bobcats. It had got so during the past two weeks that the chickens knew enough to take to their roosts an hour ahead of time, because those packs of gaunt hunt-hungry hounds could not wait for sunset any more.

Jule finished lacing his shoes and went around the house. The path to the ridge began in the back yard and weaved up the hillside like a cowpath through a thicket. Jule passed the well and stopped to feel in his pockets to see if he had enough smoking tobacco to last him until he got back.

While he was standing there he heard behind him a sound like water gurgling through the neck of a demijohn. Jule listened again. The sound came even more plainly while he listened. There was no creek anywhere within hearing distance, and the nearest water was in the well. He went to the edge and listened again. The well did not have a stand or a windlass; it was merely a twenty-foot hole in the ground with boards laid over the top to keep pigs and chickens from falling into it.

"O Lord, help me now!" a voice said.

Jule got down on his hands and knees and looked at the well cover in the darkness. He felt of the boards with his hands. Three of them had been moved, and there was a black oblong hole that was large enough to drop a calf through.

"Who's that?" Jule said, stretching out his neck and cocking his ear.

"O Lord, help me now," the voice said again, weaker than before.

The gurgling sound began again, and Jule knew then that it was the water in the well.

"Who's down there muddying up my well?" Jule said.

There was no sound then. Even the gurgling stopped.

Jule felt on the ground for a pebble and dropped it into the well. He counted until he could hear the *kerplunk* when it struck the water.

"Doggone your hide, whoever you are down there!" Jule said. "Who's down there?"

Nobody answered.

Jule felt in the dark for the water bucket, but he could not find it. Instead, his fingers found a larger pebble, a stone almost as big around as his fist, and he dropped it into the well.

The big rock struck something else before it finally went into the water.

"O Lord, I'm going down and can't help myself," the voice down there said. "O Lord a big hand is trying to shove me under."

The hounds trailing on the ridge swung around to the east and started back again. The fox they were after was trying to back-trail them, but Jule's hounds were hard to fool. They had got to be almost as smart as a fox.

Jule straightened up and listened to the running.

"Whoo-way-oh!" he called after the dogs.

That sent them on yelping even louder than before.

"Is that you up there, Mr. Jule?" the voice asked.

Jule bent over the well again, keeping one ear on the dogs on the ridge. He did not want to lose track of them when they were on a live trail like that.

"This is me," Jule said. "Who's that?"

"This is only Bokus Bradley, Mr. Jule," the voice said.

"What you doing down in my well, muddying it up like that, Bokus?"

"It was something like this, Mr. Jule," Bokus said. "I was coming down the ridge a while ago, trying to keep up with my hounds, and I stumbled over your well cover. I reckon I must have missed the path, somehow or other. Your well cover wouldn't hold me up, or something, and the first thing I knew, here I was. I've been here ever since I fell in. I reckon I've been down here most of the night. I hope you ain't mad at me, Mr. Jule. I just naturally couldn't help it at all."

"You've muddied up my well water," Jule said. "I ain't so doggone pleased about that."

"I reckon I have, some," Bokus said, "but I just naturally couldn't help it none at all."

"Where'd your dogs go to, Bokus?" Jule asked.

"I don't know, Mr. Jule. I haven't heard a sound out of them since I fell in here. They was headed for the creek when I was coming down the ridge behind them. Can you hear them anywhere now, Mr. Jule?"

Several packs of hounds could be heard. Jule's on the ridge was trailing east, and a pack was trailing down the creek toward town. Over toward the hills several more packs were running, but they were so far away it was not easy to tell to whom they belonged.

"Sounds to me like I hear your dogs down the creek, headed for the swamp," Jule said.

"Whoo-way-oh!" Bokus called.

The sound from the well struck Jule like a blast out of a megaphone.

"Your dogs can't hear you from 'way down there, Bokus," he said.

"I know they can't, Mr. Jule, and that's why I sure enough want to get out of here. My poor dogs don't know which way I want them to trail when they can't hear me talk to them. Whoo-way-oh!" Bokus shouted. "O Lord, help me now!"

Jule's dogs sounded as if they were closing in on a fox, and Jule jumped to his feet.

"Whoo-way-oh!" he shouted, cupping his hands around his mouth. "Whoo-way-oh!"

"Is you still up there, Mr. Jule?" Bokus asked. "Please, Mr. Jule, don't go away and leave me down here in this cold well. I'll do anything for you if you'll just only get me out of here. I've been standing neck-deep in this cold water near about all night long."

Jule threw some of the boards over the well.

"What you doing up there, Mr. Jule?"

Jule took off his hat and held the brim like a fan to the

side of his head. He could hear the panting of the dogs while they ran.

"How many foxhounds have you got, Bokus?" Jule asked.

"I got me eight," Bokus said. "They're mighty fine fox trailers, too, Mr. Jule. But I'd like to get me out of this here well before doing much more talking with you."

"You could get along somehow with less than that, couldn't you, Bokus?"

"If I had to, I'd have to," Bokus said, "but I sure enough would hate to have a fewer than my eight dogs, though. Eight is just naturally the right-sized pack for me, Mr. Jule."

"How are you figuring on getting out of there?" Jule said.

"I just naturally figured on you helping me out, Mr. Jule," he said. "Leastaways, that's about the only way I know of getting out of this here well. I tried climbing, but the dirt just naturally crumbles away every time I dig my toes into the sides."

"You've got that well so muddied up it won't be fit to drink out of for a week or more," Jule said.

"I'll do what I can to clean it out for you, Mr. Jule, if I ever get up on top of the solid ground again. Can you hear those hounds of mine trailing now, Mr. Jule?"

"They're still down the creek. I reckon I could lower the water bucket, and I could pull a little, and you could climb a little, and maybe you'd get out that way."

"That just naturally would suit me fine, Mr. Jule," Bokus said eagerly. "Here I is. When is you going to lower that water bucket?"

Jule stood up and listened to his dogs trailing on the ridge. From the way they sounded, it would not be long before they treed the fox they were after.

"It's only about an hour till daybreak," Jule said. "I'd better go on up the ridge and see how my hounds are making out. I can't do much here at the well till the sun comes up."

"Don't go away and leave me now, Mr. Jule," Bokus begged. "Mr. Jule, please, sir, just lower that water bucket down here and help me get out. I just naturally got to get out of here, Mr. Jule. My dogs will get all balled up without me following them. Whoo-way-oh! Whoo-way-oh!"

The pack of fox-trailing hounds was coming up from the creek, headed toward the house. Jule took off his hat and held it beside his ear. He listened to them panting and yelping.

"If I had two more hounds, I'd be mighty pleased," Jule said, shouting loud enough for Bokus to hear. "Just two is all I need right now."

"You wouldn't be wanting two of mine, would you, Mr. Jule?" Bokus asked.

"It's a good time to make a trade," Jule said. "It's a mighty good time, being as how you are down in the well and want to get out."

"Two, did you say?"

"Two is what I said."

There was silence in the well for a long time. For nearly five minutes Jule listened to the packs of dogs all around him, some on the ridge, some down the creek, and some in the far-off-fields. The barking of the hounds was a sweeter sound to him than anything else in the world. He would lose a night's sleep any time just to stay up and hear a pack of foxhounds live-trailing.

"Whoo-way-oh!" he called.

"Mr. Jule!" Bokus shouted up from the bottom of the well.

Jule went to the edge and leaned over to hear what the Negro had to say.

"How about that there trade now, Bokus?"

"Mr. Jule, I just naturally couldn't swap off two of my hounds, I just sure enough couldn't."

"Why not?" Jule said.

"Because I'd have only just six dogs left, Mr. Jule, and I couldn't do much fox hunting with just that many."

Jule straightened up and kicked the boards over the top of the well.

"You won't be following even so few as one hound for a while," he said, "because I'm going to leave you down in the bottom where you stand now. It's another hour, almost, till daybreak, and I can't be wasting that time staying here talking to you. Maybe when I get back you'll be in a mind to do some trading, Bokus."

Jule kicked the boards on top of the well.

"O Lord, help me now!" Bokus said. "But, O Lord, don't make me swap off no two hounds for the help I'm asking for."

Jule stumbled over the water bucket when he turned and started across the yard toward the path up the ridge. Up there he could hear his dogs running again, and when he took off his hat and held it to the side of his head he could hear Polly pant, and Senator snort, and Mary Jane whine, and Sunshine yelp, and the rest of them barking at the head of the trail. He put on his hat, pulled it down hard all around, and hurried up the path to follow them on the ridge. The fox would not be able to hold out much longer.

"Whoo-way-oh!" he called to his hounds. "Whoo-way-oh!"
The echo was a masterful sound to hear.

The Corduroy Pants

TWO WEEKS AFTER he had sold his farm on the back road for twelve hundred dollars and the Mitchells had moved in and taken possession, Bert Fellows discovered that he had left his other pair of corduroy pants up attic. When he had finished hauling his furniture and clothes to his other place on the Skowhegan road, he was sure he had left nothing behind, but the morning that he went to put on his best pair of pants he could not find them anywhere. Bert thought the matter over two or three days and decided to go around on the back road and ask Abe Mitchell to let him go up attic and get the corduroys. He had known Abe all his life and he felt certain Abe would let him go into the house and look around for them.

Abe was putting a new board on the doorstep when Bert came up the road and turned into the yard. Abe glanced around but kept right on working.

Bert waited until Abe finished planing the board before he said anything.

"How be you, Abe?" he inquired cautiously.

"Hell, I'm always well," Abe said, without looking up from the step.

Bert was getting ready to ask permission to go into the house. He waited until Abe hammered the twenty-penny into the board.

"I left a pair of corduroys in there, Abe," he stated preliminarily. "You wouldn't mind if I went up attic and got them, would you?"

Abe let the hammer drop out of his hands and fall on the step. He wiped his mouth with his handkerchief and turned around facing Bert.

"You go in my house and I'll have the law on you. I don't give a cuss if you've left fifty pair of corduroys up attic. I bought and paid for this place and the buildings on it and I

180

don't want nobody tracking around here. When I want you to come on my land, I'll invite you."

Bert scratched his head and looked up at the attic window. He began to wish he had not been so forgetful when he was moving his belongings down to his other house on the Skowhegan road.

"They won't do you no good, Abe," he said. "They are about ten sizes too big for you to wear. And they belong to me, anyway."

"I've already told you what I'm going to do with them corduroys," Abe replied, going back to work. "I've made my plans for them corduroys. I'm going to keep them, that's what I'm going to do."

Bert turned around and walked toward the road, glancing over his shoulder at the attic window where his pants were hanging on a rafter. He stopped and looked at Abe several minutes, but Abe was busy hammering twenty-penny nails into the new step he was making and he paid no attention to Bert's sour looks. Bert went back down the road, wondering how he was going to get along without his other pair of pants.

By the time Bert reached his house he was good and mad. In the first place, he did not like the way Abe Mitchell had ordered him away from his old farm, but most of all he missed his other pair of corduroys. And by bedtime he could not sit still. He walked around the kitchen mumbling to himself and trying to think of some way by which he could get his trousers away from Abe.

"Crusty-faced Democrats never were no good," he mumbled to himself.

Half an hour later he was walking up the back road toward his old farm. He had waited until he knew Abe was asleep, and now he was going to get into the house and go up attic and bring out the corduroys.

Bert felt in the dark for the loose window in the barn and discovered it could be opened just as he had expected. He had had good intentions of nailing it down, for the past two or three years, and now he was glad he had left it as it was. He went through the barn and the woodshed and into the house.

Abe had gone to bed about nine o'clock, and he was asleep and snoring when Bert listened at the door. Abe's wife had been stone-deaf for the past twenty years or more.

Bert found the corduroy pants, with no trouble at all. He

struck only one match up attic, and the pants were hanging on the first nail he went to. He had taken off his shoes when he climbed through the barn window and he knew his way through the house with his eyes shut. Getting into the house and out again was just as easy as he had thought it would be. And as long as Abe snored, he was safe.

In another minute he was out in the barn again, putting on his shoes and holding his pants under his arm. He had put over a good joke on Abe Mitchell, all right. He went home and got into bed.

The next morning Abe Mitchell drove his car up to the front of Bert's house and got out. Bert saw him from his window and went to meet Abe at the door. He was wearing the other pair of corduroys, the pair that Abe had said he was going to keep for himself.

"I'll have you arrested for stealing my pants," Abe announced as soon as Bert opened the door, "but if you want to give them back to me now I might consider calling off the charges. It's up to you what you want to do about it."

"That's all right by me," Bert said. "When we get to court I'll show you that I'm just as big a man as you think you are. I'm not afraid of what you'll do. Go ahead and have me arrested, but if they lock you up in place of me, don't come begging me to go your bail for you."

"Well, if that's the way you think about it," Abe said, getting red in the face, "I'll go ahead with the charges. I'll swear out a warrant right now and they'll put you in the county jail before bedtime tonight."

"They'll know where to find me," Bert said, closing the door. "I generally stay pretty close to home."

Abe went out to his automobile and got inside. He started the engine, and promptly shut it off again.

"Come out here a minute, Bert," he called.

Bert studied him for several minutes through the crack in the door and then went out into the yard.

"Why don't you go swear out the warrant? What you waiting for now?"

"Well, I thought I'd tell you something, Bert. It will save you and me both a lot of time and money if you'd go to court right now and save the cost of having a man come out here to serve the warrant on you. If you'll go to court right now and let me have you arrested there, the cost won't be as much."

"You must take me for a cussed fool, Abe Mitchell," Bert

said. "Do I look like a fool to pay ten dollars for a hired car to take me to county jail?"

Abe thought to himself several minutes, glancing sideways at Bert.

"I'll tell you what I'll do, Bert," he proposed. "You get in my car and I'll take you there and you won't have to pay ten dollars for a hired car."

Bert took out his pipe and tobacco. Abe waited while he thought the proposition over thoroughly. Bert could not find a match, so Abe handed him one.

"You'll do that, won't you, Bert?" he asked.

"Don't hurry me—I need plenty of time to think this over in my mind."

Abe waited, bending nervously toward Bert. The matchhead crumbled off and Abe promptly gave Bert another one.

"I guess I can accommodate you that little bit, this time," he said, at length. "Wait until I lock up my house."

When Bert came back to the automobile Abe started the engine and turned around in the road toward Skowhegan. Bert sat beside him sucking his pipe. Neither of them had anything to say to each other all the time they were riding. Abe drove as fast as his old car would go, because he was in a hurry to get Bert arrested and the trail started.

When they reached the courthouse, they went inside and Abe swore out the warrant and had it served on Bert. The sheriff took them into the courtroom and told Bert to wait in a seat on the first row of benches. The sheriff said they could push the case ahead and get a hearing some time that same afternoon. Abe found a seat and sat down to wait.

It was an hour before Bert's case was called to trial. Somebody read out his name and told him to stand up. Abe sat still, waiting until he was called to give his testimony.

Bert stood up while the charge was read to him. When it was over, the judge asked him if he wanted to plead guilty or not guilty.

"Not guilty," Bert said.

Abe jumped off his seat and waved his arms.

"He's lying!" he shouted at the top of his voice. "He's lying—he did steal my pants!"

"Who is that man?" the judge asked somebody.

"That's the man who swore out the warrant," the clerk said. "He's the one who claims the pants were stolen from him."

"Well, if he yells out like that again," the judge said,

"I'll swear out a warrant against him for giving me a headache. And I guess somebody had better tell him there's such a thing as contempt of court. He looks like a Democrat, so I suppose he never heard of anything like that before."

The judge rapped for order and bent over towards Bert. "Did you steal a pair of corduroy pants from this man?" he asked.

"They were *my* pants," Bert explained. "I left them in my house when I sold it to Abe Mitchell and when I asked him for them he wouldn't turn them over to me. I didn't steal them. They belonged to me all the time."

"He's lying!" Abe shouted again, jumping up and down. "He stole my pants—he's lying!"

"Ten dollars for contempt of court, whatever your name is," the judge said, aiming his gavel at Abe, "and case dismissed for lack of evidence."

Abe's face sank into his head. He looked first at the judge and then around the courtroom at the strange people.

"You're not going to make me pay ten dollars, are you?" he demanded angrily.

"No," the judge said, standing up again. "I made a mistake. I forgot that you are a Democrat. I meant to say twenty-five dollars."

Bert went outside and waited at the automobile until Abe paid his fine. In a quarter of an hour Abe came out of the courthouse.

"Well, I guess I'll have to give you a ride back home," he said, getting under the steering wheel and starting the engine. "But what I ought to do is leave you here and let you ride home in a hired car."

Bert said nothing at all. He sat down beside Abe and they drove out of town toward home.

It was almost dark when Abe stopped the car in front of Bert's house. Bert got out and slammed shut the door.

"I'm mighty much obliged for the ride," he said. "I been wanting to take a trip over Skowhegan way for a year or more. I'm glad you asked me to go along with you, Abe, but I don't see how the trip was worth twenty-five dollars to you."

Abe shoved his automobile into gear and jerked down the road toward his place. He left Bert standing beside the mailbox rubbing his hands over the legs of his corduroy pants.

"Abe Mitchell ought to have better sense than to be a Democrat," Bert said, going into his house.

The Fly in the Coffin

THERE WAS poor old Dose Muffin, stretched out on the corn-crib floor, dead as a frostbitten watermelon vine in November, and a pesky housefly was walking all over his nose.

Let old Dose come alive for just one short minute, may-be two while about it, and you could bet your last sock-toe dollar that pesky fly wouldn't live to do his ticklish fiddling and stropping on any human's nose again.

"You, Woodrow, you!" Aunt Marty said. "Go look in that corncrib and take a look if any old flies worrying Dose."

"Uncle Dose don't care now," Woodrow said. "Uncle Dose don't care about nothing no more."

"Dead or alive, Does cares about flies," Aunt Marty said.

There wasn't enough room in the house to stretch him out in. The house was full of people, and the people wanted plenty of room to stand around in. There was that banjo-playing fool in there, Hap Conson, and Hap had to have plenty of space when he was around. There was that jigging high-yellow gal everybody called Goodie, and Goodie took all the room there was when she histed up her dress and started shaking things.

Poor old Dose, dead a day and a night, couldn't say a word. That old fly was crawling all over Dose's nose, stop-ping every now and then to strop its wings and fiddle its legs. It had been only a day and a night since Dose had chased a fly right through the buzz saw at the lumber mill. That buzz saw cut Dose just about half in two, and he died mad as heck about the fly getting away all well and alive. It wouldn't make any difference to Dose, though, if he could wake up for a minute, maybe two while about it. If he could only do that, he would swat that pesky fly so hard there wouldn't be a flyspeck left.

"You, Woodrow, you!" Aunt Marty said. "Go like I told you to and see if any old flies worrying Dose."

"You wouldn't catch me swatting no flies on no dead man," Woodrow said.

"Don't swat them," Aunt Marty said. "Just shoo them."

Back the other side of the house they were trying to throw a makeshift coffin together for Dose. They were doing a lot of trying and only a little bit of building. Those lazybones out there just didn't have their minds on the work at all. The undertaker wouldn't come and bring one, because he wanted sixty dollars, twenty-five down. Nobody had no sixty dollars, twenty-five down.

Soon as they got the coffin thrown together, they'd go and bury poor old Dose, provided Dose's jumper was all starched and ironed by then. The jumper was out there swinging on the clothesline, waving in the balmy breeze, when the breeze came that way.

Old Dose Muffin, lying tickle-nosed in the corncrib, was dead and wanted burying as soon as those lazy, big-mouthed, good-for-nothing sawmill hands got the grave dug deep enough. He could have been put in the ground a lot sooner if that jabbering preacher and that mush-mouthed black boy would have laid aside their jawboning long enough to finish the coffin they were trying to throw together. Nobody was in a hurry like he was.

That time-wasting old Marty hadn't started washing out his jumper till noon, and if he had had his way, she would have got up and started at the break of day that morning. That banjo-playing fool in the house there, Hap Conson, had got everybody's mind off the burial, and nobody had time to come out to the corncrib and swat that pesky fly on Uncle Dose's nose and say howdy-do. That skirt-histing high-yellow in there, Goodie, was going to shake the house down, if she didn't shake off her behind first, and there wasn't a soul in the world cared enough to stop ogling Goodie long enough to come out to the crib to see if any pesky flies needed chasing away.

Poor old Dose died a ragged-pants sawmill hand, and he didn't have no social standing at all. He had given up the best job he had ever had in his life, when he was porter in the white-folks' hotel, because he went off chasing a fly to death just because the fly lit on his barbecue sandwich just when he was getting ready to bite into it. He chased that fly eight days all over the country, and the fly wouldn't have stopped long enough then to let Dose swat him if it hadn't been starved dizzy. Poor old Dose came back home but he had to go to work in the sawmill and lost all his social standing.

"You, Woodrow, you!" Aunt Marty said. "How many times does it take to tell you go see if any old flies worrying Dose?"

"I'd be scared to death to go moseying around a dead man, Aunt Marty," Woodrow said. "Uncle Dose can't see no flies no way."

"Does don't have to be up and alive like other folks to know about flies," she said. "Dose see flies, he dead or alive."

The jumper was dry, the coffin was thrown together, and the grave was six feet deep. They put the jumper on Dose, stretched him out in the box, and dropped him into the hole in the ground.

That jabbering preacher started praying, picking out the pine splinters he had stuck into his fingers when he and that mush-mouthed black boy were throwing together the coffin. That banjo-playing Hap Conson squatted on the ground, picking at the thing like it was red-hot coals in a tin pan. Then along came that Goodie misbehaving, shaking everything that wouldn't be still every time she was around a banjo-plucking.

They slammed the lid on Dose, and drove it down to stay with a couple of rusty twenty-penny nails. They shoveled in a few spades of gravel and sand.

"Hold on there," Dose said.

Marty was scared enough to run, but she couldn't. She stayed right there, and before long she opened one eye and squinted over the edge into the hole.

"What's the matter?" Marty asked, craning her neck to see down into the ground. "What's the matter with you, Dose?"

The lid flew off, the sand and gravel pelting her in the face, and Dose jumped to his feet, madder than he had ever been when he was living his life.

"I could wring your neck, woman!" Dose shouted at her.

"What don't please you, Dose?" Marty asked him. "Did I get too much starch in the jumper?"

"Woman," Dose said, shaking his fist at her, "you've been neglecting your duty something bad. You're stowing me away in this here ground with a pesky fly inside this here coffin. Now, you get a hump on yourself and bring me a fly swatter. If you think you can nail me up in a box with a fly inside of it, you've got another think coming."

"I always do like you say, Dose," Marty said. "You just wait till I run get the swatter."

There wasn't a sound made anywhere. The shovelers didn't shovel, Hap didn't pick a note, and Goodie didn't shake a thing.

Marty got the swatter fast as she could, because she knew better than to keep Dose waiting, and handed it down to him. Dose stretched out in the splintery pine box and pulled the lid shut.

Pretty soon they could hear a stirring around down in the box.

"Swish!" the fly swatter sounded.

"Just hold on and wait," Marty said, shaking her head at the shovelers.

"Swish!" it sounded again. "Swat!"

"Dose got him," Marty said, straightening up. "Now shovel, boys, shovel!"

The dirt and sand and gravel flew in, and the grave filled up. The preacher got his praying done, and most of the splinters out of his fingers. That banjo-playing fool, Hap Conson, started acting like he was going to pick that thing to pieces. And that behind-shaking high-yellow, Goodie, histed her dress and went misbehaving all over the place. Maybe by morning Hap and Goodie would be in their stride. Wouldn't be too sure about it, though, because the longer it took to get the pitch up, the longer it would last.

A Short Sleep in Louisiana

JIM WORTH and his wife sat down and ate their breakfast of finger-thick slices of bacon, deep-pan cornbread, and coffee after waiting nearly half an hour. The sun was more than an hour high by that time, and the bacon and bread had got cold. It had been at least ten years since Jim Worth was as mad as he was that morning.

"Maybe the poor old man is sick and can't move," Jim's wife said timidly, being careful not to make him any more angry than he already was. "He didn't look any too well when he came to the door last night and begged for a place to sleep."

Jim swung his arms over the table, knocking over his cup of coffee. His wife set things straight and poured fresh coffee into his cup.

"I asked him an hour ago if he was sick and needed a doctor," Jim said. "He told me he felt as good as he ever had in his whole life."

"But I heard him say you could send for the doctor if you'd pay for the visit," his wife said.

"That's proof enough he ain't sick," Jim shouted at her. "When a man's sick enough to die, he'll say he'll pay his own doctor's bills."

Jim's wife sank back into her chair. She was careful not to make him any more angry than he was already, and she prayed under her breath that he would not get into a violent mood this time. As it was, she was fearful that he would take it into his head to do something harmful.

When Jim Worth finished eating, he got up and went to the back door. Then, stepping to the ground, he looked through the open window into the bedroom where the old man was wrapped in a blanket and sprawled comfortably on the bed.

189

"You're the last human that'll ever beg a night's sleep out of me," Jim shouted through the window. "A man my age ought to know better than let a no-account tramp inside the house, anyway. I don't give a hoot in hell if you are eighty years old—or even ninety years old. I wouldn't let you inside my house another time if you got to be a hundred and eighty years old and came begging on crutches for a place to sleep."

Jim Worth had got up in the morning before sunrise ever since he was old enough to remember. When he married his wife, Sophie, she had begged him to let her sleep at least until the sun had risen, but Jim had made it clear that anybody who slept in his house was going to be up and dressed before the sun reached the horizon.

The night before, Jim had let Sophie talk him into letting the old man sleep in the extra bed. It had been a cold damp night outside. It had been drizzling rain since morning, and when night came, the rain settled down to a steady fall. The old man had been struggling through the sticky Louisiana gumbo all day, and he appeared to be on the verge of falling to the ground at any moment. Jim said at the time that he had never seen a more pitiful old man in all his life.

The old man had said his name was Humphrey Fallon, and that he had no home and no known relatives. He said he had been tramping the road through one state after another for the past forty years.

Jim stood at the window and looked at the old man in the bed.

"That bed tick has got insects in it," Jim shouted through the window.

"What kind of insects?" Humphrey Fallon asked, lifting his head from the pillow.

"Bugs and lice, to name some," Jim told him, at the same time wondering what Sophie would say if she had heard him. "Once they get on you, you'll never get rid of them. They'll plague you the rest of your life."

"Maybe so, but they haven't bothered me yet," Fallon said. "I'll stay till they do."

Jim went to the barn and carried out a long scantling. He took it to the window and poked and jabbed at the old man several times.

Fallon rose up in bed enough to look at Jim Worth through the window.

"Durn if you ain't the most anti-hospitable creature I ever ran into," Fallon shouted at him.

"You get out of my bed," Jim said.

"I'll get out when I finish my rest and sleep," Fallon told Jim. He lay down again and pulled the blanket under his chin. "For all I care, it might just as well be night as day. When I want to rest and sleep, I don't care which it is. Now, leave me alone. I'll get up when I'm good and ready."

Jim went to the back yard and got the mosquito smudge-pot. Then he filled it with pine lighters and set it afire. When the smoke began boiling upward, he carried it to the bedroom window and put it inside on the floor. Presently the room began to fill with black smoke, and Fallon sat up to see what was happening. In a few moments he began coughing.

"You folks here are the most anti-hospitable on the face of the earth," he shouted at Jim. "I always had a good respect for Louisiana folks till I ran into you."

It looked for a while as if the smudge-pot would drive Humphrey Fallon out of the bedroom. However, he lay down again and spread the blanket over his face. After the smoke had filtered through the blanket, it was not strong enough to affect his breathing.

Presently Fallon sat up in bed and looked at Jim.

"I've been living in this world for eighty years, but I've never had such a short sleep in my life before," he said. "What time is it, anyhow?"

"It's past time for you to get out of my house."

"You ought to be ashamed of yourself to treat strangers so anti-hospitable," he told Jim. "You'll suffer for it, though, somehow or other."

Jim went to the barn and got an armful of straw. He piled the straw against the side of the house and set fire to it. As soon as Sophie saw what was happening, she ran out of the kitchen with a bucket of water and tried to throw it on the fire. Jim grabbed her and held her with all his might. She began screaming and yelling, and after a moment Fallon came to the window.

"Now you'll get out of my house!" Jim shouted at him. "You'll get out, or be roasted alive!"

"You folks in Louisiana are just plain damn fools," Fallon said. "Anti-hospitable ain't nowhere near the right word for you."

He stood at the window watching the flames and smoke against the side of the house.

"Maybe you don't know it," he said to Jim, "but I'm just as hard-headed as they come. Don't be surprised if I stay right where I am."

"Maybe you're going to stand there and let the house burn down, but I'm not," Sophie told Jim. She ran to the pump and got a bucketful of water. After several trips to the pump the fire gradually was stopped.

Going to the window, Jim looked inside to see if Fallon had left the room. Instead, he saw Fallon getting back into bed and pulling the blanket over his head. Before going to sleep, he sat up and looked at Jim standing at the window.

"If I don't get the rest of my sleep now," Fallon said, "the next time I come this way I'll go through Arkansas and not put foot in Louisiana. Besides, I've heard that the folks up there ain't nearly so anti-hospitable as you folks down here."